4 Shots

Murder in Mormondom

The Amazing True Story of Mary Stevens' 1908 Murder

Roger Blomquist Ph.D.

Cover Photos by Roger Blomquist and BQ Photography

BQ Publications

Provo, Utah
Copyright © 2016 Roger Blomquist Ph.D.

ISBN: 154125421X
ISBN-13: 978-1541254213

CONTENTS

Preface

This is a true story that should have never happened.

Oliver Stone once said that sometimes you need to tell a lie to tell
the truth. That is what has been done here. The *true* story, without
the lies, is available in the Spring 2016 issue of the *Utah Historical
Quarterly* under the title of "A Most Horrible Crime." I used the
same research I used for that article to serve as the foundational
basis for this book.

This story came to me through the past mayor of Kanab City,
Utah, Nina Laycook, by way of my fellow filmmaker, Nathan
Riddle. Nathan and I had worked with Nina on a documentary,
celebrating the centennial of America's first All Women Town
Council. The sleepy village of Kanab surprisingly holds that
honor, and she was doing all she could to bring this little-known
fact to light. As Nathan and I were completing the documentary,
Nina and her troupe presented their historical skit, honoring the
town council at the university where I was teaching. She was
excited about the documentary we were finishing and had another
project she wanted us to do. She brought a packet of information
about the 1908 killing of Mary Manerva Stevens in the small
Orderville hamlet some twenty miles north of Kanab.

Nina claimed it was a movie waiting to be made, and all we
needed to do was to spice it up a little for Hollywood and a
general audience. Reading it with naturally skeptical eyes, I found
she was right, and I became a believer. I enlisted my
upperclassman students who needed research ideas for my
classes, and the research began. While the information they
brought was not of scholarly article quality, it still served to give a

broad spectral understanding of the events. I spent the following summer delving into all the newspaper articles and legal documents I could find. I was able to piece together a fairly accurate picture of what happened.

Nathan and I bantered around various ideas of how to get a script written from the stack of information I had accumulated and created. We decided to hold a script-writing contest. We set up a similar scenario for the contestants to write about and, after reviewing all the entries, settled on a winner. I met with him and gave him a copy of all the information he would need to put something together. We had been judges in a film competition he had entered, and we were both impressed with the script he had written. We were very excited to see what he would create.

It turned out that even though he had a great talent for writing, his strengths did not lend to period pieces. I took two or three elements from his original submission and completely rewrote it, not only to be more accurate to the story, but to the historical setting as well. Like any good script, it is still undergoing modifications and improvements and will someday see the light of day.

I worked with the *Quarterly* publishers to rewrite the historical article, once I completed it, to fit within the designs of their journal. I decided to combine that article and the script into one. I spent eight hectic days transferring all that information into this book.

Instead of writing a historical monograph of the events surrounding April 20, 1908, I wanted to tell the story the best and most accurate way that was easy to read. In order to do that, I had to make up realities that may have never happened. I also added dialogue that was never uttered, so I could convey what I could see between the lines of the historical documents. Everything fictional that I wrote was calculated to accurately explain the what and why of Mary's death. I know there are gross inaccuracies here, and that is why I published it under historical fiction. However, by reading my article in the *Utah Historical Quarterly*, it will be evident that I went to great lengths to remain as true as I could. Where I could, I used the exact words of the characters, as stated in the court records, legal documents, and newspaper accounts. Except for a few deviations for literary interest, one could overlay this story with the academic version in the *Quarterly* and see that they do line up well.

I have changed the name of one of the key players because the alleged actions of his youth do not coincide with the exemplary way he lived the rest of his life. This means one of two things, either the journal account that named him as a participant was incorrect, or he repented of his transgressions and changed his life. In either event, I do not wish to malign his character, especially without concrete proof. The other person's name I changed was because I used him to fuel the story, and I do not know if he acted in that way or not. He was the oldest of the trio, so I decided to make the literary assumption that he was the leader. There are one or two others I have changed as well, because their microcosmic involvement in this event was not enough to show their true character. In order to allow the story to progress, I deviated from what some have perceived as a differing personality, meaning that I did not write them as they actually were in history.

One other name I changed was coffee. I wrote several scenes wherein the characters drank coffee. The LDS Word of Wisdom did not become the strict hard and fast rule it is today overnight. It was an evolutionary process, and during this time good and faithful Mormons could still drink coffee even though there was an advisory against it. My grandparents, who were from this part of the state, drank coffee and, later in my lifetime, I remember them drinking Postum. Therefore, I decided to tongue-in-cheek change the coffee scenes to Postum scenes. I did not do this because I was afraid of offending some overly pious Saint, but from twisting up some non-LDS readers who could not get over the fact that history is pliable. So read those parts and chuckle at it, and think coffee instead of Postum if you like.

For all its historical faults, I have tried faithfully to portray Mary and Alvin to the best of my ability with a severe lack of resources. Read it for the story it is and save the historical criticisms for the article. This story is so fascinating that it needs little embellishment to make it interesting and readable. This is not a story of Good vs. Evil, but of two fallible people, whose decisions led them to a deadly outcome.

Foreword

by Lois D. Brown

A few years ago I taught a writing class at our local university where I had the pleasure of meeting Roger Blomquist, Ph.D. During the class, he told us of the horrific murder of 18-year-old Mary Stevens at Orderville, Utah, in 1908. Initially, I was surprised. I have studied that part of Utah quite extensively for research on my own books and I had never come across any mention of such an event. Later, when I was given the opportunity to read the book in its entirety, I immediately became engrossed in the story. My reactions ranged from shock at the well-respected individuals involved in the murder, to amazement at the level of detective work that was performed. However, nothing prepared me for the tragic end to the Killer's story, the man who was convicted for Mary's murder. His fate is poetic justice at its finest. Had the story been fiction, readers would declare it too outlandish to believe. But these are real events that actually occurred and were hushed up, not to be brought to light for decades until the sordid details were uncovered by Roger, and he simply could not forget them.

It's stories like that of Mary Stevens that eat away at authors until they finally give in and dedicate countless hours, and many late nights, to researching and revealing the truth.

Evil. Ignorance. A disregard for life. We know the dark side of humanity has been around for years. Yet we tend to romanticize the past. As a society, this does us no favors. Instead, let us learn from those who have gone before. In today's world, we discuss what the consequences might be on the rising generation who has been subjected to indulgent parenting. We do not need to wonder. The family of the killer demonstrates in full color what entitlement does to an immature mind with narcissistic tendencies—lies, deceit, and … yes … even murder.

After all this time, Roger has finally given the young Mary Stevens a voice and brought her back from obscurity. Her tale of loneliness, of hope, and of ultimate loss is, at last, going to be heard. This is a story that needs to be told, and Roger has accomplished this in a historically accurate and gripping fashion.

Many thanks to the talented Roger Blomquist, Ph.D. for bringing this piece of history to light.

Lois D. Brown received her bachelor's degree in journalism and worked as a news correspondent in Washington, D.C. She later completed a Master's degree in communications and started her own freelance writing business. She is the author of six legend-based mystery novels, two non-fiction books, and nearly fifty magazine articles and short stories. She worked as the chief editor to former New York Times best-selling author Dr. Neil Solomon, and she co-wrote a book on time management with former Miss America Sharlene Wells Hawkes. Find her online at loisdbrown.com.

Roger Blomquist Ph.D.

Chapter One
Life as Usual

This story is true. You can look it up. You'll find it all there and you can read it, but it won't give you the whole story, not as I can tell it. There are some things that never made the papers and things that some swore they would never tell.

Yet somebody did.

I was ten years old when I heard the shots on that fateful day. My name is Merlin Brinkerhoff, and I was the only one who heard them, except for the shooter...and the girl who was shot in the back. I've had a lot of time to sort through the confusion of what happened over the years, and what I am about to tell you has never been told before...at least not like this.

The town took an unspoken vow to go on with our lives and pretend this horrible event never happened. After it was over and he went to jail, we buried it in our past. I'm only telling you now because it's been over fifty years, and someone needs to know. As I tell you Mary's story, some of my memories have been clarified with time, and some are just as if I was ten-years-old again, experiencing them for the first time.

I was tending sheep in the fields just outside Gardner Hollow that April afternoon, when the reports of four gunshots rang out through the Orderville hills. Since it was 1908 in rural America, and hunting was common practice, I gave it no thought. I mean, really, who would have ever thought that murder would have been part of the southern Utah landscape? The Mormons had worked so hard to create a desert utopia, that the idea of someone killing a teenage girl never entered our minds.

No one except the gunman witnessed the grizzly crime, not even the victim.

But let me start at the beginning. . . .

Orderville was a very special place. It was the crown jewel in the Mormon United Order program; it is crucial to remember this as I tell the story.

Orderville is situated in Long Valley about thirty miles north of Kanab and the Utah/Arizona state line. Long Valley is narrow and not as suited for large-scale farming and ranching as the Kanab area, so we did not prosper as well as they did. This kept our communities, such as Mt. Carmel, Glendale, and Orderville, small and intimate.

Highway 89 runs through the valley but at the time of the murder, we had yet to see an automobile travel down along the wagon road. However, we did have the telephone. Back in '05, Hyrum Cameron and his sons from Panguitch built a telephone line from their town, down through our valley to Kanab. This single line serviced Glendale, Orderville, and Mt. Carmel among others.

One of our claims to fame was the novelist, Zane Grey, had

just been introduced to our county the previous year by a local man, D. D. Rust, which began the storied writing relationship Grey had with Southern Utah.

Asphalt was several years from making an appearance in our town and the first automobile would not come through until a year after the killing, in the summer of 1909. Even though the Wright Brothers were perfecting their flying machines, we were still years away from seeing man in the air.

The United Order system, for which the town was named, was a very special program that made all the members of the Church of Jesus Christ of Latter-day Saints equal. The philosophy behind it was all members in the Church held everything in common. It virtually eliminated the idea of personal or private property and had all people working in exchange for goods to meet their needs, not gain temporal possessions.

Just down the road from Orderville, a couple of miles, was the town of Mt. Carmel. They fell into the same difficulties as other towns that tried to practice the United Order...human failings. Regardless of how well the Order was planned out and presented, practical application always met with someone's greed.

For centuries, the European driving force had been greed. The landed gentry had more and always wanted more. The Spanish came to the Americas, looking to take gold away from the indigenous peoples who owned it. The French came over to take fortunes in furs, and the English came over to find gold but took land instead. To further their money-making schemes, Europeans purchased human labor forces from the West Coast Africans who went further inland to capture others, and then sold them to the Portuguese, Dutch, English, or any other European country who would buy them. If Euro-Americans could shuck this attitude of greed and take on the philosophy of many Native Americans, then our United Order would have worked. Many

Native Americans believed the richest man in the village was he who gave away the most, not he who accumulated the most. Nomadic tribes had no need of gathering worldly items for riches, because they would need to transport all of them when the village moved.

For us as Mormons, what typically happened was that we entered into the United Order as an established community, and all would be well for a time. Our doctors, teachers, farmers, ranchers, and shopkeepers would all work in unison, with all their earnings going into the Order, to be redistributed to the members according to their needs. Those who were unmarried needed less than families with children, so they received less. Economically speaking, it was a system of fairness and left no one wanting.

The problem arose when a man with talent, intelligence, and ambition noticed he was paid the same to work and live as the man who was dumber than a post and just swept the boardwalks in the mornings. The talented man (or the wife behind him) would demand more because he (she) felt he worked harder than the sweeper and deserved more.

Ultimately, he would pull out of the Order, and others who also felt they deserved more for their labors, followed suit. Soon, the Order would collapse in that town. They would be back to the normal farming and ranching economy the rest of rural America practiced.

This brings us back to Orderville. Mt. Carmel was in the throes of arguing about how the Order should be practiced in their town or if at all. This caused a permanent rift among the community members. Those who wanted to practice it in its purest form moved north a couple of miles and established Orderville in 1875. Obviously, the town's name came from the idea that they wanted to live the United Order the way it was intended from its conception. As I said before, we saw ourselves

4

as the crown jewel of the United Order in the Mormon empire, and we've held that close to our hearts as a badge of honor for generations.

Regardless of how hard we tried to live the Order, the same selfish elements crept in and caused contention among us, until the Brethren in Salt Lake City finally decided to end the practice church-wide in 1890. Even though it was brought to an end, we had practiced it more devoutly and longer than any other community in Zion had. We were very proud of this, and the fact that our town was the only one established with the United Order squarely as the core of the community.

Another key element that does not need to be discussed in detail but cannot be ignored was the practice of polygamy. Our town Fathers, such as Thomas Carter, practiced plural marriage that, combined with their adherence to the principles of the United Order, added to their piety. We were a light on a hill for the rest of the Mormon kingdom, and indeed the world, to look upon and to follow our example.

This gives you a better idea of what our small town was like at the time of the murder. We were tight-knit, religious, and proud of our place in Mormon history.

So if our town was so near perfect, how is it that the most horrible crime of our time happened there?

Ezra and Edith Stevens moved to Mt. Carmel, after birthing twelve children. Mary Manerva Stevens was born on July 2, 1889, in Shunsberg, Utah, near the wintering town of St. George. She was the second youngest of the lot and very academically minded.

For the people of Orderville, Mt. Carmel was "the other town," where the Mormons lived who were not righteous enough to commit to the United Order in its fullest form. The Stevens lived in "the other town," but when Mary's older brother, Joseph, married Orderville's Francis Heaton, he moved there to find work. Joseph was two years older than Francis and six years Mary's senior.

"I want you to take Mary," Ezra told Joseph one day. "She needs to finish her education, and Orderville is the place to do it."

"You want her to live in town with me?"

"It makes more sense than having her walk three miles back and forth each day," Ezra pointed out.

"Yes, that makes sense," Joseph agreed. "I certainly don't mind, but I'll have to check with Francis before I commit. I'm sure Mary could be a big help with our two kids, but I feel like it also needs to be Francis' decision."

"Can't you just tell her that this is the way it's going to be? Tell her Mary is moving in with you and that the decision has been made. Be the man of the house."

"Sure," Joseph responded, "and if I do that, I'll find I'm the man of the chicken coop. Francis is a loving Saint, but she is also a strong-willed woman."

"So you let her run your household then, son?" Ezra accused as he leveled his gaze toward Joseph.

"No, Father," Joseph said in defense. "We're trying to share the burdens and decisions of the house, like the Brethren have admonished us to do. You know, like a righteous couple; 'neither is the man without the woman or the woman without the man in the Lord,' and all that."

"Well, as the man, I think you need to be the more assertive one. She is just a woman after all."

"A woman who packs the kids around and works beside me in the fields," Joseph defended. "Say what you will, but I'll not say yes to taking Mary until Francis has had her say and feels like it's a good idea. I can either call, or let you know when we come down for Sunday dinner."

"No need to use that telephone gadget any more than we have to," Ezra stated. "Just let us know at dinner. School's not for several more months. A few days to find out won't hurt."

"Your father said what?" Francis asked in surprise.

"He said I should be the man of the house and assert my authority," Joseph explained, "and make the decision about Mary living here with us."

"And just what did you tell him?" Francis demanded, cocked and ready to get furious. "Did you agree with what he said?"

"No, of course not! I told him I would have to discuss it with you first, and then we would make the decision together. Did you really think I would make that kind of decision without you?"

"Normally, I wouldn't think so," she said, "but when it comes to your father, I've noticed he still has quite a hold on you sometimes."

"He's still my father and only lives a couple miles away. It's hard to be a righteous Saint and not honor him or my mother, for that matter, at least not the way the scriptures say. I feel duty bound to do what he says…most of the time. There are times I think he interprets the scriptures in the old ways, and thinks all women should be doing what the men say. My poor mother has had to live with that her whole life because her father tends to think the same way."

"How is it you broke away from that point of view?" Francis wanted to know.

"To be honest with you, I never gave it much thought. If I look back, I would have to say I never made up my mind about

7

his views on women, until I met you. After I fell in love and really got to know you, the scriptures made more sense when you look at an equal couple running the household. I can't believe my father doesn't see that."

"That must be why I fell in love with you," Francis said. "That and because you were the only boy in town old enough to marry me."

"Oh, stop it," Joseph said in mock scorn. "There were lots of boys to choose from. I just happened to be the best one."

"You know I asked all the other boys first," Francis teased him, "but you were the only one who said yes. So have you decided that Mary is going to move in with us?"

"No, of course not," he repeated. "It's as I told Father, this is a decision for us to discuss and make together. I'll not make it without you."

"Do I get to have her as a live-in nanny, so she can help with Edith and Joseph Junior?" she asked playfully.

"I think you can work her as hard as she'll let you. I just can't guarantee how much that will be."

"As long as I get to try," Francis chuckled. "Yes, of course she can come live with us. Your father just needs to learn how we do things in our house and the best way to ask us for something."

"And I suppose Mary will too," Joseph mentioned. "She's lived with our folks all of her life and only knows their ways. I suspect it will take her some time to get used to the way we do things here. Not to mention that Orderville is a different critter than Shunsberg or Mt. Carmel."

Joseph and Francis lived in a two-story house. When Mary's final year in school started, she moved in with them. Orderville is a great community but, like anywhere else, it had developed its own identity. As I said before, we were awful proud of the fact that we had the longest lasting United Order community in Zion.

We also never forgot it was Mt. Carmel that was left behind.

The folks here in town let Mary in but, even though she only came from a few miles away, she was still an outsider. She would have to struggle and become creative in finding ways to fit in. She was easy to like, and many of the girls would spend time with her to do homework or for other reasons. There were also others who did not want anything to do with her. The kids around town had developed their own social circles, and Mary did not quite fit into most of them. They did not reject her outright, they just tended to exclude her in some activities in which they were involved. I never had any trouble with her, but she was almost twice my age at the time.

She joined the other kids for frequent church activities but, even at that, there was always the invisible separation of being an outsider. The local Church leaders always made sure she was included, and the kids graciously followed suit. However, there was never a strong bond developed between them. At least, not one we could see.

"Look at the way she pines over those boys," eighteen-year-old Mamie Robinson hissed to her gaggle of girls. "She thinks she can catch their interest just by the way she looks at them. She doesn't realize it just makes her look lonely and pathetic. Any boy can see that, and I can't imagine any of them would want to be with her."

"She reminds me of an old hound my father used to have," seventeen-year-old Sally commented disdainfully. "It always laid on the front porch whenever he would leave and had that same pitiful look on his face until father came home. Maybe we should start calling her hound dog because of the way she looks with those sad droopy eyes."

"That might be taking it a little too far, girls," nineteen-year-old Etna commented. "I'm not saying we need to be overly nice to her, but we don't need to be cruel to her either. Someday, some of us may end up moving away from here and find we need to fit in somewhere else. I would hope they would be more understanding and accepting than we have been."

"Oh, all right," Mamie finally conceded, her tone tainted with disdain and disgust at the idea. "I'll try to be nicer, but I don't like the way she looks at Alvin all the time. Can't she see he wants nothing to do with her? Besides, everyone knows Alvin is mine. If all goes as planned, I will be Mrs. Alvin Franklin Heaton, Jr. before too long. When that happens, my ship will have come in."

"I wouldn't plan too far ahead yet," Etna warned. "Alvin is a great guy and from a strong Mormon family here in town, but he has a lot of growing up to do before he's ready to take on a wife and start a family."

"But he comes from a good Latter-day Saint family," Mamie defended, using Etna's words against her. "His father has two wives, and his second wife is the daughter of Brother Spencer, who ran the United Order here for a while."

"Yes," Sally commented, with a hint of desire escaping her voice, "and I would love to have his half-brother Franklin Alvin, if I had the chance."

"Did you know they were born only two weeks apart?" Mamie asked.

"I suppose that's why Alvin Senior named one Alvin Franklin and the other Franklin Alvin," Etna mentioned. "That means Alvin Jr. was the first one born, yes?"

"That's right," Mamie commented. "He was born on November 25, and Franklin was born two weeks later down in Moccasin."

"That's just across the border into Arizona, isn't it?" Sally asked.

"About forty miles from here, yes," Etna confirmed. "I'm guessing Alvin Sr. was spending too much time traveling back and forth, and that's why he moved Lucy and her kids up here to the Green, just outside of town."

"That's right," Mamie commented. "Now that the Federal Government has backed off prosecuting polygamists, he felt it was safe to move them up into the same state."

"I never did understand why the government stopped trying to destroy the Church and finally left polygamy alone," Sally commented.

"It's because we've stopped conducting plural marriages," Etna informed her. "In order to not leave a bunch of widows to fend for themselves, the government decided to sort of look the other way at the polygamist marriages that were still out there. They figured they would end soon enough when that generation dies off. Then they won't ever have to deal with it again."

"As much as I know that polygamy is from the Lord," Mamie said, "I'm sure glad I won't need to share Alvin with anyone else."

"That's if he'll have you," Etna cautioned.

"With my luck," Mamie continued, ignoring Etna's comment, "I would have to share him with the likes of Mary. Can you imagine being sister wives with her? It would be like having that old hound dog around all the time with a weepy, pining look."

Not only was Mary an outsider, but she had the jealousy of Mamie Robinson to deal with. Everyone knew she had her claim on Alvin, including Alvin. Even I knew it at the time. They were the town sweethearts, and everyone seemed to figure their future together the same as Mamie did. She definitely had a sweet spot in Alvin's heart, and she made no secret that she would do anything necessary to keep it.

Fortunately, Alvin never showed any interest in Mary, so Mamie never openly declared her an enemy. That did not mean she did not keep a close and scornful eye on her, just to make sure she didn't turn his head.

The school year went along as everyone expected. There was comfort in the usual seasonal change with the leaves turning colors and the coming of snow. This far south, the snow did not come often or stay long, but it always brought a comfortable blanket of beauty, before it melted away.

During the cold time of year, our community, much like all the others in Zion, turned to our church house for association with one other. We held plays, concerts, dances, played games, and just generally visited, so we could get out of our shut-in houses and live again with others for a moment.

As always spring came and, with it, an explosion of activity and growth outdoors. We had had enough of the cold and being cooped up inside. Even before the ground was ready to plant, we would come out and work it in eager anticipation to begin life anew.

I remember how cold I got that winter out tending sheep, and how extremely grateful I was to the Lord when the warm weather finally returned. I suppose I should feel proud my father saw fit to give me that much responsibility at such a young age, but our family had no choice. Father had to work at so many other jobs just to keep us fed, that the sheep's care naturally fell to me. I did not think too much of it at the time, because so many of my friends were either doing the same with sheep or cows or a few working the ground for crops. That's just the way it was.

Once April arrived, all the students in school were looking forward to getting out, and the seniors were preparing to take their final graduation examinations. Alvin's father was a rancher, much like most of the community, and Alvin Jr. worked with him. Still, Jr. had a fair amount of free time, so he tended to strut around town and act the tough on several occasions.

You know the old adage, "spare the rod, and spoil the child." It was painfully obvious that Alvin Sr. most certainly spared his rod. I think the fact that Alvin was spoiled may have been much of the attraction that Mamie had for him. I think Mary's attraction for him was one of loneliness and a deep-seated desire to be loved. She was a little heavier than the other girls were, but there were still plenty of men who found that attractive. I'm sure you've heard that meat on the bones means they come from a family wealthy enough to eat well. She was not an unattractive girl on the outside; I just think she was lonely enough inside that it dimmed her outer beauty. But then, what did I know, I was only ten-years-old at the time.

"I don't want you seeing her," Mamie demanded of Alvin as they stood outside the Co-op store.

"Surely you don't want me to walk around with my eyes closed," he responded. "I'm sure to run into something if I do."

Mamie slapped him across his arm. "You know full well what I mean, Alvin Heaton! I see the way she makes puppy-dog eyes at you, and I don't want you to have anything to do with her. Don't forget you belong to me, and your future is with me, not her."

"I think you are giving her far too much credit, Mamie," he defended. "I have no desire to be with her, and you have to know by now that it's you I want."

"You tell me that now, but what about when I'm not around, and *she* corners you?"

"Don't worry," he assured her, "I have no use for her. It's as I told cousin Junius the other day, it wouldn't bother me if someone stole her and sold her into slavery."

"Alvin! You don't mean that!"

"Of course I don't," he assured her, "but I wanted you to know that you have absolutely nothing to worry about. I have no interest in her and there's nothing she can do to change that."

"Don't you let anyone else hear you say that," Mamie warned. "I would hate to see you lose your standing in the Church for that kind of talk. If we're going to get married, you need to stay in good standing so you can be a Bishop or Stake President someday."

"I don't know that I need to be either one of those," he informed her, "but I will heed your warning and be careful."

Mary was always nice to me, and I enjoyed being around her. The last vivid memory I have of her was as she sat on the ledge we call The Point. It overlooks the town, and I remember she liked to sit up there and do her studies when the weather was good. I asked her about it one time. She said it gave her perspective. Her troubles did not seem to be as big from up there, where everything looked so much smaller. She liked watching Mamie scurry around town because her actions looked so comical from that distance. From that vantage point, Mamie's cruelty did not seem to hurt so much. Neither did the things the other people in town did to her.

She could also see more things. During one of her times to the Point, she could see the drummer's wagon from Monroe, selling his wares in the center of town. In-between her readings, she also noticed the townspeople walking around doing their daily business.

It seems like such a long time ago when Orderville was born

out of a desire to create a safe haven for the Saints…a community untouched by outsiders. Most of the older men and women had been persecuted for their beliefs in one way or another. They were driven from their homes in Missouri and Illinois and endured unspeakable horrors, all because of what we believed. They were all decent folk, going about their daily lives with very little interference from the outside world. Like many of the others in Zion, they shuttered their community to outsiders and the storms they brought.

As she sat at the Point that day, she looked out to the north and noticed a lone wagon in the distance. Thinking about the wagon coming in, the shortcomings of those she could see down below, and her own personal troubles, she reflected with deep thought.

I wonder if that wagon down there will get a warmer welcome than I did.

The wagon slowly rolled into town where Alvin's uncle, forty-five-year-old Constable Wilford Heaton, stood and waited by the side of the road. Being a small town and the fact that he had other jobs, he seldom wore a badge. He took a couple steps into the middle of the road as the wagon came closer and easily pulled to a stop.

Several other people stood or walked along the street. Some watched as Wilford addressed them, while the others went on about their business, unconcerned by the wagon's arrival.

At the reins of the wagon was a weather-beaten man in his late twenties. Sitting next to him was his sickly wife, covered in a blanket, shivering. By their appearance, it was obvious they had been on the road a long time.

"How are you folks doing?" Wilford asked them in his

friendliest official voice.

"I'll tell you, kind sir, we've certainly seen better days," the stranger said. "This trip out here sure has taken its toll on us, and I'll be awfully glad when it's over."

"That's about how it looks," Wilford agreed. "I can see you've had a hard go of it. Where are you coming from?"

"Back East," he responded. "We used to live in Silver Springs, back in Prince George's County in Maryland. Things weren't working out so well for us there, and we thought we might try our luck out West. We've heard so many stories about families coming out and doing really well in California. Maybe that will work for us too."

"I hear of a lot of people doing that," Wilford commented.

"We've been on the road for several months now, but my wife has taken ill. It hit her like a lightning bolt, 'bout a week back, just after we pulled out of Richfield. We'd be obliged if you could put us up for a couple of nights somewhere here in town until her fever breaks."

Wilford remained silent for a few minutes as he stared at the woman wrapped up in her blanket. She was pale and clammy, and he wondered how she kept from falling off the wagon seat. Concerned, he contemplated the repercussions of letting them stay or forcing them to leave.

Seven-year-old Jack and his five-year-old sister, Millie, slowly raised their heads out from under a blanket. They had been sleeping back in the wagon box and had been awakened by the conversation.

"Pa?" Jack asked.

His father turned his head toward his son and made an effort to comfort the children.

"It's all right there, Jackie boy," he said. "You and Millie just stay there in back. We're gonna get some help for Ma as soon as we can." Still sleepy but satisfied with the answer, Jack and Millie laid their heads back down and drew the blanket up to their shoulders.

Their father turned back toward Wilford and pleaded, "Please, sir, we won't be any trouble to you or anyone in town. My wife just needs a couple of days to rest."

Lapreal, a resident of Orderville and a leader in the women's Relief Society organization, stepped into hearing range. She stopped to watch what Wilford would do.

"You have faith, Brother?" Wilford finally asked him, wanting to know his stance regarding Mormons.

"Beg your pardon, sir?" the man responded, not realizing what Wilford was really asking.

"We've had troubled times here in Zion," Wilford explained. "Troubled times indeed, and it is hard to know who we can trust. We've trusted Gentiles before, and far too often they turned and betrayed us."

The man considered Wilford's words for a moment and, in desperation, responded, "It ain't all bad, sir. There really are many good people in the world…those who would give the shirt off their backs if you needed it, and those who would give their life for yours. That's the faith I have."

Lapreal had listened silently long enough and, when she could stand it no longer, stepped in and said, "Wilford, can't you see she needs our help? Send her up to the hotel. We have plenty of room for them there. We can get them cleaned up and give them some supper. Glory knows they could use some. We can send for the healer, too."

Wilford, not pleased about her interruption in the very public situation, was nevertheless grateful for some support in his position. With so many people watching his interaction with the family, he did not want to jeopardize his standing in the community by being too kind or accepting of these Gentiles, or non-Mormons, while they were in town.

"All right, Lapreal," he said, turning toward the couple, "but after that though, we've got to send you on your way. I'll tell you though, Kanab is only a day's ride by wagon to the south. If you head out early enough in the morning, you can make it there before dark and it gets too cool. It wouldn't do to have your Mrs. get any sicker than she already is. They have a right good doctor there, and I'm sure they can help you better than we can. All right?"

It was obvious to everyone in the street that the man was exhausted and very disappointed at Wilford's decision. However, he tipped his hat in a genuine gesture of appreciation for the small concession.

Despite her feeling ill from the flu, his wife also showed her appreciation for their small kindness.

"Thank you sir," she rasped, as she shivered under the blanket wrapped around her. "The rest will do me good, and we will be on our way, as you said, early in the morning."

"We'll be sure to get you breakfast and pack you some food to take along the way," Lapreal informed them.

Wilford grimaced and sported a look that suggested he wished he could do more for the unfortunate family, but his hands were tied. He gave them the best smile he could and waved them on toward the hotel. The wagon slowly made its way toward the heart of town. Everyone was silent as they watched it drive by, exaggerating the sounds of the trace chains, horses' footfalls, and the creak of the wheels as they rolled by.

As they slowly moved along the dirt road, they passed the traveling drummer's wagon with its variety of sundries and useful items openly displayed. The thirty-four-year-old drummer, while not an unattractive man, was unkempt and probably turned away as much business by his appearance as his trinkets and bobbles attracted. His wagon was stationed about fifty yards away from the Co-op store, because he was allowed no closer.

A short distance behind the Co-op store, three friends, Alvin, Hyrum, and Jackie sat on empty wooden crates playing cards. Hyrum Mower was eighteen, and Jackie Adler was twenty, two years older than Alvin was.

Mamie walked over to where they were playing cards and stood behind Alvin. She affectionately put her hand on his shoulder and looked at his cards. Without giving away any information to the other two players, she looked away idly toward the wagon as it drove into view.

Jackie was on the bulky side, but more reserved in his nature than his good friend, Alvin. Still, he proved to be the leader of the three. He looked across at Mamie standing there behind Alvin and idly thought to himself how slender and attractive she was, with her long blonde hair and the way she filled her dress. Hyrum was the most subdued of the trio. One would hardly construe him as a leader. He looked up as he noticed the wagon stop directly in front of the Orderville hotel. Mamie also glanced over as she watched the family climb down off the wagon and carry a few belongings into the building.

Will anyone tend to the animals? she wondered. Soon, the man returned, unhitched the mules from the wagon, led them over to a water trough, and gave them the chance to drink. When they finished, he tied them to a nearby tree with plenty of grass underneath while he stripped off their harnesses. The animals had been tended, so she turned back to Alvin and the game and gave the man and his situation no further thought.

Later that day, Mary emerged from the Co-op store with her brother Joseph. In her hand, she carried a paper bag filled with candied popcorn and peanuts.

Joseph turned to her with a loving smile. "Candied popcorn and peanuts make a spring day even better, don't they? What a beautiful day for a walk."

"Yes," Mary agreed, "but I can hardly wait for summer. I have so many things planned, and I know my life is about to change forever."

"It'll get here soon enough, you'll see. Then you'll get so hot and pestered by deerflies that you'll be wishing we were back here in early spring."

Mary laughed at his comment and ate a handful of her treat. "Who am I to argue with my big brother? I'm sure you're right. I will probably find myself so uncomfortable this summer that I will be begging for the cooler weather. I may even have to move up to Salt Lake City to get out of the heat." She paused for a moment as she ate another handful, sharing this quiet moment with her brother.

"I'm going over to Alice Gould's tonight after supper." she finally stated, breaking the silence. "I promised to go and see little Darlene,"

"She'll love that," Joseph commented with a smile. "I know she loves you so and loves the way you dote on her. Will you be out late?"

"No, she's been down sick the last couple of days, and hasn't been able to get out at all. I just want to stop over to poke my head in and see her for a moment. Maybe I can help cheer her up." Mary paused ominously for a few minutes, wistfully looking off in the distance. "I can't wait to have one of my own like her."

She turned back and once again focused her attention on Joseph as he spoke.

"You're really good with kids, I've noticed," he observed. "Much better than I am, that's for sure."

Mary looked concerned. "Don't sell yourself short, brother," she admonished. "I've seen you play with your children, and they absolutely adore you. You make a wonderful father. I see it every day."

"Yeah…well…," Joseph muttered. "Oh, shoot!"

Startled, Mary looked at him to determine what had caused the outburst.

"What is it?" she asked him, full of concern.

"I promised Francis I'd walk her home from checking the sheep in the fields. I completely forgot, and I'm very late. I have to go."

Mary chuckled at his outburst and said, smiling, "That's what happens when you have a wife who is with child; she has you chasing all over the place."

He started to walk away but turned back, returning her smile. "Why Mary, what are you implying, that I love spending time with my wife? How could you?"

Mary laughed at his antics. "I know you do, Joseph, I know you do."

She could tell he was anxious to be on his way to see Francis, so she quickly gave him a deep hug.

"Thank you for always watching out for me," she continued. "Thank you for letting me live with you, so I can go to school. And thank you for being my brother." She paused then, letting go of the embrace, leaned back with a smile, "Oh, and thank you for the Cracker Jacks."

"I'll always be there to protect you, you know that," he said, smiling. "And you're welcome."

"So I'll see you two at supper?"

"Yes, ma'am," Joseph said, as he tipped his hat to her and

sprinted up the dirt road.

He ran off toward the sheep fields on the outskirts of town, hoping he had not missed his wife.

Mary stood there for a few minutes and watched him, while she continued to eat her treat. While she did, she mused over how much she loved him, and how much he had done for her over the course of the last year.

Chapter Two
Small Town Paradise

A few people, gathered near the drummer's wagon, caught Mary's attention. Noticing the items displayed there, she decided to stroll over and take a closer look. Finishing her candied popcorn and peanuts, she walked casually as she wiped off her hands and stepped in among those who stood near the drummer, examining his wares.

While she spent a few minutes looking, her mind drifted back to the last few months and how much her life was about to change. She would turn nineteen in a few months and, with graduating from school, things would never be the same. At the moment, she had no idea what she was going to do or how to support herself until she could find someone to marry. There were so many responsibilities as an adult. She did not know how she could possibly take care of everything that would be laid down in front of her. Anxiety began to set in as she dwelled on these thoughts for too long, then her eyes landed on the jewelry displayed for sale.

"Good afternoon, ma'am," the drummer opened. "Can I interest you in anything today? I have many beautiful items befitting someone such as you."

"Not today, thank you," Mary responded as much to herself as to him. "I'm just..."

A lovely locket on a necklace caught her eye. It was silver and had a small clasp that allowed it to open. She removed it from its display hook to look closer at it. Carefully opening it, she saw it was designed to hold two photographs facing each other.

This would be perfect for pictures of a mother and her child, she thought to herself, *and the scrollwork on the outside is absolutely exquisite.*

"Oh, my...," she muttered involuntarily.

Unbeknownst to Mary at the time, Alvin was behind the Co-op store and idly watching her at the wagon. He had the look of someone who was very bored and was watching ants, walking along the ground. He stared longer, as she looked at the drummer's items, but showed no emotion or great interest. He glanced down the road and saw Jackie and Hyrum standing together, engaged in conversation. They were engrossed in their topic enough that they did not notice him. Nor did they seem to pay any attention to the happenings over at the drummer's wagon and Mary, as she continued to stare at the locket she was holding.

"It's lovely," she continued, as she fondled it a moment longer, realizing she could not afford to buy it.

"Not as lovely as the woman holding it," the drummer flattered her. "I should think it would look beautiful on you. Why don't you try it on? I have a mirror over here; you could see how it looks on you. What could it hurt?"

Feeling a little uncomfortable, Mary awkwardly smiled at his kind words while fighting the desire to go ahead and try it on. She shifted back and forth on her feet for a minute while the drummer smiled back at her. She was about to hand it back to him when Alice Gould addressed her.

"Oh, Mary," she said, "it's beautiful. You should buy it."

Mary quickly turned her head in surprise to find her there.

"Oh, the thought…" Mary started, but trailed off, as she knew she did not have the money for such an extravagance. She sheepishly turned back toward the drummer.

It was clear to Alice and anyone else standing close by, even Alvin, that the drummer had been overcome by Mary's looks. Alice watched carefully, curious if the drummer would stay within the laws of socially acceptable behavior, or if he would act untowardly. As much as he was drawn to her, the drummer had no place in her life. He was several years her senior, and lived the life of a traveling salesman who could offer her no stability. Decorum dictated he remain silent over his feelings, and so he did.

Afraid of the answer, Mary timidly asked, "How much?"

With a gentle smile, he responded. "It is my gift to the lady."

Without processing the ramifications, Mary blurted out, "Oh, thank you!" Then she paused as her better sense returned, and she corrected herself. "But I shouldn't, thank you."

"I would be honored if you would accept it," he insisted. "A woman of your beauty deserves such lovely adornments."

Mary paused for a few minutes as she debated whether she should accept his offer or not. She realized it was probably not appropriate to accept this token of his admiration, even if he did not mean it as such, but her heart ached to accept the gift, and she was very grateful for the attention this man was giving her.

He sensed she was about to return it and gently repeated, "A woman such as yourself deserves a small ornament to enhance her beauty."

Not used to such praise of her appearance or not even used

to praise since she had moved to Orderville, she did not want to encourage him, but did want his kind words. She looked around to see who was near while she considered the situation. She looked at Alice briefly, then at the others standing nearby. She widened her view and noticed Jackie and Hyrum were engaged in their conversation, and Alvin was standing at the back of the Co-op building.

She decided that she really could not accept the locket when Alice persuaded, "Oh, go ahead Mary. It's just a friendly gift."

She turned to the drummer. "Isn't it?"

"Of course," he assured her with a genuine smile.

"Really, Mary," Alice coaxed, "what could it hurt? And it does look lovely on you."

Mary stood still for a moment, as she skeptically tried to determine if it actually was just a friendly gift or if the drummer had devious motives in mind.

"I could save it and put a picture of me and my first child in it," she said, more to herself than to anyone else, "...when I have one."

The drummer gently urged her, "Please."

The desire to have the locket overcame her, and she decided to accept it.

Smiling with the excitement of receiving such a lovely and unexpected gift, she said, "Thank you, sir. I am ever so grateful for your kindness."

She turned to Alice and quickly embraced her. "Thank you, Alice, for talking me into accepting it. It is so lovely!"

"It was my pleasure," she responded. "It is the least I could do for all the wonderful things you've done for Darlene."

"I do love her so. I'm planning to come over after supper to look in on her."

"I know she'll love that," Alice affirmed. "Speaking of which,

I must get back to make her something to eat. I promised her I wouldn't be out too long."

After another quick embrace, Alice walked away just as Alvin walked by the wagon.

Mary turned to show him her new gift. "Alvin, look what the drummer just..."

Alvin refused to acknowledge her and walked by without stopping. She visibly shrank back from the pain of the public rejection as she watched him walk over to where Mamie was waiting. When he reached her, she took his arm and they continued walking together.

Tears began to well up in Mary's eyes as she slowly reached out to hand the locket back to the drummer. All of her excitement and desire to have it had drained from her soul.

He held up his hand to stop her and assured her it was all right to keep it.

"A boy such as that has no right to your attentions," he wisely said. "You deserve someone who will provide you with praise and attention. He has no business being part of your life."

"Thank you," she said, fighting back the tears, "I wish it was that simple."

During this exchange, her father, Ezra, looked on from the saddle and harness shop that tended to be a place of gathering. People traveling through, who needed a saddle or harness repaired, spread news of other places while they waited. He was in good spirits, yet his bearing showed someone who had worked hard all of his life in the fields. His demeanor suggested disapproval of what he saw between his daughter and the drummer. He watched as Mary tried to engage Alvin in friendly conversation. When he saw Alvin walk past her and over to Mamie, he shook his head in disgust.

"How dare he shun her like that?" he muttered.

From a few feet away, sixty-year-old Sarah Foote had noticed his demeanor and asked, "Disapprove, Ezra?"

She was there to pick up a harness she had repaired by Clifford Rogers, the saddlemaker.

He quietly growled to himself as he realized he had been caught, and an explanation was now due.

"I don't like the way that scrawny Heaton boy treats Mary. He's got a false sense of superiority because of who his family is, and it's not right. Of course, I don't like the way the drummer is making eyes at her either."

"She is eighteen," Sarah said without accusation, "and she is a woman."

"No, not yet," Ezra rebutted, a slight growl in his voice. "She's still just a schoolgirl, not at all ready for the advances of men in her life. Besides, eighteen is too young."

"Take it easy, Papa Bear," she chuckled. "If Edith's father had looked at you like that, I'm sure the two of you would've never survived the first time you went calling on her."

"Yeah, well…" he stammered, "Alvin's still no good for her. She needs to give him a wide berth and have nothing to do with him."

He paused for a minute as he collected himself. "Anyway, thank you for looking after her."

"It is Joseph who you should be thanking, not me," she commented. "He's done right by that girl. He's always looking out for her and protecting her. With him around, I can't imagine that any harm will ever come to her. He's as much a papa bear around her as you are."

"He's a good boy and a good son," Ezra admitted. "I'm lucky to have him. He's been a fine example to his brothers and sisters."

"And I'm glad to see it turned out better for him than for Joseph of the Old Testament," she chuckled.

"Well, maybe that's because I never gave him any fancy coats," Ezra stated in jest. "Besides, he was named after Joseph Smith, not the one in Egypt."

After a moment of thought, he returned to the earlier subject at hand, "I worry about her setting store by the likes of boys who treat her the way Alvin does. She deserves so much better than them." He looked back out the window as Mary strolled away from the drummer's wagon.

"Edith and I miss having her around," he said, "and so do her brothers and sisters."

"Oh, for Pete's sake, Ezra," Sarah scolded. "You're only a couple of miles down the road. You can come up and see her anytime you like. You shouldn't be so sad over this."

"I know, but it's still not the same as having her under my roof," he said, "and I worry for her."

"She's doing fine up here with Joseph and Francis. They are taking great care of her, and she is taking great care of their children, Christina and Little Joseph."

"Yes," he admitted, "but it isn't in me to not worry over her until she's married off, and I know she has a man, giving her his attention and protection."

"Just like if she was still living with you?" Sarah commented.

"Exactly."

"You should hang around a little longer," Sarah suggested, "and stop by their house for supper. Spend a little more time with them, especially your grandchildren, before you head back to Mt. Carmel."

"I'd like to, but I promised Edith I'd be home in time for supper," he replied. "Maybe we can come up and visit one of these weekends…"

"I'm sure they'd enjoy that."

Ezra turned his attention to a saddle he had his eye on and

examined it. He thought how nice it would be to have a new one that did not have rotted fleece and broken tie strings, like his old one did. With the life that was still in it though, he could not justify the added expense of a new one…at least not at this time. Maybe he should bring it in and have it fixed.

"Hi, Papa," Mary said as she walked through the door. "I thought I might find you eyeing that new saddle."

"Hi, Sweet Pea, how are you and your brother doing? How're Francis and the children faring?"

"We're all doing well," she responded, "you just missed him."

"I saw the two of you visiting through the window."

"We weren't visiting through the window," she teased him.

"You know what I mean," he scolded lightly. "I was looking through the window when I saw you and Joseph come out of the store and visit on the walkway for a few minutes."

"Yes, we had a lovely visit. It was such a nice day for it that we just had to enjoy the warmth. As a matter of fact, it was so warm this morning, I couldn't resist going up the canyon to study."

"I know you've always loved that," Ezra replied. "I also know a lot of the other kids around town like to do that too. Did you see anyone else up there?"

"No, not today, it was just me. That suited me fine, since I was in a reflective mood and wanted to be alone."

"What is it that has you so reflective today?" he asked her.

She paused for a breath and to decide how much she wanted to reveal to him at this moment, "I have a poem to write for graduation, so I was thinking about the events of the last year and all I've been through."

"The hollow does seem like a nice place to go think and study," he admitted.

"It reminds me of home," she stated, "without all the noise of brothers and sisters of course."

There was a moment of silence between them as neither was sure what to say.

"Well...I guess I best be going on back home," he finally said, a little discomforted. "Mother's expecting me for supper."

"Will you be sure and tell her I love her?" Mary asked. "And please tell her Joseph and the family are doing well. I would hate for her to worry."

"I'll be sure to do that," Ezra assured her.

He stepped closer to her and gave her a sideways one-armed hug and a kiss on the forehead.

Ezra truly did love her deeply, but he was from a hard generation that refused to show too much emotion, especially in public. That led to the awkward moment of silence between them; he desperately wanted to show her how much he loved her, but could not do it. His upbringing would not allow it. Maybe if he had been able to show more emotion toward her, things would have turned out differently, but then again, maybe not.

"Come home and visit us one of these weekends soon, will you?" he asked her. "How would that be?"

"I'd love to do that, Papa," she said as she wrapped her arm in his, standing next to him. "Final examinations begin next Monday, and it will be nice to have a break from studying. Maybe I will slip over for supper one night this week to clear my head. Besides, you never know, after graduation, you may have me back in your house again whether you like it or not."

"We'll do whatever we need to," he said. "It's what we do."

He briefly dropped his guard and looked lovingly at her for a moment.

Clearly, Mary had something else she wanted to say to him, but she remained silent. This was not the place to carry on that conversation, nor was it the kind of topic they ever talked about.

It would have to wait until she went home and could confide in her mother first.

Ezra, as men tend to be, was completely oblivious that Mary had more on her mind than exams. He had no idea she was keeping a deep secret.

Ezra turned to Sarah and tipped his hat as he started to the door, "Afternoon, Sister Foote."

With one last quick smile toward Mary, he walked out of the saddle shop and mounted his horse. Turning it south to go home, he walked him down the road. Mary stood at the window and watched him ride away. She was saddened as she left and fought back the urge to weep.

"That's a lovely locket," Sarah said, suddenly gaining her attention.

Unconsciously, Mary reached up, touched the locket around her neck, and smiled. "It *is* lovely, isn't it?"

Sarah smiled and playfully said, "And who would give you such a lovely gift, Miss Stevens?"

Mary's smile continued as she contemplated the answer, "The drummer at the wagon..."

"Oh, does he fancy you?" she asked, as if she had not watched the earlier exchange between them.

"I don't know...," Mary said as she took a moment to relive the conversation and contemplate Sarah's question. "He's sweet, but I hardly know him. He travels around so much, and he lives up to Monroe. That's two counties to the north and seems so far away."

"Your father seems to think he does."

"Father has always been a little overprotective," Mary said, more intently than she had intended as she slightly blushed. Perhaps she liked the drummer, or at least his attentions, more than she had realized.

"Now, now Mary," Sarah cautioned, "he just wants what's best for you. He has your protection and best interests at heart, even if he has trouble showing it."

"I know he does," Mary conceded, "but I'm afraid I'm going to make mistakes, and that he's not going to like it."

"Like Alvin?"

A shocked look of horror crossed over Mary's face; suddenly her secret was out.

"I saw how he ignored you as he walked right by you, and then went directly over to Mamie. Don't waste another thought on the likes of that boy. You deserve better than him, much better."

Mary's face and body relaxed; her secret was still safe, at least for the moment. "Yes, he's a mistake all right."

"You have a long life yet to live, young lady," Sarah advised, "and it's important you always learn from your mistakes."

Mary smiled uncomfortably at her comment but said nothing.

"Now, what do you say about me walking you home?" Sarah asked, more as a statement than an actual question.

Mary smiled more comfortably this time as they walked out of the saddle shop.

Six-year-old Darlene was lying in her bed, holding her precious cloth baby doll in a motherly way. Slowly, her bedroom door opened and her mother, Alice stepped in. Darlene was obviously having a difficult time getting to sleep, try as she might.

"You have a visitor, sweetie," she said. "Are you feeling well enough?"

Darlene looked beyond her loving mother into the hallway as Mary stepped into the room.

"Mary!" Darlene said excitedly. "I'm so happy to see you!"

Alice smiled at the exchange and stepped out of the room as she closed the door.

Mary walked to the side of her bed, leaned in, and gave Darlene a kiss on the forehead and a big hug.

"I thought you'd never get here," Darlene said in dramatic exasperation. "I've been waiting FOR-EVER."

"Sorry, little lady," Mary apologized. "I was helping Francis with Christina. I came as soon as I could get away."

"I'm glad you're here now," Darlene informed her. "I haven't been feeling well, so Mama and Papa kept me home. Did you play with Christina for me?"

"I sure did," Mary responded with enthusiasm. "We played knucklebones and talked to a boy."

"Yuck!" Darlene said again in dramatic exasperation. "Why did you do that?"

"Some day, when you're older, you may think differently," Mary promised her, "and we can talk more about it then."

"I don't think so," Darlene said with conviction. "Boys are awful."

"Yes," Mary responded with a tender smile, "boys are awful. Let's get you tucked in and off to sleep."

"I've tried to sleep," Darlene assured her, "but I've been having too hard of a time doing it. I'm never going to be able to sleep again."

"Really?" Mary asked with mock concern.

"I hear noises in the dark," she responded, "and they won't let me get to sleep."

Darlene beckoned her to move in closer, so she could whisper into her ear.

"I think a monster lives under my bed."

"Oh, sweetheart," Mary said as she wrapped her arm around

her, "you have nothing to worry about. There aren't any monsters in Orderville but, if it helps, I have just the thing for you."

"You do?" Darlene asked with wide eyes, full of anticipation.

"Yep," Mary nodded, "a lullaby. It was written especially to keep little girls safe from monsters."

Darlene smiled broadly and deeply as Mary tucked her in. She scooted to the other side of the bed and turned onto her side. Mary lay on the bed next to her and gently stroked Darlene's hair. She began to sing a slow lullaby to the tune of Amazing Grace.

> "It's time for sleep, my precious one,
> "It's time to drift away,
> "Lay down your head and dream of God,
> "And wake another day."

Mary continued with the second verse as she noticed Darlene was lying very still.

> "May angels come and sleep by you,
> "And keep you safe tonight,
> "And always stay and comfort you,
> "Until the morning light."

Darlene was fast asleep and breathing deeply.

Mary slowly sat up next to her and looked down at her lovingly. As she watched the sleeping youngster, she drifted off deep in thought, thinking about her own future. A solitary tear rolled down her face. After a moment, she wiped it from her cheek and smiled once more at little Darlene as she slept.

"How was school today?" Joseph asked as his sister walked in the door.

"Ciphering, reading, history…the usual," she answered. "With exams coming up next week, we are spending a lot of time in review. We tend to spend as much time at the chalkboard figuring out answers as we do in our seats. So, to answer your question, it was as fine as it could be with all that."

"Well, it will all be over soon," Francis consoled her through the open doorway as she kneaded dough in the kitchen.

She wiped the flour from her hands on her apron and walked to the doorway where she leaned against the jamb.

"Will you stay here in town with us when you're done, or will you go back to your folks?" she asked.

"I haven't been able to catch the eye of any of the young men around here yet," Mary confided, "so I don't know what I will do."

"Now that I'm pregnant again and getting ready to have another baby," Francis began, "we certainly could use the extra help, if you wanted to stay."

"Yes, that's right," Joseph added. "Even if we weren't expecting our third child, you would be welcome to stay."

"I may have to do that for a while, at least until Francis has the baby. Then I may have to move to St. George to find someone to marry."

"You could go north to Panguitch or Richfield," Joseph added. "I'm sure there are a lot of good and righteous men up there who would love to have you for a wife."

"You'd have me going all the way up to Salt Lake before long," she said in mock exasperation, "just to marry me off."

"Oh, don't be silly," he teased in return, "I'd be happy with you going to Provo."

"Enough you two," Francis interjected. "Joseph, you go

check for eggs, and Mary, why don't you come in here and visit with me while I finish up dinner?"

"Is there no one here in the valley you have an interest in?" Francis asked her, after Joseph left the house.

"I've thrown looks at Jackie Adler, Hyrum Mower, and Alvin Heaton, among others, but none of them seem to notice or take me seriously."

"I certainly hope you're talking about Alvin Jr." Francis said with feigned concern. "It certainly wouldn't be appropriate if you were ogling Alvin Sr. He already has two wives."

"It would certainly be acceptable," she countered sardonically, "if the government hadn't spent so much time and energy to bring an end to polygamy. Then I would have a much better chance of finding someone; it wouldn't matter if he were already married or not. That way, I could throw looks at both the son and his father and see who I could catch. I guess I was just born twenty years too late."

"You'll find someone who is right for you," Francis assured her, "I know it."

"What is it you know?" Joseph asked, returning with a wire basket full of brown eggs.

"That there is a man out there waiting for Mary, just like there was for me," Francis informed him.

"That's right," Joseph assured her. "Francis was older than you are now when we met. Don't lose heart; you'll find him."

"I certainly hope so," Mary replied. "I hate the thought of spending my whole life wondering why I couldn't find him. I don't like being alone and would certainly love to have a husband around."

"We would all like that for you, dear," Francis assured her. "How are your studies coming along? Will you be ready for your exams next week?"

"I do believe I will. However, I should go and study now for a while. I've been asked to write a poem and present it at the graduation ceremony, and I haven't even started. I need to go and think on it for a while and see if I can't decide what I want to say. It sure would be embarrassing if I got up in front of everybody and didn't have a thing to read to them."

"Best of luck to you then," Francis said. "I'll let you know when dinner is ready."

A bunch of the older kids had a chicken roast out at the mouth of Gardner Hollow the Sunday night before the killing happened. I think everyone was there except Mary. These were common occurrences, both to have a chicken roast and not to include her. Nobody knew it at the time, but this was the last night of normal innocence our town would ever have. After that, we would be stained forever with the crimson memory that a horrible crime had been committed in our small piece of Zion. However, we did everything to avoid talking about it or admitting it ever happened in later years.

"I sure hope you're planning to take me to the roast tomorrow night," Mamie said to Alvin as they walked along the street.

"Hmmm," Alvin said, to throw her off track, "I'm not sure who I'm going to ask to go with me. There are so many available girls here in town, I may have to line them up and look them over before I choose."

"You want to ask Mary, don't you?" Mamie teased.

"Hmmm," Alvin said again.

"Tell me you're not really thinking about taking her," Mamie demanded, suddenly worried he may not be teasing her anymore.

"Oh, don't be so dramatic," Alvin laughed a hard-edged laugh, "I wouldn't be caught dead out in public with her, and I know you girls feel about the same way. Of course, you'll be going with me. Who else would I take other than my best girl?"

"I'd better be your only girl, Alvin Heaton, or we'll be having some harsh words. I've not given you my heart lightly, so you better take care of it."

"Easy, girl," Alvin cautioned, "you'll get yourself all worked up into a lather. What say I take you over to the Co-op and buy you some hard rock candy?"

"If you keep treating me like a horse, I'm going to kick you until you're senseless," she warned him with a menacing smile. "But as long as you're offering, who am I to disappoint when sweets are involved."

"That's why you'll always be my sweetheart."

"You're not nearly as funny as you think you are," she warned. "One day, you'll really hurt my feelings if you keep joking around like that. You need to tell me you love me because I'm a wonderful person, not tease me about other girls or talk to me like I'm an animal."

"Even if I like animals more than many of the people around here?" he asked somewhat teasing and somewhat seriously.

"There you go again. Now you're going to have to buy me a full bag of candy to make it up to me. Then you're going to have to promise me that I'm the only one you want to take to the chicken roast."

"I'll buy you as much candy as you want," he smiled. "You know my uncles work there and will get us whatever we want."

They walked a few more steps in silence and then, as they reached the base of the steps leading up to the entrance, Alvin stopped and turned to Mamie.

"Yes, of course, I will be taking you to the roast," he said with a warm smile. "There is no other girl I have any interest in, only you. We may joke around a lot, but you are the one who has my heart, and I love you."

"You better, mister. Everyone in town is expecting us to get married, including me."

Suddenly Mamie heard her father call from across the road.

"Mamie girl," he called, "I need you to come home for a spell and tend to some chores while I run out to the north pastureland."

"Yes, Papa," she said, "I'll be right there."

She turned back to Alvin and said, "Looks like you'll have to go in there and buy that hard candy alone. You'll just have to bring it to the roast and give it to me there. Can you come calling on me later?"

"I have to tend to the cows and sheep later tonight, but I will see you in church tomorrow," he replied. "Goodnight."

"Tomorrow, then," she smiled warmly at him. She leaned in closely and said, "I wish I could hug and kiss you right here in front of all these people."

"Me too," he responded. "Too bad it's not appropriate."

She pulled back and trotted off after her father on their way home.

"Have fun mucking stalls," she shot back over her shoulder.

Alvin smiled and stepped up onto the Co-op landing and entered the store.

"Hello, Alvin," Edward Carroll said as he saw him walk through the door. "What happened to Mamie? Didn't I just see you two through the window, walking over here?"

"Yeah, but her father called her home for chores just as we got to the door. I promised her I would get her some hard candy, so don't let me forget before I leave. I also have a hankering for some of those candy coated peanuts with popcorn; remind me to get a bag of those too."

"I'll be glad to sell you those when you're ready to leave."

"Thank you, Uncle Edward," Alvin replied.

"What else brings you in here then?"

"I made a trade with Johnny Healy the other day," Alvin began. "I swapped him a deck of playing cards to use his revolver at the next roundup, so I could shoot rabbits. I need to pick up some shells, so I can practice before that."

"Sure, do you want a whole box or just a few cartridges to hold you over?"

"Six will do right nice for the time being. I didn't bring enough money with me for candy, peanuts, and a lot of shells. I'll get some now and buy more when we get closer to the roundup. These will give me a chance to get a feel for the gun."

"Sure enough, son," Edward agreed. "What caliber do you need?"

"Johnny's gun is a Smith and Wesson .38, so give me six of those."

"Of course," Edward said, "let me open up a box here. Are you going to the roast with Mamie tomorrow night?"

"Yes, and I thought I would do a little target practicing while we were there."

"Ah, showing off for the girls," Edward chuckled, "or at least for one girl in particular. A time-honored tradition ever since there were girls and boys in the same vicinity. I wouldn't be surprised if Adam spent much of his time trying to figure out how to show off for Eve while they were tending the garden."

"Like the rooster pheasants out in the field, wouldn't you say?"

"Just like that," Edward agreed. He reached under the counter and retrieved an unopened box of cartridges. "Let's see, six you said, correct?"

"That's right."

"Okay, one, two, three…ah, four, five, and six," he counted as he pulled them out of the box and set them out on the counter. "Okay, here you go, six .38 caliber cartridges."

"Alvin!" Hyrum Mower called as he and Jackie Adler walked into the store. "We've been looking for you."

"Hey, guys. I'm just buying some cartridges for target practice tomorrow night at the roast," Alvin said with a smile. "Why were you looking for me?"

"We're headed down to the crick to do a little fishing and came to see if you wanted to come along," Hyrum said. "Maybe we could plan some kind of prank for tomorrow's roast."

"I'd love to, guys, but I have to go home and tend to the animals. Mother would have my hide if I took off fishing before I got done chorin'. You two go on without me, but I'll see you in church tomorrow and then later at the chicken roast."

"I didn't know you had a gun," Jackie commented as he looked at the bullets on the counter.

"Borrowed it from Johnny the other day for the roundup…swapped him a deck of cards for it. I'll give it back to him as soon as it's over."

"Do you get your cards back from him when you do?" Hyrum asked. "That's about the only thing that keeps us entertained on boring days."

"I suppose so," Alvin responded. "To be honest with you, I never gave it much thought. I guess I could always get another deck from Uncle Edward, if I don't."

"Maybe Johnny'll bring them to the roast," Hyrum said, "and we can play with them for a while."

"You can play with them all you want," Alvin said, "I'll be busy with Mamie. She'll have us visiting with all the other girls there, all night long. I'll be lucky to get away to do any target practicing."

"We can try and help with that," Jackie stated. "We know how a guy needs time to do his target practice."

"No, it wouldn't do to be a bad shot when you're hunting rabbits," Hyrum added.

"Come on, we'll walk you back home on our way to get our fishing gear," Jackie suggested. "We can make some more plans for tomorrow night."

"Sure, let's go," Alvin said as he grabbed the shells from the counter and started to follow them out.

"Before you go," Edward said, "you're not done here yet."

"Huh?" Alvin stopped and turned back around.

The other two young men continued out the door.

"Your hard candy and candy coated peanuts," Edward reminded him. "Plus you need to leave me some money. I don't think your father would be too happy if I put it on his account."

"See?" Alvin said. "That's why I told you to make sure I didn't leave without them. Those two boys get me sidetracked easier than slipping on the ice in wintertime. How much do I owe you?"

"Two cents apiece for the shells, and a penny each for the hard candy and peanuts. Be careful with that gun out there; I would hate to face your father if anything happened. He would not be too happy with me for selling you the shells."

"I've hunted with you plenty," Alvin defended, "and I've always been careful."

"I know, that's why I'm selling them to you now," Edward said. "I'm just saying, be careful, that's all."

"Fourteen cents," Alvin said, as he counted out the change and slid it across the counter to his uncle. "Mamie owes you a debt of gratitude for reminding me about her candy. I'll make sure she knows it was you who reminded me to get it for her."

"I don't need any credit, son," Edward commented. "I know it's important that we keep our women happy. A lesson for you that would be well learned. Be off with you now."

"I'll put it in my memory and keep it locked away, so I don't forget it. I've got to run, but thanks again," Alvin said over his shoulder as he walked out the door to join his friends.

"Get all squared away with the Co-op there, did ya, Alvin?" Jackie asked.

"That I did. It wouldn't do to owe the store when my uncle runs it, especially when he is the Justice of the Peace in town. I'd end up in the pokey for sure."

"Naw," Jackie corrected him, "he would just take it out of your hide in lashes. Come to think of it, I wouldn't mind being around for that."

"Some friend you are," Alvin spat in pretended anger. "I hope you never have to defend me in any trials, I'd surely hang."

"Relax, my boy," Jackie said, "it would never come to that. You are too well connected throughout the county for anything bad to ever happen to you."

"I'd defend you if it came to that," Hyrum said. "I'd swear to your innocence."

"What if he's not so innocent?" Jackie asked. "Then what?"

"I'd still testify on his behalf. Alvin's been too good of a friend to leave him hanging in the wind."

"That sounds rather scary," Alvin chuckled, "but I guess it makes me feel better that I have your support."

"Go take care of your chores, ol' boy, and we'll go down to the crick and get some fishin' done," Jackie said, feeling the need to be on his way.

"Yeah, and I need to get to them before mother comes after me with father's razor strop. I'll see you two tomorrow at the roast."

"Unless you see us in church first," Hyrum said.

"Of course."

"I don't know why I'm so excited to go tonight," Mamie said as she and Alvin walked arm in arm to the roast. "Things just feel different this evening for some reason."

On a subconscious level, she believed this was a turning point in their relationship. Not that Alvin was going to propose marriage to her but, with graduating from school, perhaps he would decide it was time. If you asked her to explain her feelings, she honestly would not be able to do it. Sometimes, folks just get a feeling. Maybe, part of her excitement was knowing that only the upper class kids in town were invited to the roast, and she would not have to deal with the inferiors, such as Mary.

"You're sure in a good mood tonight," Alvin commented, "maybe I'll have to try and kiss you a little later."

"You will do no such thing, Alvin Heaton," she protested. "It would not do to have anyone in town see us kissing without a proper chaperone."

"I completely agree," he chuckled, "we need to make sure no one sees us."

"That's not what I meant, and you know it. We must observe proper decorum until we are married."

"I didn't want anything beyond a few simple kisses," he defended, "but if it's that important to you, then I'm happy to wait."

"I see we're the last ones here," Mamie said as they arrived in the hollow. "What do you want to do first?"

"I don't know, maybe a little target practice before we eat."

"From what I can see, the chicken looks like it's about ready," she observed as they walked closer.

They walked over to where Sally and Hyrum were laboring over the fire.

"How's dinner coming along?" Mamie asked as they watched. "Is there anything we can do to help?"

"Grab some water out of the jug and a plate from the buggy, and let's eat," Sally said, as she and Hyrum both straightened up from the fire. "We are ready to go."

"All right, everybody gather around," Hyrum called to the others. "Food's all cooked and ready for eatin'. We just need a blessing on it before we dig in and devour. Hey, Etna, what's the chance we can get you to say the prayer and get us going."

"I'd be glad to."

Everybody bowed their heads as she pronounced a fine yet simple blessing over the food, and then as soon as she was done, they all started to eat.

"Now this is what I call timing," Alvin whispered to Mamie. "We no sooner arrived here than they started serving us food. I could stand going to a few more parties like this."

"You know I hate to be late," she whispered back, "but you're right, this did turn out quite nice for us. I was sure hungry and ready to eat."

They all ate as much as they could and then sat back and visited for a while. As the sun went down and the sky started to darken, Alvin pulled out the .38 caliber Smith and Wesson and proceeded to make a show of target practicing. He walked down and set a large branch between two trees, then walked back to where the other kids were talking, and visited with them for a moment. He moved a safe distance away from them, took a single shot at the branch, then returned to the group and continued in the conversation. He visited with the group again for several minutes and then stepped away and fired another shot.

Once again, he returned to the group and the conversation. He spent the rest of the night by the fireside, visiting Mamie and friends, until they all went home for the night.

Everyone had a good time, and no one got hurt.

Chapter Three
The Deed

The first day of exams for graduation started on Monday, April 20. The school kids worked hard in the morning as they were given different problems in arithmetic. Many of them were fairly simple, but to separate out the better students, they became more and more difficult.

Mary did about the same as the other students on the simple ones, but she was able to excel and to show her skill on the harder ones. I remember how pleased she looked with herself when she left the building at midday. My end of the year exams were more difficult for me than hers seemed to be for her, but maybe that's because I did not get as much time to study out tending sheep.

I was outside the schoolhouse when she came out that afternoon, and she seemed to be in a particularly good mood. She skipped for a few steps as she reached the ground, so I figured she must have done quite well. There were still a lot of other students in the schoolyard at the time, but I seemed to be the only one to notice her come out. Alvin and Mamie were sitting together under the cottonwood tree reading from their schoolbooks. Mary was wrapped up in her own delight, enough that she did not seem to notice them or any of the other students for that matter. As I was whittling on a stick, I watched as she walked up the road toward her brother's place, and then I lost sight of her.

"Hi, Francis, I'm home," Mary called out as she walked into her brother's house a little after four o'clock. "How are the kids?"

Francis, three months pregnant, was in the kitchen when Mary came in. She had just finished making sandwiches. She had a bundle for Joseph, wrapped up in flour-sack cloth on the cutting board and was in the process of wrapping Mary's in another one.

She handed the bundle to her. "I thought you might like something to eat as you're working on your examinations. Here is a sandwich and two cookies to keep your energy up. I have some for Joseph here, too. He's out working in the garden area, and I have to run it out to him. He's trying to get it ready to plant, now that the weather has warmed up a bit."

"Thank you for lunch," Mary replied, "I became powerful hungry during that last hour of the test. I'm planning on taking the afternoon off and going up the canyon to study. I can run his food out to him on my way."

"That would be wonderful. Little Joseph made such a mess while I was baking, that it will take me 'til summer to get it all cleaned up. Are you going up to The Point by Gardner Hollow?"

"Same as always," Mary confirmed. "None of the other students mentioned anything about going, so I should have plenty of time to study without interruption."

"Are you going to spend all that time studying up there?"

"Well, since it is warming up so well, I thought I might sneak in a nap so I don't get too bored with studies," Mary told her. "And who knows, I may take a walk up the hollow, just to clear my head."

"Be sure and tell your brother where you are going when you get out there. It wouldn't do to have him worry about you."

"He is a protective one, isn't he?" Mary noted. "It's nice to know I have him so close, and he will do whatever he has to, to make sure I'm safe."

"Safe and loved," Francis added. "I know you've had your struggles with the town, and my cousin Alvin and his girlfriend haven't made it any easier. No matter what happens with them, always know that your brother and I love you very much, and you are always welcome in our home. I know Alice and many of the other women in town think very highly of you. Now that you'll be done with school, I'm sure you'll find things will become better."

"Thank you, sister," Mary said with great appreciation. "Things may be looking up in that regard."

"Oh, really?" Francis asked with great interest. "Pray tell, and don't leave out any detail."

"I'll know more for sure later on, so I'll wait to fill you in on everything then," Mary said tentatively. "I would hate to speak out of turn, and then not have things work out the way I hope."

"Is that why you seem to be in such a good mood today?" Francis asked. "I thought it was because the weather had turned for the better."

"Yes, and it could be very exciting. I can't wait to tell you all about it, but like I said, I need to wait until I actually have something to tell you."

"Fair enough," Francis said with understanding. "I'll wait with great anticipation to hear your girl secret, when you can finally tell me about it."

"It will be worth the wait, *sister.*"

"I'm glad we're family and will always be sisters," Francis said. "Now run along and take this to Joseph, before he falls over faint for lack of food."

"He's too strong for that," Mary chuckled, "but I'm ready to go. I'll see you later this evening."

"Any idea how late you'll be?"

"I might be back too late for dinner, so don't wait on me," Mary instructed her. "There's a chance I may be going back into town for a bit when I'm done at The Point."

"That doesn't sound like you," Francis said with a cryptic smile. "Could this have something to do with what we were just talking about?"

"It could," Mary said without further explanation.

She gathered up and bundled her brother's lunch. Smartly, she turned around and, with her books in her arms and her hat with the blue ribbon on her head, walked out the door. She walked up behind Joseph as he worked on clearing his irrigation ditch with a shovel. She stopped beside him to watch while he finished cleaning out some debris.

When he finished, he stood up to face her and leaned on his shovel.

"I'm going up to The Point to do some studying and take a break from the exams. I've been doing quite well, but I want some time to clear my head before I finish them tomorrow."

"Sounds like a fine idea," he said. "Study hard. I'll see you when you get back. Watch out for lions, tigers, and alligators."

"Oh, you're funny," Mary scowled. "You know we don't have any of those around here."

"You know we have mountain lions," he reminded her. "Well, regardless, be careful."

I saw Mary up at the Point as I walked to the fields beyond town. I waved as she glanced down and my dog, Griz, ran part way up to investigate. Satisfied she was not a sheep or a threat, he trotted back to walk by my side once again.

While the rest of the townsfolk went about their business that afternoon, I tended the family sheep. It was a pleasant afternoon and the sheep were in no hurry to go anywhere. I think they were just happy to have a warm afternoon. My dog slept beside me, except when he lazily lifted his head to watch the sheep for a moment. When he was sure they were settled and he did not have to round up any strays, he put his head back down.

Suddenly, two shots in the distance broke the silence, and the sound reverberated throughout the hollow. Griz's head shot up and he looked in their direction. After a short pause, a third shot rang out and he stood up. Then finally, a fourth shot caused him to give a short bark. There was a man and a woman further down closer to town who looked around after the shots, but they were far enough away that there's no way they could tell for sure what they were, or that they even heard anything. I was the only one close enough to hear them and to know what they were.

Slowly and without alarm, I looked over toward the hollow, thought about it for a moment, and turned to Griz. "I wonder who's out hunting." Griz looked at me but did not say anything as he lay back down. It made me figure that he didn't know either.

Since hunting was very common…and murder was not…I did not give the shots a second thought. Well, maybe a second one as I wished I could be off hunting too instead of tending sheep.

I figured Griz felt the same way.

Early the next morning, Joseph walked into his house after working in the garden. He rinsed his hands in the basin and wiped them on the white flour-sack dishtowel hanging by the door. Francis was making breakfast, while Christina and Joseph played in the other room. She had flour all over the side of her face from making biscuits. It made Joseph chuckle.

"I sure love you," he said as he used the towel to wipe her face clean.

"Thank you, honey," she said after he was done.

"Mary up, yet?" he asked. "I'd like to know how her studies went last night."

"She didn't come home last night, I noticed," she responded. "Her bed was still made up this morning."

"She probably spent the night with girlfriends again or walked over to Mt. Carmel to stay with the folks. I'll check in on her at school when I drop down to the Co-op."

"You're probably right," Francis agreed. "I know she's had a hard time with some of the kids here in town, so I'm glad she has a couple of girlfriends who treat her well. I know Mary is smart, and she really helps the others with their studies."

"You don't think they're being nice to her just because she can help them get good grades, do you?"

"No, of course not," Francis replied. "They are genuinely good girls, and are the few who have always treated her well. For now, however, gather up your children in the front room and bring them into breakfast."

"What if they don't want to come?" Joseph joked. "What do I do then?"

"How much grief can a five and three-year-old give you?" she chuckled in return.

Joseph walked into the other room as he laughed, scooped up his young son in his arms then reached down and took his daughter's hand. They all walked together back into the kitchen.

Later that morning, down at the schoolhouse, Joseph quietly stepped into the building. David Smith was officiating the exams and looked up as he saw Joseph.

"Sorry to interrupt, David," Joseph began as he looked around the room, "I just stopped by to chat with Mary for a moment. I don't see her here; didn't she make it in this morning?"

"Sorry, I haven't seen her yet." He turned to the rest of the class and asked, "Has anyone seen Mary this morning?"

Everyone in class, including Alvin and Mamie, shook their heads.

"We've not seen her yet, sir," one of the students said.

We all thought for a moment, but none of us could come up with any ideas. The gunshots I heard the evening before never even entered my mind.

"Sorry, Joseph," David said, "nobody's seen her. Everything all right?"

"Oh sure, she's probably down to the folks," he said, dismissing any concern. "I'd imagine she'll be in soon to finish up her exams. No need to worry."

"We'll keep an eye out for her," David promised. "If any of us see her, I'll send a runner over to let you know. Merlin here is pretty fast; maybe I'll send him."

I felt mighty pleased to be singled out like that.

"I'd be much obliged if you would do that. I'm going to run over to the Co-op and use their telephone to ring the folks. I'm sure that's where she ended up."

He gave David and the students a half wave as he turned and left the room. He crossed the street and walked down the road to the store. Wilford Heaton was minding the store when he entered.

Joseph set a handful of change on the counter. "Need to use the telephone, Wilford."

"I imagine the operator is up and working this morning," Wilford said. "Give her a try."

Joseph walked over to the phone on the back wall and picked up the earpiece. He rattled the receiver hook a few times and then waited for a response.

"Yes, Ellie, this is Joseph Stevens over to the Orderville Co-op store... Oh, yes, I guess you would know where I'm calling from. Yes, anyway, this is Joseph and I need you to ring my folks over there to Mt. Carmel... No, I would imagine there is someone over there, minding the store this morning who will answer the call. Pa's probably out working the flock, but Ma should be home to go over and get the call.... Yes, I'll wait on the line."

After he stopped talking for a moment, Wilford asked him, "Everything all right?"

"Sure, Wilford, I'm just checking in. Trying to track Mary down and see how her studies went last night."

"Where did she study at?" Wilford asked him.

"Up the Hollow."

"What time did she come down?"

"That's just it, I don't know," Joseph said, still without concern.

"How's the garden coming along? Are you getting ready to plant?"

"It's still early, but it's coming together right nice. I think I'm a little short on corn seed, so I may come back..."

There was a slight pause as he listened to Ellie announcing the arrival of his father on the other end and then he spoke.

"Hey, Pa, did Mary stay out to your place last night?"

There was another pause as he listened to his father's response.

"No, probably at a girlfriend's. See you this weekend."

With a slightly puzzled look, Joseph returned the earpiece to the receiver hook. After a momentary pause, he turned to walk out.

"Thank you, Wilford. Let me know if I owe you any more for the call," he said as he walked out the door.

"Of course she came down from the hollow, Wilford," Joseph carried on an argument with himself that never happened as he walked up to the Point. "What do you think, that she spent the night up there? That's absurd. Unless of course…she studied real hard and real long and just fell asleep."

He reached the Point where he knew Mary had gone, stopped, and looked around.

He was an experienced hunter, and the first thing he did was crouch down on his heels and take in the scene. There was the trail leading up to the Point from near his house. It was the one Mary took up the day before. There was also another trail that converged with it from another part of town. He looked over to where he knew Mary liked to sit as she read her books or to look over town. He looked out toward the town and again talked to himself as he processed the situation.

"This is what she would have seen while she sat here. You can see the road going north for several miles and right down into the middle of town, before the side hill blocks your view." He stood back up and walked over to where Mary had sat and looked at her tracks as he separated them out.

"Okay, I see you walked up the trail a bit. How far did you go?" He started to follow her tracks for a little while, until they merged with the other trail…and another set.

"What's this, girl, another set of tracks?" He paused as he considered them. "Boy's tracks… Did you arrange to meet someone up here, or did he stumble upon you?"

He continued to follow the tracks up the hill and into the hollow. The two sets of tracks, Mary's and the other person's, walked side-by-side, not single file, so he knew they were walking together at the time. It would appear she knew this boy, who was likely in our small town.

"Who is this you're walking with? Was this a pre-planned meeting? It's obvious you know this boy or at least trust him."

By walking along the side of the trail so he did not disturb the tracks, he followed them into Gardner Hollow to a wide spot in the trail. When he arrived, he found large pools of blood that had soaked into the sandy soil.

"Oh, dear…."

He looked around quickly but could not make sense of the confused and scrambled tracks. It was obvious some kind of altercation had happened there but, from the visible evidence, he could not tell what. Careful not to obscure any of the tracks, he trotted back toward town beside the trail. When the ground leveled out, he started to run and soon made it back to the Co-op store.

Wilford was out front sweeping the boardwalk.

Out of breath, Joseph gasped, "Wilford, something terrible happened up in the hollow. You're the constable; I need you to gather up a posse so we can go back up and look."

"What is it, Joseph?" Wilford asked, confused. "What's happened?"

"I don't know for sure," he answered, still gasping for breath, "but there's an awful lot of blood up there, and I'm scared it might be Mary's."

"Are you sure it's not from an animal?" Wilford inquired before he got excited.

"Yes. There were no other signs typically associated with harvesting wild game, and there were no animal tracks up there."

"Okay, let's get everybody gathered up."

Wilford called on Justice of the Peace, Edward Carroll, and Nevin Luke to help find her.

Jackie Adler and Hyrum Mower stood in the background behind the Co-op where they liked to play cards, but made no move to help.

Wilford turned back to Nevin, "Go get Wallace Adair and David Esplin; come back and join us…quickly!"

Nevin immediately ran to where he knew he could find the two men working, informed them of the situation as best as he knew, and took them to meet up with Wilford at the Co-op. Once all was ready, they started back toward the hollow at a jog. When they reached the trail, they too were mindful to stay away from the tracks and not run over the top of them. When they arrived at the clearing where the blood-soaked sand was, they stopped and looked to Wilford and Joseph for direction.

"Spread out from here and look for anything that will tell us what happened to Mary," Wilford instructed, "but be careful not to disturb any signs that might tell us what transpired here."

Suddenly, David called out, "Hey, over here."

The five men rushed over to his side where he stood above a small ravine filled with dirt and brush. There they could see a dust-covered blue ribbon sticking out of the dirt.

"That looks like…" Joseph began, but panic choked off any further comment.

"Everyone move back while I step down there," Wilford

commanded. "Let me see what we have here."

Joseph was overcome with absolute horror and could no longer stand back and wait. He lunged forward in hysterical panic. Wallace and David Esplin grabbed him in an effort to keep him from jumping down into the ravine. Wilford stepped down and carefully pulled on the ribbon. It did not come easily, so he began to clear the dirt away and dig down around it. As he cleared away the brush and debris, he uncovered a straw hat.

Instantly, Joseph became sick to his stomach.

"Oh, my, that's Mary's hat. Where is she...?" He could speak no more as heaves wracked his body.

Wilford quickly cleared away more brush and dirt and found a woman's body buried face down.

Wallace and David continued gently to hold Joseph, more to give him emotional support than physically restrain him from going down into the ravine. Truth be told, at this point, Joseph hardly had the ability to stand, let alone to fight and to jump down in the draw.

"Joseph," Wilford said tenderly, "come down and help get her out."

"I can't, Will, I don't have the strength."

"She needs you," he said. "Find the strength."

Joseph choked back the tears and stepped down into the ravine. Cautiously, he helped Wilford uncover Mary's body. They gently lifted her back up to where the other men were waiting and carefully laid her body on the ground.

"Brethren, you are now part of a coroner's inquest," Wilford stated in his role as constable. "This is now a legal proceeding. Take note of all the blood-soaked dirt caked to the back of her dress," he continued as he examined her. "Roll her on her side and let's examine the front and back together for a moment. I see blood on the front here too, but not as much as on her back. Lay her down on her chest, so we can clear away her dress and examine her back."

After they carefully moved her, Wilford unbuttoned the back of her dress and exposed her bare back, enough for them to see four bullet wounds.

Wilford touched each one with his right index finger as he slowly counted aloud for the record, "One…two…three…four. I count four bullet wounds in her back." Dirt from his finger mixed in with the tacky blood on her skin.

"Joseph,…," he paused for a long moment while the other men all stood silent, "Mary was murdered."

Unable to contain himself any longer, Joseph erupted into bitter tears. "Who could have done this?"

Edward turned toward David Esplin. "Quickly run into town and call Sheriff Brown down to Kanab. If he can leave right away, he can make it here by tonight."

"Yes, sir," David said. He ran down the mountain.

Edward turned back to the others, "Let's lift her gently and take her down the mountain."

"No," Joseph said quietly but with great determination, his strength returning, "I'll take her."

"As you wish," Edward acknowledged. "We'll walk along as you take her home."

An emotionally distraught, but eerily calm Joseph walked beside the trail back toward Orderville, cradling the body of his dead sister in his arms.

Townsfolk, including Alice and Sarah, had gathered near his house for any news of her discovery. They watched in a helpless state of complete and utter disbelief. Hyrum Mower and Jackie

Adler were among the onlookers as they were on their way from the Co-op. Alvin and Mamie were also present, as they walked arm in arm toward Hyrum and Jackie. The one person who was obviously not present was the drummer and his wagon.

Tears flowed down Joseph's calm face as he looked neither to the right nor to the left, but dead ahead without seeing where he was going. He was walking on pure instinct, using muscle memory to make the way back to his house. Behind him, at about a dozen yards, walked the remainder of the posse, respectfully and quietly. Joseph stumbled and fell to his knees. The posse hurried to his aid.

"No," he said. "I will do it."

Nevertheless, it was obvious to them he could not stand back up on his own. Two men lifted him by his upper arms while he continued to cradle his lifeless sister. Back on his feet, the posse again stood back for a moment to let him proceed. As they approached the house, Wilford quickened his pace so he could open the front door for Joseph.

The children were asleep and Francis was sitting quietly inside, mending a shirt when the door slowly opened. She looked up as Wilford stood aside to reveal Joseph with his younger sister in his arms. She covered her mouth, shocked. Quickly, she came to her senses and jumped to action, clearing off the kitchen table. Joseph carefully set Mary down, still cradling her head and torso against his chest.

He turned toward Francis but could not look her in the face. "I couldn't save her…" Tears started to choke off his words again, but he hoarsely fought through and whispered, "I couldn't keep her safe." He turned back to Mary as he continued to hold her, choking, "I'm so sorry, Mary…"

Sarah touched his hand. "Joseph…Joseph? You need to let her go, honey."

He refused to move, looking down toward the floor as if in a trance.

"Joseph?" she quietly whispered.

He slowly came out of his trance enough to look at her absently. Tears still streamed down his face as he opened his mouth to speak, but the words would not come. Finally, he nodded his head and tenderly laid Mary's lifeless body on the table. Intently, he stared at her for a moment, then gently cupped her face with his hand.

Sarah turned toward Wilford who stood a short distance away, watching with his hat in his hands. She motioned for him to come over and take Joseph.

He stepped over to Joseph and pressed his hand on Joseph's back. "Come along, son."

Joseph looked up at Wilford without moving.

Francis was frozen as she stood back out of the way. She watched the ordeal with the look of someone who was completely lost and had no idea of what to do.

Slowly and quietly, Joseph turned and, without a word, walked out the door.

Wilford quietly walked over and closed it behind him.

With him gone, Sarah turned to the kitchen counter, picked up the white enameled basin, and filled it with some water. She looked for a clean cloth to wash Mary.

Francis, suddenly realizing what Sarah was doing, reached into the cabinet and produced some clean white flour-sack-cloth towels.

Sarah took them back to the table and set them down. Carefully, she began to remove Mary's blood-soaked and dirt-encrusted clothes from her body. She stopped for a moment, once the clothing had been removed, and looked at the new locket around Mary's neck. She took it off and handed it to

Wilford.

"She got this from the drummer," she said and turned back to the pile of clothing she had just removed.

As she laid the clothes out on the floor, she discovered a .38 caliber bullet stuck in the still-wet blood of the clothes. She handed the bullet to Wilford. "This also might be from the drummer."

He took it and wiped the blood from it, placing it in his vest pocket along with the locket.

Sarah started to lovingly wash the dirt and dried blood from Mary's body.

"Oh, sweetheart," she said to herself and Mary, "this never should have happened to you."

Still in a partial daze, Joseph walked with determination into the Co-op and headed straight back to the phone without acknowledging anyone in the store. Ella Chamberlain was working behind the counter at the time. Knowing Joseph well, she simply watched him go by without comment, as he made the long walk across the floor to the telephone. By this time, everyone in the store knew something was happening, but no one knew what for sure.

No one approached him.

No one spoke.

Sitting in the background of the store were Alvin, Mamie, Hyrum, and Jackie, eating an early lunch. Not one of them made any movement when Joseph walked in.

He picked up the telephone's earpiece and harshly rattled the cradle.

"Ellie? Joseph Stevens. Ring my folks….Okay."

He hung up the phone and sat down on one of the cane-back bentwood ice cream parlor chairs. Everything about his posture and countenance said he was defeated. Still, no one approached him. He sat there for several minutes without moving, just staring at the floor.

The telephone finally rang. He stood up and answered it. "Joseph here….Mary's dead. You need to come right out…murdered."

The word "murdered" reverberated through the room, hitting each person with an unbelievable force.

He hung up the telephone and walked back out of the store without saying a word to anyone.

Greatly concerned, Ella watched him as he walked out the door. The others looked at each other in disbelief.

Ella muttered to herself under her breath, "Murdered? Here?"

Mamie's expression was one of shock that anyone would be killed around Orderville. It was well known that she did not like Mary, but she certainly did not wish her dead.

Jackie stood up and walked to the doorway, watching Joseph walk back toward his house. "The town will never be the same now," he said to himself. "My, how things have changed."

Soon, three determined riders were coming up the road from Kanab to our town. They were thirty-five-year-old Sheriff James A. Brown, thirty-year-old Dr. Andrew John Moir, and thirty-year-old County Attorney Harmon Scott Cutler. Even though they were riding at an easy lope, they carried with them a heavy sense of urgency. They pulled their horses up along the river and dismounted to let the horses catch their breath and take a drink.

"I can't believe a murder in Orderville," James said. He shook his head in disbelief.

"I can't believe a murder in the southern part of Utah anywhere," Andrew added. "In all the time I've been coroner, all I've seen have been accidents and natural deaths. Never did I think I would be faced with something like this, as long as I stayed down here away from the city."

"The days of the Wild West are long over," Harmon agreed, "and, at that, even Butch and the Wild Bunch never bothered anybody when they rode through."

"What time do you think we'll make it to town, James?" Andrew asked him.

"Somewhere around ten or eleven o'clock tonight if we keep on at the pace we're going," James said as he looked at his pocket watch. "I'm afraid the girl won't be any less dead if we pushed harder to get there sooner. No sense in killing the horses, too."

"Oh, I don't know," Harmon said with a frustrated laugh, "this one is being a knot-head."

"Don't think you'll be riding double with me," Andrew declared. "Anything happens to your horse, you're trotting alongside us. Just something to keep in mind, Counselor."

Once the horses had finished drinking, the three men remounted and turned them back north. When they regained the feel of their saddles, they broke back into an easy canter.

While they were riding north, we were still in shock back in town.

Joseph's house was still. With small quiet movements to complete the necessary tasks, Sarah had laid Mary's blood-soaked clothes on the floor and smoothed them out the best she could. Wilford had examined the necklace very carefully for any sign of the perpetrator, but it looked just as pristine as when she had received it. Pristine, except for the blood-soaked dirt caked on it. He rinsed it off and then cleaned the last of the blood from the bullet. He dried them both meticulously without saying a word. Walking over to the kitchen counter, he carefully laid the necklace out with the chain in an oval as if Mary was wearing it. He slipped the bullet back into his vest pocket.

Her naked body was still on the kitchen table, lying face up, with a shroud covering her.

Her face was still exposed.

Joseph was sitting in the corner with his wife. He was staring at the floor while she was looking at him with love and concern. She had loved Mary as a dear sister-in-law. She did not have the blood connection her husband did, nor did she carry the same sense of guilt and responsibility. She gently placed her hand on his knee, but he showed no indication he felt or even noticed it. With all the activity coming in and out of the house, the kitchen door stood open, letting in the warm afternoon air.

Outside, Francis could hear the sounds of a horse racing up to the house and then coming to a quick stop. She glanced out the door but did not see anything yet. She looked back at Joseph, but he still showed no sign that he was aware of anything taking place around him.

Loudly, Ezra burst in, bouncing the water on the washstand with each step. He stopped in horror as he saw his daughter's shrouded body laid out on the table. Her once vibrant face was a grayish-white, and it was painfully obvious she was no longer in there. Shaking violently, he slowly walked over to her in disbelief. Tears began to run down his face. Tears like Joseph had never seen from his father, ever.

Still shaking, Ezra almost fearfully stepped over to the table and firmly grasped the edge, as if he was going to break it in anger. After a few tense moments, he relaxed enough to gently stroke her face and lovingly move a lock of hair away from her eyes. He carefully put his trembling open hand on her left cheek and slowly bent down to kiss her on the forehead, then slowly stood back up. Nobody dared move toward or speak to him. Everyone, including Ezra, stayed motionless for a few minutes, suspended in time, until he abruptly turned to Joseph and growled with anger, not directed toward his son.

"Show me."

Ezra waited for a response from Joseph but received none. He shook with anger, tears welling up in his eyes again. He took two determined steps toward Joseph and demanded, "Show me where it happened."

Joseph painfully and listlessly stood up, as if in slow motion and, without a word, led his father out the door. Ezra, anxious, frustrated, and overtly angry, held back all his hostile emotions to allow his son some space while they walked up the trail to the Point.

When they arrived, Joseph pointed to the ground without looking up at his father. "Tracks start here."

Ezra, with an intuitive understanding of his son and the extreme emotional turmoil he was experiencing, did not press him to explain more; the tracks would do that for him.

They started to follow them up the hillside, father in front, son following behind. Ezra moved out with an angry purpose. Joseph had to struggle, in his grief, to keep up. However, Ezra's determination to know the complete story out distanced Joseph's ability to keep up, and he fell behind. He continued to follow, but with his head hanging down in a devastated and defeated posture. He was a man who had failed his father and every part of his body testified to it.

As the two men reached the site of the struggle, Joseph pointed toward the ravine. "This is where we found her."

Ezra looked down the ravine for a long moment as he imagined his daughter's lifeless body being dumped and buried there. Slowly, he turned and looked at the blood-soaked sand, squatting down on his heels to examine the tracks more closely. "Who in town walks toed-in?"

Joseph had returned to his daze while his father looked around. The question finally reached him. "What?"

"Who in town walks toed-in?" Ezra repeated. "The tracks coming up with Mary were of a man who walks toed-in. They lead off that way." He indicated where the man's tracks left the area going cross-country alone, avoiding the trail. He stood up and looked directly at Joseph. "You didn't do this, son, this was someone else. Let it go out of your heart and help me catch this man."

"And what if we find him?" Joseph asked. "What then?"

"We'll turn him over to the law, so justice can be served," he stated with authority. Then his voice turned hard as he continued, "That is, of course, if he survives the capture. One way or another, we will get him to the authorities."

Ezra began to follow the tracks again and motioned to Joseph to come with him. At times, the tracks disappeared in the rocks, and he had to struggle to find them again. They followed them to the edge of town.

"We'll lose them here in everyone else's tracks," Ezra stated. "Now, we just need to find who came back into town last night from here, and we will have our killer."

"Then we turn him over to the law," Joseph said in an almost accusatory tone.

"We turn him over to God and the law, son," Ezra reminded him. "It's not our job to risk salvation to seek vengeance."

"What about that comment you made about 'if he survived the capture'?" Joseph asked.

"I was looking at the ground where my little girl was killed," Ezra countered as he fought to answer in a level tone. "Make no mistake, we will capture him and bring him to the law. Whether he is dead or barely alive when we do, is up to him. That's not vengeance; it's justice."

Joseph looked away from his father; he did not know what to think. He wanted the killer dead for what he had done to his sister, and he wanted to be the one who did it, but he did not think he had the strength to do it and did not want to risk eternal damnation. Still, he had to find a way to redeem himself in his father's eyes. Even though Ezra did not blame him, Joseph felt an overwhelming sense of guilt, because he felt like he had let Mary and his family down. The two men walked silently back into town and to Joseph's house. Even though he was adamant about turning the killer over to the law, Ezra thought about all the ways he could kill the man who had taken his daughter's life. He was careful not to let his son see the internal struggle between what he knew he should do and what he desperately wanted to do.

Joseph thought about how he had disappointed his father. They entered the house to find the somber spirit still hung heavy in the air.

"Anything?" Wilford asked.

"Maybe," Ezra responded.

About ten o'clock that night, several of the townspeople gathered in the saddle shop. Wilford walked in and addressed the saddlemaker, Clifford Rogers, and David Smith and the others.

"The sheriff just passed through Mt. Carmel a bit ago," Wilford mentioned as he took a seat. "He'll be here any minute."

"That's a pretty good prediction, Willy," Clifford said.

Wilford looked over at him quizzically.

David looked out the window. "Sheriff and two others just

rode up to the Co-op. Your telegrapher in Mt. Carmel is a little slow."

"Telephone," Wilford corrected as he walked back out of the shop, followed by the others.

James, Andrew, and Harmon dismounted and walked stiffly as they tied their horses to the hitching rail of the Co-op.

"Hello, James." Wilford called out as he left the saddle shop and walked toward him, "Thanks for coming up so quickly."

"Sorry for the circumstances that brought us up," James stated, then, after a pause, continued. "You remember Andrew and Harmon. Figured it would be a good idea to bring a doctor and a legal mind to help us out."

"Of course," Wilford agreed.

"Where's Ezra?" James asked.

"Over to his son's place."

"We'll have to go over there and pay our respects," James said, "then I'm afraid I'll have to ask him some questions." He paused for a moment, "Is she still in the canyon?"

"No," Wilford informed him. "We held an inquest and Joseph brought her home. Sarah's got her all cleaned up."

"Well, then I guess there's another reason I need to go over to the house."

"Just so you know," Wilford said, "we've been talking about it, and not only are we greatly shocked and agitated over Mary's violent death, but we're committed to doing everything we can to find this killer and bring him to justice. We figure he probably has about a day's head start on us but, as soon as you're ready to go, we'll be in the saddle."

"As soon as I'm ready then."

Back at Joseph's house, there were many candles and lamps burning to brighten the room. The heat from the flames hung heavy in the air. Sarah gently wiped away another imaginary smudge of dirt, as she emotionally tried to prepare Mary's body for her final rest in the grave. After a tender pause, she delicately brushed the lifeless teen's bangs out of her face. She continued to stare lovingly down at Mary and quietly wept as she mourned a girl she had loved as a daughter.

Ezra had slipped into a quiet state of disbelief as he stared off into space, while he stood next to his lifeless daughter. He thought of nothing in particular, but drifted from one thought to another, each one avoiding the reality of her death. A light knock came at the door as it slowly opened. Wilford, James, Andrew, and Harmon entered with their hats in their hands, a sign of respect for the deceased. Space was limited in the room, so Sarah, Francis, and Harmon moved into the parlor. Joseph sat motionless in the corner again, staring at the floor. Wilford, James, and Andrew walked over to Ezra and stood near Mary's body.

"Ezra, you know Sheriff Brown," Wilford said.

"Of course," Ezra said. "Hello, Jim. Thanks for coming. I'm sorry it had to be under these circumstances."

"I'm the one who's sorry about the circumstances," James stated. "I wish we were here for happier reasons."

Ezra turned to Andrew, "Hello, Doctor."

"Andrew, please," he insisted.

"We're so sorry for your loss, Ezra," James said barely above a whisper as he rolled the brim of his hat in his hands. "I couldn't endure losing one of my children. I can't imagine how you must feel right now."

"Thank you to the three of you for coming. It means so much to me that you are here to find the monster who did this."

"Yes, and we best be getting started," James said. "Wilford, what can you tell us?"

"Let me show you," he said as they turned to the table.

"Help me move her onto her side," Wilford instructed as they repositioned her body. He removed the shroud covering Mary's upper body and continued, "Four shots, all in the back."

Andrew stepped in to take a closer look as Wilford explained. "Two came out the front, I noticed."

"Yes," Wilford confirmed. "She was running away from whoever did this." He reached into his vest pocket and retrieved the lead bullet. "Sarah found this slug in the girl's clothes when she was cleaning her."

"Mary," Ezra corrected barely loud enough for them to hear.

"What?" Wilford asked.

"Sarah found a .38 slug in *Mary's* clothes," Ezra insisted.

"Of course, Ezra, I'm sorry," Wilford apologized. "Sarah found this .38 bullet in Mary's clothing when she was cleaning her."

James turned to Ezra and, with a quiet confidence said, "What I can tell you, Ezra, is we will find out what happened here. You have my word that we will expend every bit of energy we have to bring this killer to justice."

Ezra just nodded in acknowledgment.

Looking at his watch, James continued, "It's after midnight. Let's call it a night and get an early start in the morning. We're tired from our long ride, and I'm afraid we might miss something important in the dark."

Turning to Wilford, he asked, "Any chance there are some vacant rooms in the hotel tonight?"

"I've already seen to that," Wilford assured him. "I have a room set aside for you. It shouldn't be too much trouble to get two more. All we need to do is get the keys from the front desk, and you can get some sleep."

"Sounds like it'll work just fine," James said. "Ezra, let's have you and Joseph meet us in front of the Co-op just after first light, and we will dig in with everything we've got."

"The Co-op then," Ezra confirmed. "Good night and thank you again for coming."

James, Andrew, Harmon, and Wilford walked out into the night's darkness.

"Any ideas of who may have done this, Will?" James asked as they walked toward the hotel.

"My money's on the drummer at this point."

"What drummer? We didn't notice any wagons when we came into town."

"He left without saying much of anything to anyone," Wilford said. "He lives up to Monroe, and I know he was headed toward Circleville after this. No one's quite sure when he left, and we know he was sweet on the girl. He gave her a necklace with a locket on it, and we think he may have made advances toward her after that."

"We'll keep it in mind when we're looking things over tomorrow. If what you say is true and it turns out to be him, he won't be too hard to find driving that big ol' wagon and everything."

Chapter Four
To Track A Killer

Early the following morning, the men all met outside the Co-op store. It was still early enough in the spring that there was frost on the ground, and the men could see their breath.

Wilford pointed off toward the canyon. "That's where it happened. What I want to know is, how did an outsider know about the clearing up there?"

"Anyone snaking through here on the dodge could easily run into it, if they were trying to escape detection," James said as he looked off to where Wilford pointed. "It could be that whoever did this passed through here months or years ago and stumbled upon the site. They could have passed by the edge of town, undetected by anyone here, and Mary bumped into him. Maybe it had nothing to do with her. Perhaps he killed her to avoid being turned into the law. We'll be sure to look for two sets of horse tracks."

"Why two sets?" Wilford asked.

"Because he would have been leading a pack horse," he

answered, "with plenty of supplies so he wouldn't have to stop in town. That way you would never know he was in the area."

"Are you giving up on the idea that the drummer did it?" Ezra asked.

"No, not at all," James responded. "I'm just looking at all the possibilities, so we don't miss something important. The drummer could have overheard folks talking in town, or maybe Mary herself told him about the hollow."

"Do you want some of us to go up there with you?" Wilford asked.

"No, I don't think so," James said. "What I want is for you, Ezra and Joseph, to explain to us in detail what happened, and then I want the doctor to walk it with me. Let's use this area here beside the store to act as the area where Mary was killed."

Wilford turned to Joseph. "Let's begin with you, and take it through the same order as it happened."

Joseph briefly began with the conversations he and Francis had with Mary before she left for the Point. He continued with his search for her around town and then following her tracks up to the hollow.

"When I found the blood pools, I knew it was time to get the law involved, so I ran back down here and got Wilford and the posse."

Wilford took over the narrative at that point. "I gathered up several men to help us look, including Edward, because he is the Justice of the Peace. We went back up there as quickly as possible, until we got to the clearing. We tried to be as careful as we could about obscuring the killer's tracks, but things became rather hectic once we found Mary buried in the ravine."

"As I can well imagine," James said.

Wilford continued, "Once we found her, we dug her out and held a coroner's inquest to confirm that she met a befouled fate, and it wasn't an accident. Then we brought her back to Joseph's house and called you."

"Father also noticed the killer has a size six shoe and walks toed-in," Joseph added.

"Excellent," James said. "I think we have a pretty good idea of what happened. Andrew, do you have any questions before we walk up there?"

"No, I really don't," he answered. "I figure I will have plenty though when we return. Are you working the store today, Wilford?"

"Later this afternoon. Edward is working it this morning. I'll be up to the house if you need anything when you return."

"And I suppose you and Joseph will be up to his place?" James asked Ezra.

"That's right," he confirmed.

"We'll be back then."

James and Andrew left the group and walked up the road to where the trail took off toward the hollow. Like the others, they walked alongside of the trail, so they would not obscure the killer's original tracks. When they reached the clearing, they looked around trying to separate the tracks of the murder from those of the posse.

"What do you think?" Andrew asked after they had a few minutes to formulate a theory.

James reached up and scratched at the beard stubble on his face that was starting to be itchy. "It looks premeditated and cold-blooded."

"Who do you think it was?"

"First thing is, we have to find out who else came through town besides the drummer in the last few days."

"You don't think it was the drummer?" Andrew asked, surprised.

"I'm sure it very easily could have been him and probably was," James responded, "but like I said before, I hate to get our sights set on him and miss an important clue."

"Ah, of course," Andrew commented, "due diligence and all."

"Precisely."

"Do you think we can catch whoever did this, if they have a couple of days' head start on us?"

"If it's the drummer, we know where he's headed and where he lives," James observed. "He doesn't move very fast. If it's someone else, then it could be quite a bit more difficult. It all depends on who it is, but it looks like the shoe print is a size six or so. Not many men wear that small of a shoe. His feet aren't much bigger than Mary's." He indicated the ground and continued, "She was shot here first, while she was walking away." He stepped over to the side, moved forward a step or two, and continued. "The killer stepped over here and shot her again." He stepped around again. "After the fourth shot, the killer dragged and dumped her into the ravine and knocked a bunch of dirt and brush on her from the sidewall."

"That must have been when he noticed the hat," Andrew added.

"I believe you're right," James agreed. "This is where his plan broke down. He quickly threw the hat on top of the rubble and kicked dirt on it."

"But not enough, since the ribbon was still visible when the posse got here," Andrew observed.

"That's right," James stated, "but in his haste, he didn't notice. Looking around, it's obvious if he hadn't made that mistake, we never would have found her body. It was the perfect place to hide her."

"When the best plans run into reality…." Andrew muttered.

"And thank goodness," James immediately added. "That may be the only way we can solve this case. Otherwise, they may never have found Mary, and the killer would have slipped through our fingers, never to be found." He paused for a moment as he looked around at the scene one more time and looked back at Andrew. "Have you been keeping track how long it took us to walk up here from town?"

"Yup, we've been going for about a half hour so far," he responded. "That includes the ten minutes we spent looking over the murder site."

"Excellent," James said as he kicked a rock on the ground. "Let's see how much longer it takes us to get back to town."

"Do you think we will be able to identify the killer by his tracks?" Andrew asked him as they walked alongside the trail.

"Two things we have going in our favor is that we know he wears about a size six shoe, which is uncommon for a full-grown man. The other thing is that sometimes he walks pigeon-toed. That narrows it down a lot."

"Why do you think it's only sometimes?" Andrew wondered.

"Well, Doctor, I was hoping you had an idea on that. Surely, there has to be a medical reason why it is intermittent. If we can't figure out why he's doing it, we will have a harder time figuring out who he is."

"One of the things we know about him is he is a thinker," Andrew reasoned, "because this was obviously a premeditated crime. The killer chose this place because it was the perfect place to hide the body."

"I would have to say," James corrected, "he thinks himself a thinker but, in reality, isn't as smart as he thinks he is. That may be the key element we need to look for as we question suspects."

"You mean because, even though he planned the perfect place for the murder, he panicked when he committed it and left the ribbon exposed?"

"Exactly," James confirmed. "That may be the way we catch him by getting him flustered and making him trip himself up. Or maybe we can get him bragging, and he'll slip up and give us a direct confession."

When they arrived back at the edge of town, James asked Andrew how long it took them to walk back.

"It took us twenty minutes at a walk to get back here from the clearing," Andrew stated, looking at his watch. "That means it took us fifty minutes overall; twenty up, ten to look around, and twenty back."

"Okay, now we have a timeframe of how long it took the killer too, if he left from here."

"So, if it was the drummer," Andrew said, contemplating the situation, "he could have locked up his wagon and easily slipped up there and back."

"Yes, and if it was a stranger who came through town," James said, thinking about it, "he would have done some quick scouting around to locate the clearing up the hollow.

"Maybe he heard about it from the locals on a previous trip and had it planned out before he ever returned to town."

"Quite possibly so," James agreed, "or he could have been walking up the canyon, looking for a place to lay low for a while and ran into her. It might have just been a plan of perfect convenience and not premeditation after all."

"But someone would have seen his horses tied off somewhere," Andrew noted. "Maybe we need to do some asking around about that, too."

"It looks like everyone is in the saddle shop," James observed. "Let's go in there and tell Wilford and the others what we've found."

They entered the shop to find Harmon, Wilford, Ezra,

Joseph, Edward, David Smith and, of course, Clifford sitting around the room discussing the case.

As James looked around and took inventory of those present, he felt it was appropriate to proceed. "Any outsiders come through town lately?"

"Couple of migrant workers were here for a few days," David said, "but they pushed through when they finished all the work we could give them."

"They work for families in Kanab sometimes," Wilford pointed out.

"They were there working when Mary was killed," James said. "I remember running into them at the Co-op down there when I stepped in to take your phone call."

"What made you notice them?" Wilford asked. "Were they acting suspicious or something?"

"It's really rather embarrassing. I wasn't watching where I was going and I ran into one, knocking the bag of grain out of his arms onto the ground. Otherwise, I wouldn't have thought anything of them."

"The peddler came through a few days back," Clifford mentioned, "and left right after it happened."

"That's right," Wilford confirmed, "that's where she got the necklace. Didn't you say he was sweet on her, Ezra?"

"Yes, and he was paying a lot of attention to her just before the..." he trailed off for a moment and then recomposed himself. "He gave her the necklace as a gift."

"Could be it was just his way of advertising, you know, trying to drum up a little more business," Harmon suggested. "Maybe there was nothing romantic behind it after all."

"No...no, judging by the way he looked at her, I think he indeed had intentions, romantic or otherwise," Ezra refuted.

"You don't suppose he followed Mary up the canyon and

killed her when she refused him, do you?" Joseph asked.

"I'm starting to think so," Ezra commented, anger beginning to edge into his voice.

"I'm starting to think so, too," Wilford added.

"Sounds like we should look into him," James admitted. "Any idea where we can find him now?"

"He was heading up through Panguitch after his stay here," Wilford mentioned. "If we hurry, we can catch him."

"All right," James said. "Harmon, let's gather up a few men and ride north to find him."

He turned to Andrew. "I suppose you should stay here and do an autopsy. I want to know exactly what killed Mary."

"You mean besides the four bullets fired into her body?"

"Careful," Ezra growled, "that's my little girl you're talking about."

"I meant no disrespect, sir; I was speaking in a strictly medical capacity."

"I'm sorry," Ezra said, softening his tone. "I'm afraid this is going to take me some time to come to grips with."

"It's understandable," Andrew stated. "I deal with loss a fair amount and, believe me, you have every right to feel the way you do. I imagine it will take you quite a while to get over it."

Ezra nodded without comment.

"What I'm wanting," James said, bringing the conversation back on track, "is to know exactly what happened. Which of the four shots were fatal, which ones she could have survived, and in what order were they fired? Answer as many of those questions for me as you can. That's what I want you to take care of while we ride."

"It just so happens that's exactly what I had in mind to do."

Harmon turned to Joseph and Ezra and said, "I suppose the two of you will want to ride with us."

"Try and stop us," Ezra said, with less growl in his voice than he had previously used.

"Had no intention."

"Once we have our posse selected," James began, "I want to spend some time investigating things here before we go. I want a better feel for the situation before we ride off after him."

Harmon nodded, "Good, let's do it."

All the men, except the saddler, exited the building. After a moment, James walked back in the room.

"Are you not joining us, saddlemaker?"

"Do you need me?" he asked. "I figured you had plenty of riders to go with you."

"I could always use another level-headed man along for the ride."

"You have some good men out there. Take a look at them again, and if you still feel like you need me to come along, then come and get me. Otherwise, I'll stay here and keep working."

"I imagine you're right. After all, we're only going after one man."

Outside the Co-op later that afternoon, Harmon and several other men were waiting for the sheriff with their horses tied to the hitching post. Among the posse were the men from the saddle shop, Jackie Adler, Hyrum Mower and other townsmen.

As James stepped out of the building, Jackie asked, "Sheriff, shouldn't we head out and catch up with the killer before he gets away?"

"No hurry. He's slowly heading back toward Circleville with a heavy wagon. We know right where to find him."

James paused for a minute and took inventory of the men he had around him.

"But we are all here and ready to go," Hyrum said, too emphatically for James' taste.

"Let's get our affairs in order before we go off all half-cocked. We'll head out at first light in the morning."

"First light?" Jackie asked, obviously disgusted. "What is wrong with going right now? We need to get out there, catch the man who did this, and bring him to justice. Zion cannot stand if we let corruption grow within and take over."

"Zion will stand for another day," James assured him. "It will take far more than one guilty man experiencing an extra day of freedom to bring down the Lord's people. Leave 'er be, young man."

"At least tell us what you have against going out this evening," Hyrum insisted.

"I'll give you two very good reasons. First, I do not relish the idea of riding into this man's camp in the dark. If he did indeed shoot Mary, then that means he has a gun and is willing to use it. The second reason is even simpler; if we wait until morning, I can sleep in a soft bed tonight. Otherwise, we're sleeping on the hard ground."

"The hard ground is what you based your decision on to let the killer get away?" Jackie asked with a flavor of disrespect.

"No. I base it on darkness and safety. I don't want to explain to my wife why I'm coming home dead. Now that's the end of it. Besides, it will be easier to find him in the daylight."

"The sheriff's right," Ezra said. "We know who he is and where to find him. Let's walk into his camp in the daylight with an advantage."

Jackie and Hyrum continued to grumble such things as they should be riding off to catch the killer and not waiting around to let him get away, but no one came to their aid to challenge the sheriff.

The crowd dispersed and James walked back over to the saddle shop. "Please reconsider my request. I have several unknowns and a couple of hotheads. I could sure use another level-headed person to help keep them in line."

"Are you headed out this evening?"

"No, not until first light," James explained. "Don't want to catch him in the dark."

"Ah, wise move," Clifford complimented him. "I take it you are a chess-playing man."

"Never developed much of an interest in it. Why do you say that?"

"You are trying to outmaneuver your opponent. It is a good chess move."

"It is also a good sheriffin' move," James said.

"I'll give you that; it certainly is," Clifford said as he considered the sheriff's request. "Will you deputize me and give me a badge?"

"I didn't bring any badges with me. Didn't know I was going to be deputizing a posse."

"That's okay, I can make one out of leather," he quipped.

"You'll come with us, then?" James inquired.

"Haven't decided yet, but I'll let you know by first light tomorrow. If I'm there, I'm going. If I'm still home in bed, then I'll be staying behind."

"Oh my, a comedian. Maybe I was wrong about wanting you to come along," James laughed.

"Let me think on it overnight."

The next morning, as the black sky began to give way to dark blue, the men of the posse started to gather outside the hotel. The sheriff was up early, sitting on the hotel porch drinking a cup of Postum. One by one, the posse men walked over with their horses in tow, ready to head north. Clifford walked over without his horse.

"You planning to run alongside of us, saddlemaker?" James joked as he remained seated.

"Went to clean out the hooves of my horse and found he had thrown a couple of shoes. I'm going to have to fix them before I ride. Go ahead, and I'll catch up as soon as I get shoes on him."

"I was afraid you were going to tell me you couldn't find a saddle to ride."

"Oh, you're funny," Clifford said.

"Catch up as soon as you can, then. I don't suppose we'll get too far ahead of you."

Clifford nodded his head in acknowledgement and then returned home to shoe his horse.

James took one last drink of his Postum and tossed the rest out. As he walked over to his horse, he could hear Jackie and Hyrum muttering something about getting on their way so they could catch the killer and dish out some justice.

This is going to be a wonderful ride, he thought sarcastically to himself as he swung into the saddle. *I wonder if there is any way we could ditch the troublemakers and leave them behind.*

He turned his horse north onto the road and headed out at an easy canter. "Easy does it, everybody. Let's not get too worked up before we get there, and let's keep an easy pace for the horses."

As they rode along, they passed Alvin as he walked with a bundle on his way to the Co-op store. He only gave them a passing glance as they rode by.

I should have gone with them, Alvin thought to himself. *I wonder if it is too late to saddle up and join them.*

After the posse had loped along for several miles, James gave the command to let the horses walk for a while and catch their breath. Harmon and James were several horse-lengths ahead as they walked along, so Harmon began the conversation.

"How much chance do you think there is that the drummer is the killer?"

"I don't know," James responded, "but I'm not ready to rule out any possibility."

"The town seems pretty dead-set, if you will pardon the expression, that he did it."

"That's because it fits into the scenario of an elevated Orderville in Zion," James explained. "If the killer is an outsider, then the town can rest at ease with themselves, because somehow evil snuck in when no one was looking and took one of our own. Otherwise, they have to take a long hard look at themselves and admit they aren't as righteous as they like to think they are."

"But the drummer's not an outsider," Harmon corrected. "He's one of us."

"Yes and no," James stated. "He is a Saint and lives up to Monroe, but he is somewhat of an outsider because he isn't from Kane County. He's from Sevier County. This is probably the best scenario for the town, because while he is somewhat of an outsider, he's not a Gentile outsider, so the greater evil out there hasn't broken through our protective shell. It is a lesser evil *if* he's among the disaffected Saints."

"You don't think that one of our own is the greater evil?" Harmon cornered him. "You know, more of a betrayal, unexpected, and all that?"

"There's far more evil out there than killing a girl," James responded without further comment or explanation.

Harmon contemplated the sheriff's words and decided not to pursue his comment. Instead, he went back to the subject, which they had been talking about previously. "Do you think the drummer is a disaffected Saint, then?"

"I have no idea, but that would be what the town would want. Everything could be kept neat and tidy, and Orderville can go back to its pre-murder state of pride and innocence."

"What if we catch this man and find out it isn't him?" Harmon asked. "What then?"

"That's where Andrew comes in, to borrow a theatrical phrase."

"You working on the annual ward dramatic play, are you?"

"I'm afraid so. My wife roped me into it."

"Okay, what do you have Andrew doing, besides the autopsy?"

"Do you remember the discussion we had about the bullet holes, and which ones came first?" James asked.

"I do."

"Yesterday, I instructed him to try and determine how and why the killer acted the way he did. You know, to try to get a sense of what kind of man we are dealing with. That way we know better who we're looking for."

"I'm not sure I follow."

"Because the more I think about it, the less convinced I am the drummer did this."

"Why?"

"How many smarts does it take to realize that if you're visiting in town and you kill a girl, that a drummer's wagon is not a good way to get away?"

"Not many," Harmon confirmed, "but maybe he took that into account. Could be, he thought you'd take that into account and figured you would discount him because of that. Besides, didn't you say the killer thought he got away with the perfect murder?"

"That answer made me dizzy," James said with a half-laugh. "If I hadn't seen the murder site, I might have believed that, but Andrew and I determined he thought he was much smarter than he actually was. And the exposed ribbon kept it from being the perfect crime."

"That fits into my estimation perfectly."

"Perhaps, but I'm still not convinced. That's why I asked Andrew to consider the possibility that one of Orderville's own did it."

"Boy, they're not going to like that," Harmon said with a whistle between his teeth. "So if you think that, then why are we riding after the drummer?"

"Because there is enough evidence to suggest it might indeed be him. Also, pulling this posse away from the idea that he did it would be like turning a herd of cattle when they're on a stampede. No, we need to investigate to make sure it isn't him. Besides, let the town find out on their own without us trying to convince them."

"Right, that's too much work for us. Let's keep it simple. You would have made a good lawyer. You should think about it when you're done being sheriff."

"I'll keep it in mind, but I think one lawyer in the family is enough."

"You mean your half-brother, John?" Harmon asked.

"Yes, and a fine one he is. Shall we lope the horses again?"

The posse loped easily into the small town of Hatch. There was a local man in his early thirties, walking in the street. He carried a forty-pound burlap bag of feed over his shoulder.

James rode his horse over to the man and stopped. He

dismounted and walked the last few feet, holding the horse's reins in his hand. "Has a traveling drummer been through here recently?"

"Looking to do some shopping, are you?" the man asked.

"No, I'm the sheriff from down to Kane County, and we need to ask him some questions. Have you seen him?"

"Sure, he was just here for a couple of days," the man told him. "You just missed him."

"Know where he is now, perchance?" James inquired.

"Headed toward Panguitch if he's coming from down south, I would suppose. The storekeeper across the way would know more; he's always glad when the drummer leaves. He might as well close up shop and stay home when the drummer comes, because no one goes in when he's here. They spend all their time shopping at the wagon."

"I'm much obliged." James turned his horse and led him over to the store.

Harmon, sensing what James was doing, rode over to take his horse while he went into the store. The rest of the posse stayed mounted where they were.

"Tie off and come with me," James said to Harmon as he rode over. "I want you in there to hear what the shopkeeper may say."

Harmon dismounted. They tied their horses to the hitching rail and walked into the store.

Not happy at the delay, the rest of the posse started to grumble.

"I can't believe we're just sitting here when the peddler is so close," Joseph Stevens said, "especially after all that riding we just did."

"I say we should go get him," Jackie Adler said, "enough of this waiting around."

"Let's go," Hyrum said, then he turned to Wilford. "Stay here and let the sheriff know that we went on ahead to find the drummer."

"Since I'm the constable, I can't condone you taking the law into your own hands," Wilford said quickly before they had a chance to ride away. "If you find him, just keep him there until we can catch up."

"Not your jurisdiction!" Jackie called over his shoulder as they rode away.

The posse rode hard until they found the wagon tracks on the road.

"I found the tracks, boys," Jackie called back to the rest of the men. "Let's take it up a notch!"

The men rode harder until they found where the tracks turned off the main road to a small clearing. They could smell the campfire smoke and knew they had him. They slowed their horses down to a gentle lope as they entered the clearing. Their horses were lathered after the hard run from Hatch and were fighting to catch their breath as the riders brought them to a stop. The men were all worked into a lather themselves, ready to exact their frontier justice on this brutal murderer.

The drummer's horses were tied to a tree so they could graze, and he was casually sitting in the shade of his wagon. He was idly working on a leather holster which, when finished, would become part of his inventory. He acted very cool and calm as the posse rode into his open camp. Even though Jackie had his 94 Winchester 30-30 pointed straight at him, he made the last two stitches and cut off the excess thread.

The man acted as though he had done nothing wrong,

nothing at all.

"I've seen groups like this before and they usually had something grave in mind. Don't expect me to grovel. If you came for that, I'm afraid you will be disappointed. About all I have left is my dignity, and I don't expect to let you take that from me. Whatever you're here for, I didn't do it; I'm sure of it."

Without any introduction, Jackie blurted out, "We're here for justice!"

Unfortunately, for the peddler, he had a fifty-foot rope hanging on the side of his wagon.

Jackie hopped off his horse and grabbed the rope, and walked over to a tree with a large branch.

"I'll have to charge you gentlemen for the rope," the drummer said, a slight amount of morbid humor in his voice.

"Shut up!" Jackie threw it over a tree limb and started to fashion a crude hangman's noose with it.

"What have I done? At least according to you?"

"You killed my daughter after you had your way with her," Ezra accused, because it was the only scenario that made sense to him. "Now it's time for you to meet your Maker and explain to Him why you did it."

A look of horror suddenly came across the peddler's face as the reality of the situation settled in his mind. He knew that no matter what he might say, this situation would only end one way…with his brutal death. He had no friends in the posse; they were still back in Hatch.

"Look, friends, I don't know what you're talking about," he said, his voice beginning to tremble.

"Of course you don't, but we're here to remind you and hang you just the same," Jackie replied.

They forcibly tied his hands behind his back and pushed him up on one of his horses, bareback. Ezra and Joseph stayed at the edge of camp and watched, still on their horses. Just as they were finishing the noose and reaching for his head, James, Harmon, Wilford, and Clifford cantered up.

"I guess you needed my help more than I realized." Clifford quickly assessed the situation.

"Don't you think you ought to wait for a judge?" James asked Jackie, who still had a strong hold on the drummer.

"We got him, and we're going to hang him! We know he did it, and Mary's family deserves quick justice. Don't you, Ezra?" Jackie pushed, more as a statement and not so much as a question.

"True, but two things you should know before you finish this hanging," James said, eerily calm.

"And just what may they be?" Jackie asked, unwilling to mask his anger and contempt toward the sheriff at his interruption.

"First, the townsfolk here abouts swear he was in Hatch when Mary was killed."

"They could be lying. And what, pray tell, might the other thing be?"

"And second," James said as his hand slowly moved along his belt, closer to his revolver, "his boots are the wrong size. Take a look."

When the posse looked, it was obvious that his feet were bigger than the killer's. While their attention was diverted, James easily rested his hand on his gun.

"What size boot do you wear, peddler?" Hyrum asked.

"Ten."

Suddenly the posse lost all of their starch, mumbling some half-hearted apologies to the drummer as they pulled the rope down and untied the noose. Hyrum handed the crumpled rope back to the peddler without coiling it back up. The others quietly shuffled back to their horses and left without any fanfare. James nodded toward Harmon, Wilford, and Clifford to go ahead and ride back with the others, and then he turned back to the drummer.

The drummer stood there for a moment, speechless, with the rope in his hands. He was not quite sure what he was supposed to do at that point.

After he had a chance to collect himself, he was finally able to say, "Thank you, Sheriff."

He set the rope down near the wagon and picked up the holster he had just finished. He handed it to the sheriff. "Here, take this."

James took the holster.

"Fine piece of work there," he said, examining it closely. "I will use this with pride."

"You deserve it," the drummer said. "You saved my life."

"I'm just glad we got here when we did. It could have been a whole lot worse."

"Yes, for me it would have been," he said. "I never realized how frightening it can be, being that close to a wrongful noose. By the way, what exactly was it that had everyone so worked up? I know someone died, but I couldn't figure out who."

"It was Mary Stevens."

"Mary?" the drummer asked, thinking about the name. "You mean the lovely girl I gave the locket necklace to? That Mary?"

"She's the one."

"She's dead?" he asked with disbelief. "Please tell me it isn't so. Are you sure you didn't make a mistake?"

"No mistake, it was her."

"Oh...," the drummer trailed off as the enormity of the situation finally hit him. His strength suddenly left his body as his legs gave out, and he forcefully sat down on a stump. "I really liked her. She was a nice girl. Why did they think it was me?"

"Some of the folks down in Orderville thought since you fancied her, you may have made advances toward her. They also felt she may have rejected your affections, so you killed her for it."

"How could they think that?" The drummer shook his head and looked back up at James.

"Because you were gone shortly after you gave her the necklace. They thought it was a sure sign of guilt. They couldn't get it through their heads that maybe you left because it was time for you to move on to Hatch and Panguitch."

"From their side of it, I can see why they would think that," the drummer said slowly nodding his head, as his strength returned and he stood back up and looked James in the eye. "What about you? Did you think I did it?"

"I was never convinced, but I had to follow through and find out," James explained. "Besides, I had to come to make sure the others didn't get out of hand and do something rash. The more I looked into it, the more it seemed like a local did it because of where she was killed, but they weren't ready to hear that. Maybe now we can start looking for the real killer."

"And I'm eternally grateful that you came along."

James nodded his head in acknowledgement.

"I should be riding on now and catching up with the others," James said, turning his horse. "I best be there when they start thinking again and set their sights on someone else."

"Best of luck to you, Sheriff."

For most of the posse, the ride back to town was one of shocked silence. I've never known them to be so quiet outside of prayer time in church meetings. They were all so convinced it was an outsider who killed Mary, they never even considered anyone else. They figured since the peddler was the only outsider who had been through town lately, it had to be him.

But it wasn't.

With each step the horses took, the stark realization sank into each of the townsmen that it had to be one of their own. Unless, of course, another outsider had slipped in and committed this heinous crime. But no, somebody surely would have seen him, or at least some sign of him where he stopped to camp. The news these men were about to bring back to town would be the hardest for us to bear.

Did I forget to mention that while she was alive, Mary never quite fit into town with the arrogant elite, but once she had been killed, she instantly became one of Orderville's beloved daughters?

So, not only was one of our own killed, but now it would seem one of our own did the killing. Our reality was about to shatter, and our world would never be the same. How would we be able to live with ourselves?

The demeanor of each of the vengeful posse members was completely crestfallen, which spoke volumes about the great failure they had just experienced. The rest of the posse showed outward signs of concern. The town may now become hostile toward them because some of them were also outsiders.

Francis was out waiting for the men when they returned from Hatch.

"Any luck?" she asked Joseph and Ezra as they rode close to her.

"Wasn't him," Joseph said, hanging his head low. He could not bring himself to look her in the face. The feeling of failure he'd carried for the last couple of days had become so much heavier when they could not catch the killer.

"They're holding up the funeral, waiting for all of you to

come back," she informed them. "As late as it is, they may decide to wait until the morning to have it."

"No," Ezra stated despondently, yet matter-of-factly as a tear welled up in his eye. "Let's go put my little girl in the ground then. She needs to be put to rest."

Ezra and Joseph turned their horses and followed Francis to the church house. Wilford motioned to James, Harmon, and the rest of the posse to come and join them.

I was glad when Francis brought Ezra and Joseph into the meetinghouse for the funeral, because I was awfully tired of waiting there. The whole town had turned out for this and, except for the children, everyone was patiently waiting for the posse's return. However, we were very disappointed they were not able to bring news to her services that her killer had been apprehended. That would have been sweet justice for her. As it was, she had to settle for the return of her family.

Ezra walked in, bent over as if he was carrying a large boulder on his back. He sat down heavily next to his wife, Edith, without even looking at her. She reached over and put her hand on his, but he made no move to indicate he even knew she had done it.

The Bishop conducted the services, as was customary in the Church, and he did a fine job, I suppose. He had Sister Sarah Foote stand up and read the poem Mary had written for the graduation ceremony later that week. Mary would have read it to the graduating class as the school had requested. The topic they gave her was, 'I wonder.' Sarah walked up to the podium and stood there for a moment, as she unfolded the paper Mary had written. I remember thinking it odd this was the last thing she had done that we would ever see. I don't know what made me think of that.

The *Richfield Reaper* newspaper would later publish the poem in its entirety, which may have made it the most famous Utah poem of the year.

Sarah finally started reading.

> "I wonder if they thought I could take this part,
> and I wonder if they think I know how to wonder?
> Well, I wonder if I do?
> I wonder who is the program committee?
> I wonder where their good common sense is?
> I wonder why they didn't give, 'I wonder' to somebody who could wonder?
> I really wonder if Franklin thinks that's poetry he's just been reading?
> I wonder if he could not do better with another???
> I wonder if Blanche doesn't think she's quite smart?
> Well now, I wonder if she doesn't?"

I remember how uncomfortable Franklin looked when she read his name. He quickly glanced around to see who was looking at him, and then he shot a quick glance over at his brother, Alvin. You would have thought he'd just been scolded.

Blanche blushed, and it was obvious she was unhappy at being mentioned in Mary's poem.

Sarah continued.

> "I wonder if Alvin could think of more to growl
> at? If he can't, I wonder why?

I wonder why Josie quit school and I wonder
how she obtained courage to enter school again?
I wonder, well, I wonder if she thought she was
so quick at learning she could learn it all in the
last two weeks?
I wonder if she can?
I wonder if Mamie thinks she's large enough to
be worth mentioning,
I wonder why Hyrum stands so straight and
thinks himself so great?
I wonder if it's because he's class president, or I
wonder if it's because he's so popular among the
girls?
Well, I wonder."

Alvin suddenly became angry when Sarah read his name,
looking like he was going to come right out of his seat and storm
out the door. It was obvious he was incensed at the fact Mary had
singled him out, and he had forgotten the fact that there were
many others mentioned in her poem. Ironically, he had answered
Mary's question; yes, he could find more to growl at.

Mamie, who was sitting next to Alvin and had her arm
wrapped around his, squeezed it so hard I was scared it might pop
off right there in the services. Josie did not seem to be too
offended, but did look down to avoid any of the glances from the
others in attendance. Hyrum, bless his heart, thought he was
being complimented and sat up even straighter than he had been.
He also glanced around to see which of the girls were looking at
him.

"If it wasn't for wonders, I wonder what we'd
do?

> I wonder if Hattie could become what people call
> famous?
> I wonder if she expects to cultivate her
> wonderful talent for music,
> or I wonder if she knows it all -- well, I wonder if
> she does?"

Hattie lowered her head and blushed, but I could see she was grinning from ear to ear as she thought about Mary recognizing her and suggesting she may become famous.

> "I wonder why parents and trustees don't visit
> the school?
> I wonder if they care for the dollar and care for
> their horse, but I wonder why they don't visit the
> school?
> I wonder if they think they have such a lot of
> teachers that they don't need their support?
> Well, I wonder if they do?"

This one was not too shocking to anyone in particular, but I did notice the parents looking around at each other briefly, and then back to their hands in their laps.

> "I wonder if we're all going to get a diploma next
> week?
> If not, I wonder why?
> Well, I guess it will be the biggest "I wonder" if
> we do all graduate.
> I do wonder if it would make us feel great?
> Well, there is nothing for us to do but study and
> wonder until the middle of next week.

"Then I wonder if we won't wonder how the School Board of Utah became so learned as to make questions we will all wonder how to answer.

I wonder if Brother Smith hasn't the patience of Job to teach the eighth grade for so long.

I wonder if he doesn't wonder how, where, and when he obtained his patience?

I wonder and still I wonder, but I cannot wonder what we all will become.

And I often wonder if everybody wonders at the same things.

I wonder if this audience thinks our program is worth listening to?

If they don't, I wonder why?

I wonder if they don't think I'm quite smart?"

David Smith looked as proud as a new parent at the public recognition of his great efforts, while teaching his students. He was never one to brag over the efforts he put into his teaching. For him, it was just who he was – a great teacher. However, he did not mind that his most famous, or I suppose I should say infamous, student had shouted it to the world from beyond the grave.

The applause Mary had expected to get from reading her poem never came because they were in a funeral service, and I don't think the audience enjoyed it as much as she hoped they would.

As I look back over years of time and experiences of my own, I detect a bit of a harsh voice and think she was in a cynical place when she wrote it. Come to find out, she had more on her mind to wonder about than we realized.

When Sarah finished reading the poem, a few people stood up and spoke to Mary's character and related various scriptures to her life and passing. When they finished, the Bishop stood back up and announced that the body would be buried the next morning at ten o'clock for those who wished to join the graveside service. He dismissed the funeral and tended to the arrangements for the body.

"I'm so sorry about Mary," he said, facing her family afterwards. "I've taken care of all the arrangements for tomorrow, so you can go home tonight and rest until then."

"Not expecting to do much resting," Ezra commented, "but we thank you for what you're doing. I don't know what I would have done without you."

"You've had a lot to take care of in the last couple of days, and I'm just glad I could be here to help you. Now go home and see if you can get some rest."

"Thanks again, Bishop," he said. He, Edith, Joseph, and Francis walked out the door.

Still to this day, I remember how defeated both he and Joseph looked. I don't remember seeing anybody that disheartened ever since. But, then again, I've not seen anyone who'd just had their daughter or sister murdered and followed after the wrong man, thinking he was the killer. Of course, Edith looked like she was somewhere else. She had cried so hard since her daughter's death and then again, in the funeral, I don't think she had the strength to try to address those around her. She was merely following Ezra at this point, not thinking for herself. She was numb with grief and only a shell of her normal self.

Instead of going home, many of the townspeople drifted over to the Co-op store and gathered inside. They began to discuss this change in thought. They were trying to regain their bearings.

Their idea of reality was not what the situation really was.

Because the drummer did not commit the crime, who else could it be other than one of our own? But then again, how could it be one of our own?

"Who else came through town?" David Smith asked in denial, searching for any other possibility than the elephant in the room.

"No one," Clifford commented.

"Someone had to," David argued.

"No," Clifford repeated, "but that means…"

"It was one of our own who did it," Wilford said, finally saying it aloud for all to hear.

"Who in town has a size six shoe and walks toed-in?" James asked.

"No one I can think of," Wilford responded. "Gentlemen?"

There was a long pause in the room as each of the men present thought about the question and tried to remember if they had seen anyone walk pigeon-toed. None of them could, so they each shook their head.

"I guess I need the night to think on it," James said as he stood up. "I'm going back to the hotel. See everyone in the morning. Andrew? Harmon?"

"Us too," Harmon said. "It was a long ride today, and my mind could use the rest."

"Yeah," Andrew said, "long day autopsying too. I wish I could have been on the trail with you too; my back and feet are killing me."

After they left, Clifford asked the obvious question. "How could it be one of our own?"

Everyone in the room looked perplexed, but no one answered.

Outside, as the sheriff and others were returning to the hotel,

Andrew spoke in a careful hushed tone to the other two men.

"Jim, there's something you need to hear away from the others." He glanced around to double check that no one else was within hearing range.

James and Harmon stepped in closer to hear him better.

"Mary had intimate relations with someone before she died."

James stopped up short as he contemplated this new development. After processing for a minute, he looked back at the other two. "That would answer a lot of questions. How soon before?"

"I'm afraid I can't tell," he responded. "Our modern medicine is still so limited in many ways. However, with that being said and with the report of Mary's activities in the few days before she died, I would *guess* it was right before she was killed."

"You mean to say she had relations with her killer just before he shot her in the back?" Harmon asked.

"That's merely speculation, without any evidence yet to substantiate or disprove it. I'm just saying maybe. It's something to keep in mind."

"Which is speculation?" James asked. "That she had relations just before she died or that it was with the killer?"

"The killer part," Andrew clarified. "The other part is scientific fact."

"Not a word of this, mind you, to anyone," James ordered. "I don't want Ezra hearing rumors and accusations about this until we know what it means to our investigation. If it doesn't mean anything, then tell no one, ever. Let him have his daughter the way he remembers her."

"I think that's a good idea," Harmon said. "There's no reason the law should get involved over this. She has been brutally assaulted with the result of death. The County has no desire to sully her reputation after that."

"I agree," Andrew said. "Let the family remember her the way they knew her."

"Then so be it," James said.

This, what Harmon was talking about, was perhaps the most critical piece of this whole mystery puzzle. The Utah State Government made intercourse with a single, unmarried woman between the ages of thirteen and eighteen a felony. Perhaps, whoever was having relations with her killed her to avoid going to jail.

Back in the saddle shop the following morning, James, Andrew, and Harmon sat around the wood-burning stove, having Postum. The pot was on the stove heating for second cups. Clifford was across the shop working on a saddle and paying them no mind.

"After thinking on it," James said thoughtfully, "I've come up with a plan."

"Thank goodness," Harmon said. "I've been racking my brain all night and haven't been able to come up with a thing."

"What's your plan, Jim?" Andrew asked.

"I've studied the tracks around town, and none of them are toed-in."

"So, how are you going to come up with tracks that aren't there?" Harmon asked. "Remember, I'm the county attorney, and we need to keep this legal."

James responded, "Of course, it will be legal. Because none of the tracks around town are toed-in, it had me greatly perplexed. Just as I was drifting off to sleep last night, it dawned on me that all the tracks we were looking at around town were of people walking alone."

"Are you trying to say that Orderville is truly a lonely place?" Andrew asked. "It sure seemed to be for Mary."

"No, but remember, our killer walked…"

"Side by side with Mary," Andrew cut in and finished the sentence. "Ah, I see now."

"Exactly."

"What are you planning to do then?" Harmon asked.

"I think what we're going to do is get some of the young women in town to walk arm in arm with the boys who wear about a size six shoe," James explained. "And then we'll see what we can come up with."

"Why not just focus on those boys who wear a size six?" Harmon asked.

"There goes that fine legal mind of yours again," James said with mild humor. "That sounds like a great courtroom solution, but since we don't want to spook the killer, we want to herd him in a group and not single him out yet."

"That way he'll feel more at ease and walk normally," Andrew observed, "making it easier for us to catch him."

"That's right."

"I think it just might work," Harmon confirmed.

"What do you think, Clifford?" James asked. "You think we can catch him like that?"

"Not that I was listening to your conversation, mind you," he said, "but it sounds like it might be the only way to find him, unless you want to walk around for the next month, following couples and looking at their tracks."

"My wife would have my hide if I did that. She hates it when I have to go sheriffin' out of town for a couple of days. A month would never do."

"Then I say you have a plan there."

So later that day, the sheriff, doctor, and lawyer gathered up all the youth in town they could, making sure they had all those with smaller feet. Just to divert suspicion, they did include Hyrum, who probably had the biggest feet in town.

It was rather comical to watch all of the young ladies in town walking around arm-in-arm with the boys. The sheriff made sure to instruct the girls to walk them on both the lawns and out on the dirt road but did not tell them why.

The sheriff made sure to put Mamie with Alvin in the beginning, but then had the girls rotate their boys. She obviously enjoyed the task as she walked arm-in-arm with her beau, but she also enjoyed the attention when she walked with the other boys. Had she realized the sheriff's endgame, she would not have enjoyed it as much.

The sheriff, doctor, and lawyer milled around as all this was going on, glancing at the ground from time to time to watch the boys' feet as they walked.

"Gotcha," James said out loud to himself.

He walked back to Andrew and Harmon. "It's the Heaton boy."

"Alvin or Franklin?" Andrew asked.

"Alvin Jr." James clarified.

"I don't believe it."

"When he sidled up to Mamie, he walked toed-in, and he's a size six. Did either of you see anyone else it could be?"

The other two men shook their heads and Andrew said, "From what I gather from the folks around town, he didn't have anything to do with Mary."

"That's right," Harmon said. "Her father mentioned how he even shunned and ignored her after she got the locket from the drummer."

"Think about it," James said. "If there was nothing going on between them, then he wouldn't have shunned her. He would have stopped and politely listened to what she had to say and then been on his way. Ask yourself, in her excitement, why did she choose to show it to Alvin?"

"I just figured it was because he was the first person walking by," Andrew said, "and she was excited to show it to someone…anyone."

"Perhaps, but if it was Alvin who was secretly seeing Mary, then it would all make sense."

"But why didn't anyone in town tell us it was him she was seeing?" Harmon asked.

"Because they didn't know she was seeing anyone," Andrew stated. "After the autopsy, I asked around a little to see if I could figure out who she was having relations with but, as far as anyone here knew, no one was calling on her."

"That would certainly explain Alvin's behavior then," James said. "Let's gather up the couples and let the girls go home."

He released the girls and brought the boys into a group around him. "Do any of you have a .38 revolver?"

Alvin and another boy raised their hands. The other boys just looked at each other and shrugged their shoulders.

"I have a .45," one of them said, "Does that help?"

"No, son, thank you," James said. "I'm only looking for a .38 caliber."

He turned to Alvin and the other boy. "Go get them."

They trotted off home to retrieve their guns.

"Thank you, gentlemen, for helping us today," James said to the others. "You may now go back to your chores. You've been a great help."

The three men stood, waiting for the two boys to return.

"Looks like you're on to something," Harmon said. "You may have just broken this case wide open."

"Maybe," James said, "I hope this will tell us."

"What are you going to do, if it's not him?" Andrew asked.

"Make my wife mad by staying here until I figure out who did it."

"Oh, she'll love you for that," Andrew retorted.

"That's why I'm going to blame it on you."

"Some friend you turned out to be," Andrew said, giving James a wry look.

The second boy returned with his revolver and handed it to James who took a minute to look at it and chuckled. "This gun doesn't even work. How long has it been broken?"

"All my life, sir," the boy said without a hint of guile. "That's why my pa let me have it. He said I couldn't hurt anyone with it unless I hit him over the head. He also said that a bat or club would work better for that."

"Why do you keep it then if it doesn't work?" Harmon asked, his lawyer mind beginning to take over.

"Always figured I would get it fixed someday when I grew up and had a good job of my own," the boy said. "Or when I needed to use it for something."

"Something like what?" Harmon said, almost as if in cross-examination.

"What he means, son," James stepped in to soften the tone of the conversation, "is why do you think you might need it?"

"Mostly for wolves and coyotes when I'm out herding sheep, but we usually use the lever gun for that. That's why I never worried about getting it fixed."

James dismissed him to go back about his business. Alvin was in sight. He and Mamie were returning with his gun, and James did not want the other boy there when he questioned Alvin.

Alvin handed his gun to James. "Is this your gun then, son?"

"Sure, to shoot rabbits at the roundup," Alvin explained.

"How long have you had it?"

"A couple of weeks, maybe. I traded my deck of cards to Johnny Healy to use it until the next roundup. I thought I might impress Mamie with my shooting skills."

"We're going to have to arrest you and take you down to Kanab to ask you more questions," James said. "We'll take you back to your folks first, so you can let them know what's happening. We also need to have a look around while we are there."

"Arrested?" Alvin asked in bewilderment. "For what? I haven't done anything."

A look of complete surprise, terror, and disbelief crossed over Mamie's face as she heard the accusation.

"For the murder of Mary Stevens."

"I don't believe it," she said. "There has to be some mistake."

Chapter Five
Confession is Good for the Soul

Most of the town gathered down by the Co-op; we all wanted to see Alvin one last time before he was taken away. He looked surprisingly calm as he sat in the wagon box, his hands cuffed together. Except for his restraints, he could have been going off to the county fair, for all the emotion he showed. On the other hand, Mamie was a complete mess. She was crying to beat the band and trying to stay close to him. She was also promising to write if she could not come down and see him.

Thinking about it all these years later, I would really like to know what he was thinking as they took him away. His face showed no fear or concern. As a matter of fact, he almost wore a pleasant expression as he left.

The wagon left town with James, Harmon, and Andrew riding their horses alongside. There was a driver with a guard seated next to him. By the driver's feet was a double-barreled coach shotgun. It was broken open with the shells lying next to it. That way, the bouncing of the wagon would not accidently make the gun go off.

The guard had a long gun. His was a standard Winchester '73 with an octagon barrel, and very reliable. He rode with it cradled easily in his arm in a nonthreatening way.

As long as Alvin behaved, he was treated as well as anyone could wish to be treated. The handcuffs were merely a precaution to prevent two things: one, Alvin getting a wild notion and trying to jump out of the wagon to run away, and two, in case Ezra or someone else decided they did not want to take a chance on the justice system breaking down, and letting him go. James could argue it was just as bad to shoot a chained-up man as it was to shoot a young woman.

Fortunately, neither Ezra nor anyone else tried to take the law into his own hands. Nor did Alvin try to make his escape. Ezra did, however, quietly ride his horse behind the wagon with a revolver holstered on his hip.

James pulled up gently on his horse and dropped back to where Ezra was riding. "You planning to use that gun?"

"Not unless he tries to run," Ezra explained, "then it's coming out like greased lightning. Vengeance of the Lord and all that."

"That's my job, Ezra," he warned. "You best not be clearin' leather."

Ezra stared hard at the sheriff as he weighed his options and next words carefully. Finally, his face softened and he said barely above a whisper, "My daughter…"

"Ezra, look me square in the face," James commanded as they rode together.

Ezra locked eyes with James and waited for his next words.

"I give you my word of honor; he will not get away, dead or alive."

"Then I give you my solemn oath that my gun will not clear

leather…unless you miss," Ezra promised.

James held his stare for a minute as he debated the wisdom or necessity of forcing the issue with Mary's father. As the horses walked, James finally looked toward the wagon to glance at Alvin and see what was ahead on the trail.

Ezra said nothing, as he patiently waited for James to contemplate the situation and how he would respond. He respected James as a great man of honor and knew when he gave his word, you could take it to the bank. For that reason, Ezra wanted to be upfront with him, so he could also keep his word to the sheriff.

As James thought over the probabilities of Alvin escaping, or even trying, he realized they were minimal. He decided pushing the law at Ezra would serve no useful purpose.

Four hundred yards later, he finally spoke. "Okay, if I miss."

"Good enough," Ezra said. "My word of honor."

"Welcome along."

Andrew pulled his horse up and joined James and Ezra. "We're not going to make Kanab tonight."

"No, we're going to have to stop along the way," James agreed with him.

"Sounds like you've been contemplating on this for a while," Andrew said. "Where are you figuring to stop?"

"Same place we stopped for water on the way up. When we were there, I noticed it would make a good camping spot, if we had to stop on the way back."

"Good thinking," Andrew said. "It shows you've spent a lot of time on the trail. I'm glad we're traveling with you and not trying to figure out logistics on our own. I may be a good doctor, but I'd never make a good cowboy."

"You sell yourself short, Andrew. I've seen you at work, and you have a keen eye for detail. That's why I brought you and had you perform the autopsy. If you had to turn your hand at cowboying, you would pick it up in no time. Much better than I would pick up doctoring."

With a laugh, Andrew responded, "You're too kind, Jim, but you may make a better doctor than you think. Much of it is listening to patients and then performing surgery, even when you don't know what's wrong with them."

"I sure hope you're joking," Ezra said, "or I'm never going back to the doctor again."

"Of course I'm joking," Andrew laughed. "It is amazing how rapidly modern medicine is discovering new cures to keep us healthy. You'll be in good hands if you go back, especially if you come see me."

"Maybe I'll do just that," Ezra stated without humor, "the next time I need a sawbones."

"Oh, now that was just hurtful," Andrew laughed.

"How's Alvin doing up in the wagon?" James asked him.

"He's doing alright," Andrew responded. "He seems to be in good spirits, and I don't think we will have any trouble from him along the way."

"Did you hear that, Ezra?" James asked, not letting his relief sound in his voice. "Looks like neither one of us has anything to worry about."

"Does that mean you're not itching to use that new holster you've been sporting around?" Ezra asked.

"Oh, I'm using it right now. It's keeping my gun safe while we ride. If you mean am I itching to draw my gun out of it, I never itch to do that. That has to be the worst part about being a sheriff; the fact I may have to draw and shoot somebody someday. I hate the thought of it."

"As I told my boy the other day," Ezra began, "I'm all for law and order, but if it comes down to it, I have no problem taking a life to save mine or my family's."

"I hope we never have to cross each other then," James said.

"I thought we were here to take care of Alvin," Andrew stated, "not start a fight of our own."

"Ahh, we're not fighting," Ezra said. "We're just talking and supposing. I can't imagine a situation where James and I would be on opposite sides of the law…unless you're planning to go outlaw on us."

James smiled. "No, no plans to do that."

"Why do you think he did it?" Andrew asked, changing the subject.

"He hasn't admitted to doing it yet," James reminded him.

"No, but do you have any doubt in your mind that he did?"

"No, actually I don't," James admitted. "I had my suspicions from the first time we walked up the hollow that it was a local who did it. That's why I wasn't too worried about getting all lathered up about the drummer. I understand why the town wanted it to be him, but he doesn't seem the kind of man who would do it."

"I was surprised when we found out he had a wife and children back in Monroe," Andrew said, "and he really seemed dedicated to them."

"If that's the case," Ezra interjected, "why was he making advances to Mary?"

"I don't believe he was, Ezra," James said. "I truly think he was complimenting a beautiful girl and trying to drum up a little more business."

"How does he drum up more business by giving a necklace to my daughter?"

"Because she was so taken with it," James said, "that she would go all around town and show it to everybody. Some of the people she showed would become interested in what else he had to sell and would go and see. It was smart advertising, I'm just sorry it almost got him killed."

"It was lucky you got there when you did," Andrew said, "or this story wouldn't have a happy ending."

"The ending won't be so happy for Alvin," Ezra said with a certain amount of satisfaction, mixed with pain. "Or at least it better not be."

"Something I've been meaning to ask you, Ezra," James said, "but I keep getting distracted away from it. Why on earth did you and Joseph just sit there when Jackie was about to hang the drummer?"

"Wasn't my doing," Ezra stated without emotion, "and it wasn't my place to stop them. If he was guilty, then he deserved what he got."

"And if he wasn't?" Andrew asked.

"My daughter wasn't guilty of anything, and she was killed."

Andrew and James looked at each other. James only shook his head to remind Andrew that they had taken an oath not to tell Ezra about Mary's sexual activities unless it was absolutely necessary. Andrew needed no reminding.

"And you could live with yourself if an innocent man was hanged?" James asked.

"Like I said, it wasn't my doing, and I didn't know he was innocent. Maybe you should ask Jackie Adler that question."

"I don't think I have to, I saw the look in his eyes. He would act like it didn't bother him, but I think he would lose a lot of nights' sleep over the deal."

"I think I see our watering spot about a mile up the road," Andrew said. "I'll go let Harmon and the driver know we'll be stopping for the night. Any special requests for dinner?"

"What are our choices?".

"Bread, cheese, and dried meat," Andrew said, just as

seriously as he could.

"Happy days," James chuckled as he tried to stifle his humor. "That's exactly what I would have asked for. I've had a hankering for that for weeks now."

"You two have been out on the trail too long," Ezra commented with a sour expression.

"We hardly ever get out on the trail together," Andrew told him.

"Then maybe the two of you ought not be out on the trail together at all."

"Oh, don't be sour," James said, "we're just fooling about to help pass the time."

"Well, ride back up there with the wagon, if you're going to do that," he growled. "I don't want to listen to you try to be a vaudeville show out here on the trail."

"Oh, all right," Andrew said, "we'll try to curb the trail humor, so you don't have to pretend to not like it."

"I'm not pretending."

They made camp by the creek where they had planned and gathered enough firewood to last them through the cold night. They also made sure they had enough for Postum and biscuits in the morning.

After they had dinner and it was time to turn in for the night, James turned to Alvin. "If you will give me your word that you won't run off in the night, I won't handcuff you to the wagon wheel."

"Will you leave my hands cuffed together?"

"I will. As an officer of the law, I can't leave you uncuffed all together. But as I said, if you will give me your solemn word that you won't run, I won't chain you to the wagon. Fair warning though, if you promise me and it sounds phony, I'll cuff you to the highest part of the wheel, and you will sleep standing up."

"I guess that's fair. No, I'm not going anywhere. To tell you the truth, I'm more afraid of Ezra than I am of you. You're here to see that justice is served."

"So is Ezra, I assure you."

"No doubt," Alvin agreed, "but I think his idea of justice and yours may be a bit different. I also think if I ran away, he would hunt me down and shoot me like a rabid dog." The words burned in his throat as he remembered the day he took Mary's life.

"I'd say you are reading that one right. However, he gave me his solemn word that if you escaped, he would not shoot you unless I missed."

"That's not a lot of comfort. I've seen him shoot," Alvin stated, "and he can shoot the dust off a hawk in flight. I'm afraid he would shoot me one leg and arm at a time as I ran. No, Sheriff, you have my solemn word that I won't run during the night."

"I believe you. I hope you have as comfortable a night as you possibly can."

"Thank you, Sheriff. You've been as kind to me as I could expect under the circumstances."

"In all honesty, I'm just doing my job," James assured him. "You have not been found guilty or innocent yet, and it is my job to bring you to trial, so a jury can decide your fate."

"Yes, but a lesser man would treat me like the killer he saw me as," he commented. "I wonder if Ezra would be as kind as you've been."

"He might surprise you."

"Perhaps."

"Anyway, here's your blanket. Rest easy, tonight."

The next morning when they woke up, they found Alvin

sleeping comfortably in handcuffs. Well, as comfortably as he could. There was no indication that he had any intention of running. He was once again loaded up in the wagon after breakfast, and the party all started off to Kanab at an easy pace. As they rode into town, people in the streets stopped to look and watch the suspected murderer go by. News had traveled fast, and they wanted to see who he was.

"Welcome to Kanab," James said as he turned to Alvin.

"They don't look too friendly," Alvin said, his concern starting to show.

"They're not much on murder," Andrew commented.

"No, I don't suppose so." Alvin looked down at his handcuffs.

Ezra quietly smiled to himself as he heard the exchange. He thought about adding a comment, but felt these three had stated it perfectly.

The ride through town seemed like it took longer than coming down from Orderville, at least to Alvin. He was not accustomed to so many harsh stares and, oddly, it struck him that he was not sure why they would look at him that way. It seemed there was something broken with his emotions that would come over him at certain times, and this was one of them. Later, the newspapers around the state also noticed this tendency and repeatedly commented on it, most particularly when he was at his arraignment and hearing.

When they finally arrived at the County Jail, Alvin was placed in a cell by himself.

"You were good to your word that you wouldn't try to escape on the trail," James said to Alvin as he stood in the open doorway of the cell. "Will you give me the same oath about not escaping from my jail?"

"I'm not sure what you're getting at, Sheriff."

"What I'm meaning is that you've earned some credit with me. If you give me your solemn oath that you will not try to escape, I will leave the cell door open, while there are people here in the building."

"Why would you do that?" Alvin asked. "That seems like an odd thing to do."

"Two reasons, son," James explained. "First, you did right by me out there on the trail, as I said before, so I'm willing to give you a chance."

"Okay, what is the second reason?"

"Ezra is still in town, and he has his long gun with him."

"I see," Alvin said with perfect clarity. "You're not putting any limitations on him this time."

"Not only that," James warned, "I'll even deputize him if I think you're itching to run off."

"I guess staying put is going to be a good idea then," Alvin conceded.

"Think of this as your new home for a while. Better settle in and make the best of it."

James started to walk into the other room, thought better of it and turned back around.

"With all that we talked about, there is only one rule around here, if you try and run, we'll shoot you in the back…four times."

The reality of this comment really hit home for Alvin, and James could see his countenance visibly change from one of comfort to one of horror.

After a moment, his face relaxed once again. "Understood. I won't cause any problems."

"I thought not. I'll be back in the morning after I clean the trail dust off me."

"I imagine I'll be here," Alvin replied just as if the school principal had reprimanded him.

James turned around and walked into the jail's main room.

"He's all yours," he said to the jailer. "He won't be any problem."

"How can you be so sure?"

"He gave me his word."

"What if he breaks it?" he asked.

"Then I told him I would give him lead, four times over," James said evenly.

"Good enough, Sheriff," he said. "Go home and get some rest. I'll hold down the fort here and call if there's any problem."

"Good night, then."

James left the jailhouse and mounted his horse. He slowly rode home as he contemplated the events of the last few days. What a strange turn of events they had been. Never in his imaginings had he thought he would have been dealing with this kind of heinous crime.

Later, as he and his wife Pearl were getting ready for the night, she sat reading in bed. James finished cleaning up, after bathing, and put on his nightclothes. He walked into the bedroom, slid under the covers, and sat next to his wife.

"So, do you *know* Alvin killed that poor young Mary?" she asked.

"Pert near," he responded, "I'm just missing the motive yet. I'm sure I'll figure it out soon enough; I just need to give it some time and worry over it for a bit. Maybe after a night or two of sleeping in our own bed, it will come to me. It usually does."

"How far along was she?" Pearl asked as she still perused through her book. She was not really reading at this point, but used it more as a distraction.

"How far along was she, what?" James asked, completely missing what was so obvious to his wife. "You mean with her school exams?"

"With child, Jim," she said, completely surprised that such an intelligent man had missed this simple fact. "How far along pregnant was she?"

He looked at her for a minute as he tried to figure out what caused her to say such a foolish thing. "What makes you think she was pregnant?"

"Everything you told me tonight. That whole long story tells me she was pregnant. I'm surprised you didn't see it on your own. I'm probably more surprised that Andrew didn't find it in his autopsy."

"Heavens to Betsy." He sat tall in the bed. "I would have never figured that out, and Andrew wasn't looking for it."

His thoughts raced, "I must say I'm surprised none of the women in Orderville thought of it. They all knew Mary in some way or other."

"Probably because they are all too close to the situation and, like you said, because they knew her. I didn't know her all that well, so I'm not hampered by what I already know of her. Besides, the whole town was in shock over this, and probably looking to see the best in her. We tend to do that after folks have died."

"You're a genius," he said, leaning over and kissing her. "I guess we're running back up to Orderville in the morning. Andrew's going to love me for this."

Angered by the loud and incessant knocking on his front door, a tired and groggy Andrew answered it, still wearing his nightclothes. It was obvious that James had awoken him.

"What in the Sam H…," he started, until he saw it was James at the door. "What's the matter, Jim? What on earth could be so important that you've dragged me from my restful slumber? I would have thought you'd still be enjoying that comfortable bed of yours."

"We've got to go back to Orderville," James said with an apologetic look on his face. "Turns out there may be more to the story, and we missed it."

"The hell you say," Andrew complained, rubbing his eyes to try to focus on the world. "You realize I've already ridden more this week than I usually do in a year, don't you? Why are we going back? And this better be an awfully good reason."

"Looks like Mary was pregnant," James informed him without ceremony.

Andrew motioned for James to come into the house and closed the door behind him.

"I'll get dressed."

Sitting on a table near James was a book that he absently picked up and began looking through. He opened it up and read the title. It was Henry Gray's *Anatomy: Descriptive and Surgical.* He thumbed through it, while Andrew quickly changed his clothes.

"I guess this must be fascinating reading if you're a doctor," he said to himself. "As far as I'm concerned, as sheriff, I've seen enough body parts bleeding all over the place."

"What are you muttering about?" Andrew asked. He had returned dressed and ready to go.

"Anatomy, it's not for me."

"It has all the information in it that will tell us if she was pregnant or not."

"Do we need to pack it up and take it with us then?" James asked.

"No, I know all I need to for this," Andrew said. "All we need now is breakfast. Come into the kitchen and let's see what we can rustle up."

That afternoon, James and Andrew rode back to Orderville. They stopped at the Co-op store and tied up their horses.

"Is that who I think it is over there?" Andrew asked James when he saw a familiar man step out of the saddle shop.

"You mean Joseph Erickson, the District Attorney?"

"Yes," Andrew confirmed, "that's him, then?"

"It is, and we need to go over and talk to him."

The two men walked stiffly across the road, where Joseph stood waiting.

"Saw you ride into town," he said. "I've been wanting to talk to you. I'm glad you're here."

"You heard about what's been going on down here?" James asked him.

"I did and, since I was already making the circuit," he stated, "I thought I would ride down and get the scoop first hand. So what can you tell me?"

"We need to go and talk somewhere private," James said. "Do you have a hotel room we can use?"

"I can do you one better, I think," Erickson said. "Come with me."

He led them back into the saddle shop. Andrew and James noticed Clifford was the only one there. He was in the corner working on a set of harnesses that needed repair.

"Clifford," Erickson began, "any chance you can run across the road to the Co-op and buy yourself some dinner while we use your shop? I'll pay for it. We have some very sensitive issues we need to talk about, and we can't do it on the street. I hesitate doing it in the hotel room, you never know who might accidently overhear."

Clifford chuckled, "Are you trying to say there are people in the hotel, who make it a habit of listening to other people's conversations?"

"Not at all," Erickson defended. "We just don't want anyone to get wind of this until the proper time, if that ever comes."

"I'm on my way," Clifford said. "I need to stop by the house afterward, so I'll be gone for a good hour and a half. I'll put up the 'gone to lunch' sign when I go. Just be sure to pull the door shut all the way when you leave."

"Got it. Thanks."

As soon as Clifford put out the sign and left, Erickson turned to James and Andrew. "What can you tell me about the investigation?"

"The long and short of it is," James began, "we thought we might have a good suspect in the drummer from Monroe, but he had a good alibi. Then we came back to town and looked at the folks here, and we're right sure we have the man who killed Mary. He's locked up in the jailhouse down to Kanab."

"Alvin Heaton?" Erickson asked.

"Jr., yes," James confirmed.

"Well, then what brings you back up here, other than my good fortune?" Erickson asked.

"We think Mary may have been pregnant when she was killed," James informed him.

"That certainly puts a new twist in the rope," Erickson commented. He turned to Andrew. "Did you not think to check on that when you performed the autopsy?"

"Never occurred to me," he defended. "I did check to see if she had relations before her death, which she had, but since her cause of death was obvious, I went no further. At the time, we had no idea of a motive, and no one in town mentioned the fact that she had been sparkin' with someone."

"I hope it *was* sparkin' and not someone forcing his intentions on her," James stated. "If that's the case, it would explain why no one knew about it. That's the sort of thing a good girl would not want anyone to know."

"No, because it would tend to invite others to expect they could get away with the same thing with her," Erickson observed. "Unfortunately, there's no way around it. We need to know if she was pregnant."

"She wasn't forced," Andrew confirmed.

"What exactly is it that you're saying, Erickson?" James asked, afraid of the answer.

"We need to conduct another autopsy."

"She's buried in the ground," James argued. "I don't have the authority to order her body exhumed, and that is the only way we're going to find out."

"I do," Erickson said. "As District Attorney, I can order it done."

"Her family's not going to be happy about this," James commented.

"Let them know this will help us convict the Heaton boy, if it was indeed him," Erickson explained. "And if it wasn't, then knowing will help us to find out who did do it."

"Because it goes toward motive?" James asked, looking for confirmation. "And if we know the motive, then it helps us to know who to look for."

"Yes."

"It seems a shame to dig her up," Andrew said with some disappointment. "We just laid her to rest. I feel horrible that I didn't think to check when I had her on the table."

"Don't beat yourself up too much," Erickson said. "It's not the sort of thing we think to look for in a case like this...what am I saying? We've never had a case like this!"

"I've never even heard of a case like this before," James said, "not even up North in the cities."

"Still, I thought to look to see if she'd had relations, I should have thought to take it a step further."

"You were looking for forced relations and not an ongoing relationship," James consoled. "We had no idea she had been seeing anyone, so we wouldn't have thought her pregnant."

"But your wife did."

"Women are funny like that, sometimes," James sidestepped to dissuade Andrew from further berating himself anymore.

"I think I'll have Dr. Robert Garn come down from Panguitch to help you," Erickson said. "Not that I don't think you are capable, but..."

"I know," Andrew said, "a second set of eyes would be a legally good idea right about now. Besides, after my oversight, I could use the moral support."

"I was going to say, that he's had experience in looking at exhumed bodies," Erickson said, "but I like your comment even better."

"I should be the one to tell Ezra," James said.

"No, I should be the one, it was my mistake," Andrew corrected. "But you better be there with me."

"Should I come along, too?" Erickson asked.

"No," James instructed him. "I've known Ezra for years and watched Mary grow up from time to time, whenever I was up to Mt. Carmel, or they were down to Kanab. Andrew knows him too and has been a part of the investigation from the beginning, so it should come from us. He might see you as an outsider trying to intrude or take over."

"Good enough, I need to run up to Panguitch anyway. You have my order, so you can put the blame on me if you need to. Anything to smooth things over with her father."

"Safe trip and we will telephone if there's a problem or when we have an answer," James said.

Erickson walked out of the saddle shop when James suddenly turned to Andrew.

"Ezra's still down to Kanab and this is not the sort of thing to say over the phone with others listening in. We'll tell Joseph, and he can decide how to tell his folks."

The two men walked out of the saddle shop, making sure the door closed solidly behind them. They walked across the street to the Co-op and checked on their horses. They were just loosening up their cinches so the horses would be more comfortable, when they heard Clifford's voice as he stepped out.

"Get 'er all done then?"

"Sure did, the shop's all yours again," James said. "We appreciate the use of it. I sure do love the smell of leather."

"Yeah, me too," Clifford chuckled. "I'm off to home then for a bit, and I'll be back down to the shop later on. Let me know if you need anything else."

"Will do, thanks."

They walked into the Co-op to find Wilford cleaning an empty store.

"Well, hello there," Wilford kind of smiled. "Did your prisoner escape?"

"You know better than that," James returned the smile. "I'm afraid we need to exhume Mary's body in the morning."

"The family's not going to like it," Wilford commented.

"I'm not going to like it," James said, "and I don't suppose Andrew here is going to like it much, either."

Andrew shook his head to indicate he indeed did not relish the idea.

"Can't be helped though," James added. "We think she was pregnant and that provides motive."

"And you're thinking that my nephew got her pregnant?" he

asked.

"That's what it's looking like," James answered, apologetically. "At least there is an awful lot of evidence pointing in that direction. However, we're not ready to start making speculations yet. Mostly we're still trying to gather the facts."

"Does this mean we're going to have to tell Ezra his little girl was having relations with someone?" Wilford inquired.

"I'm hoping we can give them a vague reason about the exhumation, and only say something if we have a positive result."

"Let's hope for the best on that," Wilford said. "I'll bet your rooms are still available over to the hotel. You've had a long ride so go get settled in, and I'll start making arrangements. I'll also let Joseph know what we're doing, so we don't catch him by surprise with this."

"We talked about that earlier," James informed him, "and decided it would be best to let Andrew and me tell him, but we sure would be obliged if you would come along."

Nodding, Wilford responded, "Of course."

James and Andrew left the store, untied their horses and walked them around the back of the hotel to the horse stalls for the customers' animals. They took off their saddles and put them in the tack shed to keep them out of the weather. They used the pitchfork to feed their mounts some hay that had been put there for that purpose. Once their horses were taken care of, they gathered up their overnight things and walked to the hotel. Their rooms were indeed still available, so they requested to use the same ones and put their belongings in there. They returned to the Co-op to find Wilford gone, but Edward was tending it in his absence.

"Any grub left for dinner?" James asked.

"Sure, I think I can round up enough for the two of you," Edward said. "Give me a little bit to get it warmed up."

James and Andrew ate their soup-and-bread supper in relative silence; neither looked forward to the idea of what was to come next. They still needed to walk over to Joseph's house and tell him what needed to happen with his sister. They finished their meals and took the last drinks out of their cups.

"Ready?" James asked.

"If there's no way around it," Andrew said. "Let's go get it done."

When they arrived at Joseph's house, they knocked on the door. After a moment, Joseph answered.

"Sheriff, Doctor," he said, "what's wrong? Is my father all right?"

"He's fine," James said. "We're here for something else."

"Don't tell me Alvin got away."

"No," Andrew said as he and James stepped through the door, "but there is a complication."

James closed the door behind them.

James and Andrew looked around and noticed Francis and the children were not within earshot.

"I'm afraid when I was conducting the autopsy," Andrew continued, "I didn't think to check something critically important. We will have to bring her up out of the ground tomorrow, so a Panguitch doctor and I can reexamine her."

"Dr. Garn? Why would you have to do that?" Joseph asked. "Can't you leave her be?"

"Please don't ask me to explain," Andrew said. "It is a delicate matter, and one that shouldn't be discussed unless absolutely necessary. Please, let's just leave it at that."

"I don't think I like that idea," Joseph said. "What if I refuse?"

"We're working under the direction of the District Attorney," Andrew explained with great sympathy. "It's in the hands of the law at this point. There's really nothing you can do. Please understand, if there was any other way to do this, we most certainly would."

Joseph stood there and glared at them for a moment, and then softened his look.

"We need to be on our way," Andrew mentioned. "We just wanted to come by and let you know, so you didn't find out from somebody else."

"I appreciate your consideration, it does help," Joseph said. "You're right. It would have been awful to hear about this from the town."

"We'll let you figure out how you're going to tell your father," James said. "We didn't want to be the ones to tell him over the telephone. You can decide how you want to handle it."

"I'll figure something out," Joseph said. "Thank you again for coming by and letting me know. Good night."

"Good night," Andrew said. James nodded his head to convey his wishes.

The two men stepped out of the house and walked away when Andrew turned to James. "You know what we forgot?"

"No, what's that?"

"Wilford."

"That's right," James said in realization. "We were going to wait and have him go with us."

"I was so wrapped up in facing Joseph I forgot all about it until just now. I wish we had him with us, but I think it turned out as well as could be under the circumstances. Joseph seemed to understand the need for what we were doing, even if he didn't understand *why* we were doing it."

"Or like it."

On their way back to the hotel, they met Wilford returning to the Co-op.

"I guess you're off the hook for going with us to see Joseph," James said. "Andrew and I were so worked up over telling him, that we jumped in and did it, without realizing we were leaving you behind. Anyway, he knows now, and we can proceed when Robert gets here in the morning."

"How did he take it?"

"As well as can be expected," James said. "Andrew told him straight he'd missed something important and he and Robert had to go back and reexamine her."

"Did you tell him why we were going back in, and what we were looking for?"

"No. Andrew requested that he not ask, so he didn't. I'm not sure he wants to know."

"Maybe not, but his father will," Wilford pointed out.

"Andrew gave a pretty good argument. Maybe we'll let him try it on Ezra, if it comes down to that."

"Let's hope it doesn't. You two need to get to bed, so we can get together in the morning and talk about it some more. For now, it's all speculation. Tomorrow we should know something."

"You made all the necessary arrangements?" Andrew asked.

"I sure did," Wilford confirmed. "I have a feller digging her up right now and will have her ready and waiting for you where you conducted the original autopsy."

"Why do you have him digging her up right now?" James asked. "Tomorrow morning will be soon enough."

"How many people are running around right now in the dark?" Wilford asked him.

"Nary a soul," James replied.

"That's right," Wilford said. "I figured we would have a whole lot fewer questions to answer if no one knew what we were doing."

"My hat's off to you, Constable," James said. "You are a

much sharper knife than I am. I'm impressed. Maybe if we work fast enough, we can get her back in the ground before anyone else knows we've taken her out."

"Regardless of how hard we try to keep it a secret," Wilford warned, "they will all know soon enough."

"Well, maybe we can keep the why a secret then," James said. "That would be good enough for me."

"Agreed. I'll see you two in the morning. Goodnight."

"Goodnight, and thank you." James said.

The following afternoon, James was sitting in the corner of the saddle shop drinking his Postum. Clifford was on the other side of the shop working on a saddle at his workbench. He stopped for a minute, long enough to take a slow drink of his Postum, and then looked over at James. He said nothing as he looked, and then went back to the saddle. Breaking the silence, Andrew and Robert walked in. They went directly to the coffee pot, poured themselves a cup, and sat down next to James. They remained silent.

"Is it time for me to go to lunch?" Clifford asked as he wiped his hands on his apron.

"That obvious?" Andrew asked.

"Starting to get used to it. I'll be back in an hour or so. Remember to pull the door closed hard behind you."

"Thanks, Clifford. If you see Wilford…"

"Yeah, I'll send him over."

"Thanks," Andrew said.

As soon as Clifford left the shop, Andrew took a quick sip of his drink and turned to James. "I'll be jiggered if she wasn't right."

"You mean?"

"Yes," Robert said, "Mary was pregnant."

"There's our motive, boys," James said with conviction. "Thanks for coming down, Dr. Garn."

He turned to Andrew, "Looks like we'll be riding back to Kanab in the morning. It's time to get the truth out of young Alvin Heaton."

"We best be letting Joseph know what is happening and, if he hasn't told his father yet, we will do it as soon as we get back to town," James mentioned.

"That's a good idea," Andrew said. "This time…"

Wilford walked into the building. "Clifford said you made him go to lunch again and that you wanted to see me."

"This time," Andrew began again, "this time I want Wilford to come with us."

"What did I just walk into?" Wilford asked, concerned.

"Mary was about seven or eight weeks pregnant," Robert informed him. "Now you three get to let her brother know we're finished and will return her to her eternal resting place."

"I dodged it last night," Wilford admitted. "I suppose being there today is only the Christian thing to do. Are you going to tell him what you found?"

"Again," Andrew began, "not if we can help it. I think Ezra needs to know this first, because it won't be long before everyone else knows it."

"I think what I'll do is tell Ezra as soon as we get down there," James said, "and then tell him he has twenty four hours before we tell anyone else. That way, he can get back up here and tell Edith and their children first."

"Excellent thinking," Wilford agreed. "I don't believe anyone has found out we've pulled her up yet, so I'm going to wait until dark again to take her back. That will help keep this under wraps until Ezra can tell his family."

"I believe my work here is done," Dr. Garn stated. "I will be on my way back to Panguitch, now."

"You don't want to stay the night and start out fresh in the morning?" Wilford asked.

"Wife promised me pot roast as soon as I got home. I'm aching for pot roast. Good day, gentlemen."

Dr. Garn left the shop while the other three remained behind. Wilford poured himself a cup and sat down by the other two.

"Hmmm," he said.

The other two just nodded.

Nobody moved, except to sip their Postum.

James reached over to the pot to pour himself another one. "Drat."

"Gone?"

"Yup."

"Means we have to go?"

"Yup."

"We could make another pot," Wilford suggested.

"Yup, we could."

Still no one moved.

"I'll stick-pull you for it," James said.

"Naw," Andrew said. "Come on and let's get it over with. I'll tell him again like I did last night."

"Fair enough."

"We do need to fill it back up for Clifford, though," James said. "We did run him off and drink it dry."

"I'll get it," Wilford said. "I know where he keeps everything and how he likes it."

With the door pulled closed behind them when they were finished, they walked to Joseph's house to find him working in the garden area. He stood up to address them.

"This is the last place I saw Mary alive," he told them. "I'm thinking I might make a little memorial to her over in the corner by the peas. She likes peas… liked peas."

"We came by to let you know we're returning Mary to her resting place," Andrew said, "and again, how sorry we are this had to happen…any of it."

"Did you find what was so important that you had to disturb her like that?"

"We did, thank you," Andrew said. "We'll be heading back to Kanab in the morning, so we can let your father know what happened here today."

"Thank you for being so discreet about this. I walked by her grave this morning to explain to her what was going to happen, and I noticed you had already moved her. I've been watching the cemetery, and nobody's gone by there today, so nobody knows. I appreciate that. I'm sorry if I seemed hostile last night. You really took me by surprise."

"We thought you handled it quite well," James said. "Andrew was saying how impressed he was with you and your comportment. No apology necessary."

"Regardless…" he said.

"Don't worry over it, Joseph."

"Thank you," he said.

It was a long ride back to Kanab the next day because James and Andrew dreaded informing Ezra that his recently deceased daughter was pregnant. They had pretty much avoided the subject until they reached town and were riding up to Ezra's hotel.

"Maybe we could send him a telegram," Andrew mentioned as they rode.

"Won't work."

"Maybe we could write a nice long letter and slide it under the door of his hotel room," he suggested.

"Won't work."

"Maybe we could hire a special messenger to let him know."

"I like it, but it won't work."

"Maybe we could..."

"Won't work," James said, cutting him off.

"If you're going to continue to be a stick-in-the-mud," Andrew complained, "I'm going to leave you home next time."

"Won't work."

"And why not?"

"Because I brought you along," James pointed out, "not the other way around. You sure bellyache a lot for a doctor."

"Yeah," Andrew said in mock frustration. "Well, I didn't become a doctor, so I could exhume poor girls who were murdered because they happened to become pregnant. I became a doctor to help people."

"Helping us catch her killer is helping people, especially Ezra."

"I suppose so," he conceded, "but I still don't like the idea of telling him."

"We're here now," James pointed out. "We might as well knock on his door and tell him, and then we can be done with it."

"Fine, lead the way."

They tied off their horses and walked into the hotel.

"Ezra Stevens still in the same room?" James asked the hotel clerk.

"Still there," he responded. "Last I saw however, he was in the dining room eating his meal."

"Thanks. We'll go in there and check on him."

They walked into the dining room and saw him sitting at the table finishing up his meal. The two men were hungry after their long ride, but they needed to take care of the pressing business at hand.

"Hello, boys," Ezra said, as he saw them approach. "Haven't seen much of you the last couple of days. Heard you rode back up to Orderville. That true?"

"It is," James said, "and we need to talk to you straight away. Can we go up to your room?"

Ezra looked around and noticed they were the only ones there, except for the waiter, who was busy across the room.

"I think we can talk here without being disturbed," he said. "What's on your gentlemanly minds?"

"It's your daughter," James said in a subdued voice. "We had to do something drastic."

They now had his full and undivided attention. "What did you do, lads?" he asked them point-blank.

"Mary was pregnant."

"The hell you say," Ezra exclaimed, completely denying the possibility.

"I'm afraid it's true," Andrew said. "The District Attorney ordered us to exhume her and verify it."

"You dug her up?" Ezra asked in angry shock, causing the waiter to look in their direction. "Without even asking my permission?"

"We had a court order, Ezra," James said in a hushed tone. "We didn't have a choice."

"So everyone in town found out about this before I did?" he growled. "How dare you?"

"Settle down, Ezra," James said. "It was done very discreetly, and I don't think anyone even knows except for Wilford and the man hired to do it."

"How do you keep that sort of thing a secret?" Ezra demanded.

"They dug her up and moved her at night, when everyone was asleep, and then they took her back the same way. No one else in town knows she was even moved, no one except for Joseph. We let him know before we did it."

"Did you tell him she was with child?"

"No, we've told no one else. We won't tell anyone down here for twenty four hours, so you have time to get home and tell your family before it comes out in the newspapers."

"I'm not happy about this," he said, "but I do appreciate you coming and giving me this advance warning. I think if I leave right now, I have enough light left I can get a solid start on my ride. I best go square up on my room and be on my way. Twenty-four hours, you say? Do I have your word on that?"

"Twenty-four hours," James promised him, "not a minute sooner. You have our word."

"And Wilford's not going to be spreading it all over town before I get there?"

"We all took an oath not to say anything. He won't tell. It was actually his idea to dig her up and put her back at night, so the town wouldn't know."

"Again, I am obliged and in your debt. I'll be off then."

Ezra quickly walked out of the dining area and up to his room. While he packed his belongings, James and Andrew ordered dinner. They were in idle conversation when Andrew caught a glimpse of Ezra rushing through the lobby on his way out the door.

"Guess our twenty-four hours starts now."

Once they finished eating, they rode over to the jailhouse to check on the prisoner. When they saw that all was well, they went home.

"What did you find?" Pearl asked as James walked through the door.

"Ask me tomorrow night," he said. "Can't talk about it before then."

"How cryptic," she said with a knowing smile. "Why tomorrow night?"

"I gave my word."

"And you are a man of your word, so I won't make you tell me. However, while you change your clothes, I'm going to speculate for a minute, and you can just listen."

"Is this going to get me into trouble?" he asked her with a worried laugh.

"Not if you don't say anything to compromise your promise."

"All right, then, I'm going to change my clothes."

She followed him into the other room. "I'd say that after you rode all the way to Orderville, you pulled her body out of the ground. Andrew re-examined her and found I was right. Then before you told anyone else, you quickly rode back home, so you could tell Ezra who's been haunting the jailhouse, making sure the Heaton boy didn't get away. You told him and sent him home to tell his family, before you tell anyone else. Am I close?"

"What makes you think that's what happened?"

"Because that's what I would have done if I was in your position. Now you can wait until tomorrow night before you tell me if I'm close or not. It's time for you to come to bed, and rest up for your sheriffin' duties ahead of you tomorrow."

"You know why I married you, don't you?" he asked her.

"Because I'm smart and beautiful," she said, "and because I made you do it."

"Yes."

The following evening, James walked back to the jailhouse.

He stopped at Andrew's house first to invite him along. He knocked on the door. Andrew answered it.

"Don't tell me we need to head back up to Orderville," Andrew complained. "I don't think my backside could take it."

"Oh, my pessimistic friend," James said, "do you not think I could be stopping by with good news?"

"Are you stopping by with good news?"

"No."

"So, where's the pessimism?" Andrew inquired.

"All right, you win. I stopped by to let you know I was headed over to the jailhouse to interrogate Alvin. Did you want to come along?"

"I don't see the need," Andrew responded. "I can't think of anything I would need to ask him. You know all the facts I do and maybe a few beyond. You are the best sheriff we have in town and I'm sure you'll do a good job."

"I'm the only sheriff in town."

"I know. Now, who's being the pessimistic one?"

James left him there and completed his ride over to the jailhouse. When he arrived, he found Harmon was already there waiting for him. With him was Thomas Carter, a leading member of the community in Kanab and one of the former leaders of the United Order in Orderville.

"Can you let us in on the big secret now?" Harmon asked as he walked through the door. "You said you had to wait until tonight, and then you would explain everything. It's time."

"Yes, and thank you for your patience," James said. "Here is the brunt of it; Mary was pregnant."

"That's a shocker," Harman exclaimed. "Why did you have to wait to tell us?"

"Because I promised to give Ezra time to ride home and tell his family, before someone down here telephoned up to

Orderville and spilled the beans. That would be a horrible way for them to find out."

"Yes, of course," Harmon said. "You made the right choice, and I would have done the same thing if I'd thought of it. By the way, I brought Thomas here to talk to Alvin because he used to live up to Orderville. Alvin grew up knowing him, and I think he will respond favorably to a familiar friendly face."

"It doesn't hurt that he's in the Stake Presidency, either," James said. "Maybe Alvin will respond to him being his religious leader on some level."

"Maybe," Harmon said, "but I didn't bring him here for that. I brought him here for his community ties."

"Fair enough. Hello, Thomas."

"James."

"Are you ready for this?" James asked.

"I believe so. I've never done this before. Then again, neither has anyone else in the county, so I guess I'm as good as any."

"We need you to go interrogate young Heaton for us," Harmon said. "You are acting as a legal agent for the county in this, and I think he will respond better to you than he will to us."

"Let's see what we can do then," Thomas said as he headed toward the jail cell.

Alvin had been behaving well while he was locked up, so they had continued to leave the cell door open for him. The cell was typical and small with a cotton-stuffed canvas mattress on metal spring slats, riveted to the bed frame. He was sitting on the edge of the bed when Thomas entered. He drew a chair in behind him, and set it down facing Alvin. He sat down and paused for a moment.

"You know why I'm here?" Thomas finally asked him.

"Yes, and it ain't going to happen," Alvin stated defiantly.

"Confession is good for your soul, son," Thomas began, "we

will stay here all night if we have to but, mark my words, you will tell me the truth."

"You sound quite confident."

"Why shouldn't I be?"

"Because I didn't do it."

"We have far too much evidence to the contrary for us to believe that," Thomas informed him.

"No, you don't, because I didn't do it."

Back in the main room, James and Harmon visited, while they waited for Thomas to conduct his interview.

"Do you actually think he can do it?" James asked after trying to listen in on the interrogation. "Like he said, he's never done a murder interrogation before."

"He's the best in the county," Harmon assured him. "I've used him before on tough cases, and he's always come through for me. He's as reliable as they come."

"He's been in there for a long time," James said, concerned. "I'm not sure he's going to be able to crack this nut. Maybe this is why Alvin was so quick to agree to not run away. He's sure he can outwit us."

"Let's go over his alibi, once again, and see if we can find any holes in it that will help Thomas," Harmon suggested.

"All right...let's see," James thought over what Alvin had told him on the ride down in the wagon. "Monday afternoon, he went to the Co-op where his two uncles work..."

"One on his mother's side and one on his father's, correct?" Harmon asked for clarification.

"That's right, so we have verification from two different sides of the family."

"But still, they have a vested interest to see him innocent," Harmon pointed out.

"Yes," James admitted, "But one of them is the constable and the other one is the Justice of the Peace, so I'm going to tend to believe them."

"Agreed, at least for the moment. What about after the store?"

"He says he went home and ate dinner with his mother who ordered him out to do chores afterwards," James said.

"Do we know what chores she had him do?" Harmon asked, showing his skill as a lawyer.

"He said she sent him out to fix the fence. He puttered around for a while and then returned to the house. After a while, he went back out and cleaned the stable. After the stable, he went back inside and changed his clothes, so he could go down to the store and wait for his cousin, Homer Esplin to come along. When Homer finally did come by, the two of them went to his house and spent the rest of the night over there."

"Did you find any holes in his story?"

"Not that I could prove," James stated. "How can you prove that someone didn't clean the stall when the cow's still in there messing it up as soon as you're done?"

"I see your point."

"Let's hope Thomas has better luck finding the chinks in his alibi than I did," James offered. "He has been in there a couple of hours now. I wonder if he's getting anywhere with the boy."

"Have faith, Brother. Let him work his magic," Harmon suggested.

Back in the cell, Thomas was really putting the pressure on Alvin. He resisted the best he could for quite a while but, as he became tired of Thomas' continual pestering, he finally began to wear down.

"Did you do it?" Thomas asked strongly.

"No."

"We found blood on your shoes and coat," Thomas persisted

with passion. "Did you do it?"

"No," Alvin said as he continued to resist Thomas' efforts. "It was from a chicken."

Thomas felt he was getting closer to a confession, so he pushed harder.

"You had the gun! Did you do it?"

"No!" Alvin insisted, "I didn't do it!"

Outside in the main room, James and Harmon came to their feet as they heard Thomas drilling Alvin but good.

"Leave him be," Harmon said. "I can hear it in Alvin's voice. He's about to crack."

"Is he going to hit the boy?" James asked, concerned.

"No," Harmon answered. "He doesn't have to. Keep listening."

Thomas was now standing directly above Alvin, and his voice became stronger and louder. "Confession is good for the soul! Alvin! Did you do it?"

Alvin dropped his head.

"Alvin! Did you do it?"

More adamantly than before, he snapped his head up and almost shouted, "No!"

"Alvin! We know she was pregnant!"

Alvin dropped his head back down, hesitated for a moment and then, just above a whisper, finally admitted, "Yes."

Back in the main room, James leaned over close to Harmon and whispered, "Could you hear what he said?"

"No," Harmon whispered back.

"Tell him to ask again."

"Don't worry, he will."

Back in the cell, "Say it again, Alvin."

"Yes," Alvin said, more audibly than before.

"Thank you."

Thomas took a deep breath and sat back down in his chair; he was spent.

Alvin sat there listlessly and silently, his head hanging. He began to weep softly.

After he had a chance to catch his breath, Thomas slowly stood back up. He stepped out into the main room, picked up a pen and some paper and handed them to James.

"Time for you to write, Sheriff. The boy's going to make a confession."

James and Thomas returned to the cell, while Harmon brought in a writing table.

"Take it from the beginning, son, while the sheriff writes it down."

Alvin silently nodded his head as he walked back in his mind to the beginning. "She wanted me to marry her because she was..."

"Hold on a minute, Alvin," James said, "I need to write the introduction. I will say it out loud as I write it, so you know exactly what it says."

"Okay," Alvin said, waiting.

"Kanab, Kane County, Utah, May 15, 1908. With my own free will, without promise of hope of reward, or without fear or threats on the part of any person or persons, I confess with my own free will and choice that on April 20, A.D. 1908, at about 5:30 post meridian, I shot Mary Stevens to death."

He paused for a moment.

"That sound about right so far?" James asked him.

"So far... I put her in a wash in the rocks and covered her body with loose rocks and brush."

"Okay, let me write that down...all right, got it, now I'm writing more. 'The following are the facts that led up to the deed.' Okay, continue."

"I had unlawful relations with her. She wanted me to marry her and I refused. She insisted, and we quarreled. I told her I did not want to marry her, and she said she could make me. So I made up my mind to kill her if she still continued to insist."

"Are you getting all this, James?" Harmon asked him, concerned.

"Yes."

Outside in the main room, they could hear the door open. Thomas stepped out to see who it was.

"Hello, Doctor," he said. "What brings you here at this late hour of night?"

"Couldn't sleep, so I thought I would come over and see if there was any progress."

"We got it," Thomas said.

"He confessed?"

"Sure did. He's spilling his guts all over the place right now, and James is writing it all down."

"I guess it's time for Harmon to let Judge Ford know we're ready for an arraignment," Andrew said.

"Any idea who's representing the boy?"

"I heard John Brown might take on the case and be his defense," Andrew stated.

"The sheriff's brother? I can't wait to see this," Thomas said. "Let's poke our heads back in and hear the rest of the confession."

Back in the cell, James was shaking his hand from the cramps. "I've not written this much since…I'm not sure I ever have. Okay son, I'm ready to continue."

"Monday afternoon, we made an appointment on the school house porch to meet up in what is known as Gardner Hollow about 5 o'clock p.m. Then I went to the store, stayed there some time, then went home, ate dinner, got my gun out of the trunk, and came out on the porch. Mother called me to drive some cows out of the lot. I drove them out. She told me to fix up the fence, but I did not do it. I went over to the barn instead and looked at a setting hen, went back to the house, stayed there a few minutes, then went right back of our house and up on the hill, over into Gardner Hollow, waited there a few minutes, and then Mary came. We walked up the hollow to the place where her body was found. She again insisted that I marry her. I said that I would not. I said, "Won't you let me off and not make me marry you?" She said, "No. I can make you marry me by law." Then, I pulled out my gun and killed her. After covering her up with rocks, I went back down on a trot and walk. I left the wash just above the flume, went along the ditch bank to the fence, crossed the fence over into the stack yard, and went through Kesiah Esplin's barn, down through the lot to the east door of the house. I asked for Charley, then started home down the sidewalk. I ran part of the way."

"James," Harmon said when Alvin paused for a moment, "why don't you get up and walk around for a few minutes before we continue. You're starting to look like the pony that got put in with all the cows."

"Thanks, Harmon," he said. "I could use the rest. Give us just a moment there son, will you?"

"Sure," Alvin said. "Take your time. It looks like I'll be here for a while…no hurry. Besides, the longer it takes me to do this, the longer it will be before they hang me."

After a few minutes of walking around, James returned and sat down. "Any time you're ready again."

"I was on my way home," Alvin continued. "Fred and William Heaton, George Burkham, Ferry Brunham, and Uncle Fred were outside, and the others were in the house. I also saw Joe Stevens on the opposite sidewalk on his way to his mother-in-law's place. I went to the barn. I had the cartridge shells in my pocket and threw them out in the west end of the barn. I went to the house and put my gun in the trunk, changed my clothes, went to the barn and cleaned out the stable, went back to the house, changed clothes, stayed for a little while and talked to Ma. Then I went to the store, stayed there until Homer Esplin came along, went home with him, and stayed the rest of the night."

"Anything you want to add before we sign and witness it?" Harmon asked.

"No. That ought to about do it," Alvin replied.

"Good enough then," he said. "James, why don't you put our names down as witnesses, so we can sign it?"

"Sure," James said. "I see Andrew decided to join us after all. Do you want me to put his name down too?"

"You bet."

"No," Andrew interjected. "I wasn't here for all of it, so it may cause some complications down the road if we do. Leave me off of it, and you can call me in to testify on the part I did hear, if needed."

"I think you have something there," Harmon said; "good thinking to keep us in the best position we can be for the trial." He turned to Alvin and said, "This changes the whole rodeo, son. Now that we know you did it, and you know we know, you've become more of a risk for escaping. By all rights, I should be locking up the cell door and dropping the key down the well. Because you've been so cooperative with us over the past several days, I'm going to give you another chance. If you will give me your solemn oath, once again, that you will not try to escape, I will continue to leave the cell door open. If you promise me, and then escape anyway, I won't send Sheriff Brown here after you; I'll send for Ezra and deputize him. Any part of this you don't understand?"

"I understand every part of it, sir," Alvin said, glancing down at the floor to avoid Harmon's gaze. "The sheriff already gave me the same warning…"

"Are you still okay with this, James?" Harmon asked.

"I am. Alvin's always been straight with me, and I'm inclined to expect the same of him, unless *he* proves otherwise. I also think there is wisdom in sending for Mary's father if he does try to run away. He won't be hindered by jurisdictional lines, like I will be."

"Do you hear that, Alvin?" Harmon said. "Ezra won't stop until he finds you, if you run. Can you imagine what he will do to you if it comes to that?"

Alvin, still looking at the floor, said, "Yes."

"Do I have your word?"

"You do at that, sir."

"Let me hear you say it."

"I promise that if you leave the cell door open on my behalf," he slowly looked up at Harmon, "I will not run away or try to escape."

"That will do."

Thomas and Harmon gathered around the table above James and watched him sign as a witness, and then each took their turn signing the confession. Thomas started to take the chair out he had brought in at the beginning of the interrogation.

"No, sir," Alvin said in a gentle voice. "Please leave it, if you would. The table too."

Thomas looked over at James for a decision. James nodded to let him know it was all right.

"Thank you, Sheriff," Alvin said. "I thought I might like to do a bit of writing and maybe some reading while I'm here."

"You're welcome."

"Any idea when we'll go to trial, sir?"

"First we have to arraign you, son," Harmon stated. "Then

we need to have a hearing to prove we have enough evidence to proceed to trial. It wouldn't do to use the county's money to hold a trial if we don't have enough evidence."

"No, I suppose not," Alvin muttered.

"I think the answer to your question is, in a couple of days," James clarified. "We need to talk to Judge Ford in the morning and see what his schedule is, but I suspect he'll shift things around to get you in there sooner so you don't have to languish too long."

"Thank you, Sheriff," Alvin said. "I'm exhausted. Is it all right if I go to sleep now?"

"Of course," James said. "We're done here. Get a good night's sleep, and we'll try to have an answer for you in the morning."

The four men stepped outside into the main room and left Alvin to sleep.

"Let's get a copy of that confession to the *Richfield Reaper* paper, so they can print it," Harmon said. "I think we can get things to settle down quicker if they know we have the killer, and he won't be doing this to somebody else."

"I can't believe he actually walked by Mary's brother right after he killed her, like nothing happened," Andrew said, "and with her blood on his coat and shoes. As much as I know about medicine and the human body, I still can't understand how a person could be so cool and collected to do that."

"I don't know," James said. "I've often wondered that when I've been investigating other crimes. But, of course, none of them have ever been anything like this. They've all been smaller crimes, like chicken thieving, cow tipping, or fellers beating each other senseless."

Chapter Six
The Wheels of Justice

At the end of May, Alvin appeared in the Kanab courthouse for his preliminary arraignment. I wasn't there, but I heard it was very unusual for these kinds of legal events. As reported in the newspapers, interest was greatly aroused over the affair, as it hadn't been over anything in years, even more so than when Kanab elected America's first all women town council. The little courtroom was packed to the doors, and the building was entirely surrounded by those anxious to get a glimpse of the young fellow under charge of the grave crime.

Alvin appeared, as required, but he was unprepared both physically and mentally for the proceedings. One report by the *Deseret News* stated that he showed signs of embarrassment or, maybe fright in the beginning. They stated this was indicated by a slight quivering of his lower lip, but he soon overcame it. Once he mastered the quivering, they reported, he was able to maintain an appearance of indifference. This was where our townspeople became so confused. We never would have believed he would act like that if many of us had not seen it for ourselves. It was almost as if he had this whole other side to him that he kept locked away and never allowed us to see.

Once Justice of the Peace Edwin Mantripp Ford had entered and everyone had been seated, the judge looked around the room. After taking inventory of those present, he rapped his gavel.

Before anything else, the judge read the complaint against the defendant. "It has been sworn that Alvin Franklin Heaton, Jr., at the time and place of Orderville, Utah, unlawfully, willfully, feloniously, and of his deliberately premeditated malice aforethought, did make an assault in and upon the person of one Mary Stevens, causing her death on April 20, 1908. The charge is to be murder in the first degree." He paused for a minute to let the sting of the legal charge dissipate a mite.

All the while, the judge was reading the complaint against him, Alvin did not or could not focus on what was being said. Instead, he looked about the room or stared out the window.

The judge changed to a lighter tone of voice.

"Good morning, everyone," he said as he again looked around the room, this time in greeting. "I see we have Counselor Harmon Cutler present for the county, and I see the defendant, Alvin F. Heaton, Jr., is present. What I don't see however, and I find a little disturbing, is counsel for the defense. I realize the hearing and trial will go quicker if he is not represented; however, it certainly won't take."

He looked directly at Alvin. "Mr. Heaton, have you obtained counsel?"

"Yes, I have, sir," Alvin answered.

"Can you tell me where he is then?" the judge asked. "I don't see here on record where there is a defense attorney listed."

Alvin paused for a moment without answering the judge.

Judge Ford continued, "You do not need to plead right now.

You may have time to consult with your attorney and prepare your plea."

Even though Alvin was looking directly at the judge, it was obvious he did not understand or even comprehend what he was saying to him.

"You do have a lawyer, then?" the judge asked.

"Yes, I do."

"Is he in the room?" he asked.

Alvin looked around the room for a few minutes and then gave a big sigh. "I don't understand what you mean."

"Did no one explain to you that you have the right to an attorney?" Judge Ford asked in surprise.

Alvin said nothing.

"You will want to find an attorney to defend you. I will allow you nineteen days in order for you to obtain one to act in your defense. At the end of the nineteen days, I expect you to enter a plea of guilty or not guilty. If you are still unprepared at that time, the court will enter a plea of guilty on your behalf. Consult with your parents over this, and find someone to take your case. I return you to the care and custody of Sheriff Brown of Kane County. Court dismissed."

As he walked out of the courtroom, Alvin smiled at Hyrum who was standing near the door. Hyrum nodded in return. Alvin was taken back to the jailhouse and spent a comfortable couple of weeks while he waited for his next arraignment. His parents secured the services of the sheriff's half-brother, John Franklin Brown as his defense attorney.

After the charge had been reread, and all the other formalities had been addressed, Judge Ford once again asked Alvin if he was ready to proceed with a lawyer this time.

"I am, Your Honor," Alvin stated. "I have retained John Brown to be my lawyer."

"Counselor Brown, how does your client plea?" the judge asked him.

"My client pleas not-guilty for the purposes of going to a hearing and trial."

"Does that mean he may be changing his plea?"

"It means we need more time to review all the evidence before we can answer that."

The courtroom was packed on the morning of Alvin's hearing. Folks flooded in from all over. I had plenty of chores to attend to back home, but my folks had to know the outcome, so we traveled down there to see. Of course, because I was a witness, I had been summoned and did not have a choice whether I went or not. I wonder if I hadn't heard those shots, if my folks would have been so interested, or if we would've stayed home and gone on about our business.

Many of us wanted to know the fate of this killer, so we all tried to squeeze into the courtroom. Even with the windows open and ceiling fans going, all the bodies in the enclosed room made it hot and uncomfortable. Most of the spectators held hand fans and fanned themselves in an attempt to stay cool. To some extent, it helped, but mostly, it was still hot.

Sheriff Brown was seated at a table with Harmon Cutler, and they kept talking between themselves in preparation for things to come. It was interesting to watch the sheriff's wife, Pearl, sitting behind him at the rail. She looked so proud that her husband was up front and center in the biggest happening ever to come to Southern Utah. She couldn't have looked more proud if he was prosecuting one of the Wild Bunch gang.

Besides me and my family, Mary's father and brother were

there, Alvin's uncle Wilford was also there, so was Sarah Foote, John Healy, Mamie Robertson, Jackie Adler, Hyrum Mower, and Alvin's cousin, Junius Heaton as those summoned to testify.

Mary's mother stayed home to tend to the family, because it was only the hearing and not the fate-deciding trial that would soon come. Try as she might to stay away however, her need to know what was happening finally drove her to have one of her sons escort her to Kanab. She slipped in late and sat down next to Ezra.

Alvin's defense attorney, John Brown, walked in with Alvin alongside him. I don't know if he was trying to make a dramatic entrance or not, but he most certainly did. He was casually escorted by the deputy from the jailhouse who was carrying a rifle lazily cradled in the crook of his arm. It was obvious he was not concerned about Alvin trying to make his escape but merely doing his job.

Alvin was unfazed by any of the commotion going on around him and had a very pleasant expression on his face. It was almost as if there was indeed a complete break of reality between what was happening in the courtroom, and what was going on in his mind. After all that had been going on, I couldn't believe he smiled easily and greeted people he knew as he walked by. He was very casual about the whole affair. It was almost as if he were being seated in the audience of a church play or down to dinner.

His parents were there to support him through this, but he hardly seemed to notice or even recognize them. His mother tried to catch his attention with a quick wave, but he was completely oblivious to her efforts. His father, Alvin Sr., nodded to John Brown in salutation, but the motion was from across the room and did not allow for conversation. After they sat down at their table, his attorney placed his hand solidly on Alvin's shoulder. I suppose it was to reassure him that all would be fine but, in his state of mind, it was obvious to the rest of us he had no need of it.

We all stood when Judge Ford walked into the courtroom. He walked over to his bench seat and sat down. Everyone else sat down, too. He picked up the stack of papers in front of him and glanced over them. He rearranged them into a different order; perhaps to one that made more sense to him. He tapped them on the bench to straighten them out. I was surprised at how loud it sounded, while everyone was quietly waiting to hear his first words. It was just like the beginning of a horse race when the horses are anticipating the run, and the riders are anticipating the starting gun.

"We have the case of Alvin Franklin Heaton, Jr. before us with the charge of murder," Judge Ford said.

And there it was, the horses off and running in the race. Now we would see where this was going.

"We are here to determine if there is enough cause to proceed on to trial," he continued. He paused and glanced at the papers again, focusing mostly on the page he had moved to the top. We all waited again, in anticipation after the false start.

"How does the defense plea?" the judge demanded to confirm the somewhat tentative plea entered at the arraignment.

Ahh, now we were really on our way. Here it comes.

"First," Attorney John Brown said, "the defendant pleads *not guilty*. Second, we waive the right to a hearing and are prepared to move right on to trial."

What? How could he plead not guilty? I had heard the gunshots! He had confessed! It was in the *Reaper*!

There was an audible gasp throughout the courtroom. No one could believe it. We had all read his confession in the paper. How could he have the audacity to rescind it? What was going through this attorney's mind? Everyone was absolutely confused and trying to make sense of what was happening.

What about the hearing? Why was his attorney skipping that part of the process and moving right on to trial? I didn't understand it at the time, but as I've aged with many years, I realized that the county pretty much had Alvin dead to rights, with plenty of evidence, and there was no way that such a high profile case would not go to trial. John Brown realized a hearing was an unnecessary use of energy and county funds.

Alvin's mother looked relieved to think there was some hope for her son. Tears began to flow down her face as she clutched tightly to the handkerchief she held up to her face. His father sat stoically and showed no emotion.

"What say you, Counselor?" Judge Ford asked Harmon.

"Your Honor, if you please, with a trial of this magnitude, we want to make sure we have all our facts in order before we proceed. It wouldn't do, if we showed up to trial and lost or had a mistrial, because we had forgotten something."

"Let me get this straight," Judge Ford said. "The defense has given you a free pass to move straight to trial, but you want to go through your argument just for the practice?"

"It's a little more pedestrian than I would put it, but that's the gist of it, Your Honor."

"This should be interesting. Proceed."

"Thank you, Your Honor," he said, "and we will proceed as if that served as our opening argument."

The judge nodded his head in approval.

"To begin with," Harmon continued, "we have a written and signed confession by Mr. Heaton."

"Objection!" John interrupted as he jumped to his feet. "The confession is inadmissible in court because it was given to a member of the clergy."

I noticed the judge was rather confused at this outburst, since the defense had already conceded.

"How do you figure that?" Harmon shot over to Alvin's attorney. "I was present the whole time, and no clergy member was called upon or showed up, during the interrogation."

"Thomas Carter," John said with a smug and victorious smile.

"What?" Harmon asked, obviously confused.

He stood there for a moment, looking angrily at John as if he wanted to say something else, but was so mystified by what he heard that no words came.

"Thomas Carter is one of Alvin's religious leaders," John said, still with that smile, obviously very pleased with himself. "Therefore, the confession is inadmissible."

"Oh, for Pete's sake, John," Harmon exclaimed, exasperated, "everyone around here is a Mormon! There's no one in the county we could bring in that isn't Mormon. I sent Thomas in there to interrogate the prisoner and he was not there in a religious capacity."

"Did he, or did he not, tell the defendant that confession was good for his soul?" John asked him.

"Well…yes…," Harmon stammered, "but he was still there in an official capacity, not a religious one. Therefore, the confession must be allowed to stay in play. You can't, in good conscience, take this away; justice must be served."

"Sorry, Harmon," John said. "Once he was in the jail cell, he inadvertently changed roles to that of a religious leader. You need to remember Mr. Carter was Alvin's bishop at one time in Orderville and is in the stake presidency now. That kind of relationship doesn't just change overnight. The Mormon Church's teachings are so ingrained in the culture that during the interrogation, there was no distinction in my client's mind between Thomas Carter, the religious leader, and the civilian servant for the law."

"Your Honor?" Harmon turned to the judge in desperation. "Surely you can see the rightness of what we're doing? The defendant also confessed to Sheriff Brown, Doctor Moir, and myself, and we are not his religious leaders. That must account for something. It was printed in the paper, and everyone knows about it."

"I'll have to side with the defense on this one, Counselor," Judge Ford said. "The confession is no good. Present your case another way. Call your first witness."

Harmon was visibly shaken and disappointed. He was so convinced this hearing would merely be a formality that he had not even considered he would run into any opposition he could not easily handle.

Alvin's mother looked like she was about to faint. Alvin Sr. reached his arm around her to give her emotional support and help hold her up.

None of us in the courtroom could believe what we had just witnessed. To a person, we had all read the confession in the paper. There was no doubt in anyone's mind that he was guilty and would plead that very thing before the magistrate. We all felt the shock and disappointment even as Harmon did, and our hearts bled for him as he stood there. He looked just like a man standing on a lonely crossroad's corner, who just found out his true love wife was leaving him for a traveling harmonica player.

Ezra couldn't believe it either. His face hardened with anger and his whole demeanor became rigid.

John Brown, on the other hand, looked like the proverbial cat that just ate the unsuspecting canary. He knew he had staged a dramatic upset and completely overturned the County's case. For the first time, he thought he really had a chance to win.

"Very well, Your Honor," Harmon stammered, and then paused for a moment to figure out his next move. "We call Jackie

Adler to the stand."

The bailiff called for Jackie and then swore him in. He was seated on the stand.

Before he began speaking, Harmon stood silent at his table as he did his best to regroup his thoughts and composure. As long as he stood there, I was sure the judge would get after him for stalling, but I think he was being very understanding of the plight Harmon found himself in.

"Now, Jackie," He finally began, "how are you related to the defendant?"

Harmon sounded rather tentative and looked like a man who had lost all of his confidence.

"Friends, I guess you could say."

Harmon paused for another moment.

My father leaned over me to my mother and whispered, "He'd better pull it together fast, or he's going to lose by not talking at all."

Harmon finally spoke again, this time with a little more conviction, "Has the defendant ever talked to you or anyone else you know about Mary or killing anyone?"

"Objection, Your Honor," John said as he quickly stood to his feet, "too many questions asked in a roundabout way. The Prosecution has to ask direct questions."

Harmon snapped his head around and glared at John for a moment and then turned to the judge to see what he would say.

"I'm sorry, Mr. Brown," Judge Ford stated. "The defense is out of order."

"Your Honor?"

"You're out of order," he repeated.

You could see Harmon stand back straight as the judge chastised the defense attorney.

"Yes, I heard what you said, I just don't understand it."

"You waived your right to a hearing," the judge informed him. "You do not have the right to object to the questions the prosecution may ask."

I'm sure I saw a smile begin to sneak across Harmon's face as he regained the upper hand.

"But you sustained my objection about the confession," Brown pointed out. "Why are you cutting me off now?"

"It was you who cut yourself off," Judge Ford stated. "Your argument about the confession was too compelling to ignore, so I had to go along with it, but I'll not be playing this game with you. You've already conceded to the prosecution, and that will be the end of it. Now sit down in that chair, John, and just watch the rest of the proceedings like the other spectators in the room."

You could almost hear a cheer about to erupt from everyone in the courtroom. Everyone, except for John Brown, of course. He now looked like the feller standing at the crossroads. Harmon stood taller once again because he had been vindicated. Now things would proceed more as they were supposed to.

"You may proceed, Councilor," the judge said to Harmon.

"Has the defendant ever talked to you about killing Mary or anyone else for that matter?" he asked, his confidence having returned in full.

It was obvious to everyone in the room that John Brown was itching to jump up and object again. He squirmed around as if he was sitting on a red anthill. I think Harmon re-asked his question, just for this very reason. Retribution, is that the word I want?

"Yes," Jackie said. "Once as we walked past Gardner Hollow, he commented that it would be a good place to commit a murder. He said in order to escape detection, one simply needed to act natural, and he would not be found out."

"Did it sound to you like he had already planned the murder and was ready to commit it?"

"Obj…," John Brown started to say as he began to stand but quickly checked his action before he completed it.

"Good save, Counselor," the judge said. He turned to Harmon and said, "Continue."

"Mr. Adler?" Harmon urged.

"Yes, I truly believe he was ready and perhaps planning to commit the murder."

Alvin's mother looked mortified at his answer.

"Thank you, that is all," he said and then turned to John. "Counselor?"

"No questions, Your Honor," he said, sounding like a boy who had been reprimanded and sent to bed without supper.

"Next we want to call Junius Heaton to the stand," Harmon announced.

The bailiff called for Junius and then swore him in. He was seated on the stand.

"Junius," Harmon began again, "how are you related to the defendant?"

"I'm his cousin, sir," he answered.

"Has the defendant ever talked to you about Mary or killing anyone?" he repeated the same question as posed to Jackie Adler.

"Yes, sir," he confirmed. "One day, when we were down riding the range in Arizona, just south of the line, I asked him what kind of girl Mary was. We often talked about such things while we rode the miles day after day."

"And what was his response?" Harmon asked. "Did he offer some kind of opinion on her?"

"Yes, he replied that she was no good, and that he could kill her as easily as he could a dog."

Alvin's mother looked like she was about to faint.

"A dog, you say?" Harmon asked in exaggerated exasperation. "Is that all the more he thought of her?"

"Counselor," Judge Ford interrupted, "I caution you on going too far afield of proper courtroom etiquette. Regardless of the fact that the defense has laid down and given you the day, you must still act with proper decorum."

"Yes, Your Honor," Harmon said, only slightly phased by the reprimand. "I'm afraid I got rather carried away; that was quite a revelation."

"Indeed it was," Judge Ford admitted, "however, my caution still stands."

"Understood."

"Go ahead, then."

"Mr. Heaton," he said, returning to the witness, "what was your response to this statement?"

"I said, 'You don't mean that.'"

"And understandably so, did he make any comment after that?"

"He responded by saying, 'Well, I don't know if I would kill her, but that's just to show you what the boys think of her.'"

"I see. I take it there was no more the defendant had to say. Is that correct?"

Harmon, knowing full well the answer to the question, looked over at Alvin to catch his response. When he did, the rest of us followed his gaze to see for ourselves what he was looking at. Much to my surprise, Alvin showed no change of emotion.

"No, sir, there's more," Junius informed him. "After that, when we had returned to town, we were at a dance and Mary walked by. He said that someone ought to take her virtue and then take her out and kill her."

Edith buried her face into Ezra's shoulder to stifle her loud gasp and the following sobs. Ezra's face turned stone hard again.

"Why didn't you say something about it to someone when it happened?" Harmon asked.

"I didn't think too much of it at the time. Alvin often acted the tough around town, 'shootin' up the place' and all, if you will. I figured he had a burr under his saddle for her. Mostly he was just talking tough, you know, all smoke and no fire, that's all."

"Thank you," he said, and then once again turned to John and taunted, "Counselor?"

Barely able to mask his irritation, he said, "No questions, Your Honor."

"Your Honor," Harmon stated, "we are ready for John Healy."

The bailiff called for John and then swore him in, seating him on the stand.

"Now, John," Harmon began, "how are you related to the defendant?"

"Friends."

"Has the defendant ever talked to you about Mary, or killing anyone?"

By this time, no one was looking toward John Brown to see what his reaction was. We all knew how he felt, and he had finally been able to stem the emotions from visibly surfacing.

"Not to me or to anyone I know of."

"Do you own a .38 caliber Smith and Wesson revolver?" Harmon asked him.

"I do, but I rented it to Alvin for a deck of cards."

"Why would you do that?" came the obvious question.

"Well, sir, I've known Alvin all my life, and he said he wanted to use it to shoot rabbits at the next roundup. I had no idea he was planning to use it on Mary instead of the rabbits. I sure feel awful about that."

"You didn't think it was a strange request from him?"

"Oh no, sir, not at the time. We hate the rabbits up there, because they get into our gardens and eat our crops."

"Thank you." Again, he turned to John, "Counselor?"

"All right, Harmon," John blurted out, "enough of rubbing it in my face, you can let it go now."

"Counselor, I've warned you," Judge Ford said. "No more outbursts. Counselor Cutler is merely following the courtroom protocol I demanded of him. Leave him be and play along."

"Yes, Your Honor," he said with all the dignity he could muster. "No questions, Your Honor."

"Your Honor," Harmon began, with an ever so slight victorious tone in his voice, "since Counselor Brown will not be asking questions during this hearing, I am comfortable dispensing of the formality, if it suits the court."

"I'm fine with it, Counselor. I must admit, even though I demanded it, it was becoming rather tedious, and I'm sure the defense won't mind."

John quietly shook his head.

"I think we'll all be happier now; proceed," the judge instructed.

"I wish to call Sarah Foote to the stand."

The bailiff called for Sarah and then swore her in. She was seated on the stand.

"Now, Sarah," Harmon began, "how are you related to the defendant?"

"I grew up with his grandparents and have known little Alvin and his parents all of their lives."

"I guess it's safe to say you know him quite well," he commented.

"As well as anyone does, I suspect," she stated. "However, we never saw this coming."

"No, we didn't," Harmon admitted. "Did you clean up Mary's body and prepare it for burial?"

"Yes, I did," she confirmed.

"Can you tell me what you found?" he inquired.

"As I was removing her clothing, I found one of the bullets that had gone clean through the poor thing."

"How did you find it?" he asked. "I would have thought the bullets would have been lost or lodged deeply within her."

"It was caught in the folds of her dress," she informed him. "In all the moving the men did of her body, getting it up out of the ravine and getting it down to Joseph's house, it must have pushed it out the rest of the way. The blood had become sticky, and it held the bullet firmly against the fabric. No great mystery, young man."

"I see," he said. "Is this the .38 caliber bullet you gave to Constable Heaton?"

She took the bullet and examined it. "I would have to say so. I didn't clean it before I handed it to him, but I would have to say I'm sure this is it."

"Thank you, Sarah; you've been a tremendous help."

As Sarah stepped down from the stand, Harmon spoke to the judge. "I wish to call Wilford Heaton to the stand."

The bailiff called for Wilford and then swore him in. He was seated.

"Now, Wilford," Harmon began, "how are you related to the defendant?"

"I'm his uncle."

"What is your position in Orderville?"

"I'm the constable and the manager of the Co-op store."

"Has the defendant ever talked to you about Mary or killing anyone?"

"No, sir," Wilford assured him, "but he did come in to the Co-op and buy bullets from me."

"What caliber were they?"

".38 caliber."

"Did he say what he was going to use them for?" Harmon asked.

"He said he, Jackie Adler, and Hyrum Mower were going to the chicken roast. He said he was going to shoot at some tin cans for practice, and that's why he only needed six. I never gave it much thought, because he'd always been a pretty good boy and never got into any real trouble. Target practice and hunting is almost as common out here as riding your horse."

"Quite so, Constable," Harmon said to reassure him he was not the one on trial. "You were with the party that found Mary's body, were you not?"

"I was. Joseph came hotfootin' it into town from the hollow, calling for a posse. He said he found pools of blood in the sand up there, and he was sure something awful had happened to Mary. When we went up there, we found her hastily buried in the ravine, after being brutally murdered."

"You conducted a coroner's inquest there in the clearing after you uncovered her body; is that right?"

"Yes. Once we had cleared away the dirt, brush, and debris, we carefully lifted her out of the ravine and laid her down. It was then that we examined her body."

"What did you find?"

"When we opened up the back of her dress, we found she had been shot in the back four times by a .38 caliber bullet."

"How could you tell it was a .38 at the time?"

"We couldn't. All we could determine at the time was she had been shot four times from behind. It wasn't until we got back to town, and Sarah cleaned her up, that we discovered the caliber."

"I can't believe you are testifying against your nephew like this; what does your brother Alvin Sr. have to say about it?"

"I haven't much choice. As Constable, I have to testify. Besides, if he is innocent, then the truth will win out. If not..."

"Good enough, sir. I have no further questions. Thank you, and you may be seated."

The bailiff called for Joseph Stevens and swore him in. He was seated on the stand.

"Now, Joseph," Harmon began, "how are you related to the defendant?"

"Know him. I married his cousin."

"How are you related to the victim?"

"She is…was my sister. She was living with me at the time Alvin killed her."

"Well, that's what we're here to determine. Hopefully, we will be able to prove it."

Harmon paused to allow the room to drift away from Joseph's emotional accusation for a moment, and return to the direction he wanted to take the witness.

"Tell me what happened on the afternoon of April 20, this year."

"Mary had been taking her final examinations and wanted to take a break. She took the afternoon off from school and went up the hollow to study some more before she continued."

"Is that the last time you saw her?"

"Alive."

"You found the spot where she had been killed?"

"Yes, the next morning, though I didn't know it at the time. I just knew something awful had happened. That's why I scooted back into town and got Wilford and the others to come help me determine what happened and to whom."

"After you notified your father and he went up from Mt. Carmel, did you take him out and follow her tracks back to the murder scene?"

"We did. We found that a man with size six shoes joined her, and they walked together, side by side, to the clearing where she was killed."

"How many other tracks came or went from the murder scene?" Harmon inquired.

"Just his, other than Mary's, and the posse's tracks, later on of course."

"You were able distinguish his from theirs?"

"Not in the center of the struggle so much, because Alvin…the killer and Mary walked over the same ground a few times. He also brushed some of them out to hide that he had dragged her body and secreted it in the ravine."

"What about outside the struggle area?"

"Most definitely. First off, the killer had unusually small feet for a man, so it was easy to tell his from any of the posse members. Also, when I went up alone the first time and when the posse went up, we were all careful not to disturb those tracks, so we could examine them later."

"So, for clarification, besides the posse and Mary, how many other tracks came or went from the murder scene?"

"Only his. Father and I circled the clearing until we found his exit tracks and followed them."

"How did that turn out for you?"

"Difficult. He took a different route back to town than the one where he went up. The path went through some rocky areas where Father lost sight of them at times, and it took some doing to find where they picked back up again."

"Were you finally able to track them successfully back to town?"

"We were. We followed them right back to the town roads but, by then, there had been enough traffic they were lost forever."

"Did you try to look around and see if you could find them again?"

"No, it was rather like pouring a cup of water into a horse trough and then trying to scoop the same water back out…impossible."

"Thank you, Joseph, that's all I have for now. I am sorry for your loss, and you may take your seat."

The bailiff called for me and then swore me in. I was seated on the stand. I was scared to death, but I would not show it or admit it.

"Now, Merlin," Harmon began, "how old are you?"

"Ten."

"You must be very brave to be up here testifying."

"I tend sheep by myself." Like I said, I would not show it or admit it.

"Yes, you are very brave. How are you related to the defendant?"

"Not by blood; we live in the same town, and I see him at church activities and such."

"Can you tell us where you were on the afternoon of April 20 of this year?"

"That's the day Mary was killed, right?" I asked.

"Yes, son, that's right."

"I was out tending the family sheep with my dog, Griz. We were out in the field where Gardner Hollow opens up."

"And what did you hear on that afternoon?"

"I heard four gunshots."

"Were you concerned?"

"No, hunters are always out on the hunt."

"All right, do you remember what time this happened?"

"It was somewhere between five and six in the evening."

"Did you have a watch to know?"

"No," I said, "but I had been watching the sun, and I knew it was about time for Pa or someone to bring me my supper."

"Did you see anybody come or go from the hollow, while you were out there?"

"No. Before the shooting, I was sitting in some shade and couldn't see the mouth of the canyon."

"And after?"

"Wasn't worried about the shots, so I was watching the sheep, not the hollow. Am I in trouble because I didn't see who killed her?" It suddenly dawned on me that maybe I had done something wrong.

"Not at all, son," Harmon reassured me. "I just needed to ask those questions. It's as if I'm putting a great big puzzle together, and each person I bring up here has a few of the pieces. I have to be sure and ask a lot of questions to make sure I get all the pieces from all the people. I'm sorry if I made you feel bad."

"It's okay, sir."

"Thank you. Those are all my questions; you may sit back down now."

The bailiff called for James Brown and then swore him in, seating him on the stand.

"Now, Sheriff," Harmon began, "how are you related to the defendant?"

"I just know him from interacting with people at church."

"Did you have any personal contact with him before the investigation?"

"Not to speak of," James explained. "I was familiar enough with the boy that I knew who he was on sight, but I don't recall ever talking to him before the murder."

"You were called up to Orderville to investigate the murder the day after it happened, is that correct?"

"Yes, sir, that is what happened."

"Who did you go up and investigate with?"

"Doctor Andrew Moir, and yourself."

"Did you and Doctor Molr walk the path yourselves after we arrived there?"

"Yes."

"And to what purpose did you do that?"

"Sheriff investigating the crime scene."

"But why take the doctor?"

"Second pair of discerning eyes. Also, it would give him a visual understanding of the crime area for when he would conduct the autopsy."

"Understandable. What did you find as you were following the tracks described to you by Joseph and Ezra?"

"We found that a man with size six shoes made the tracks…and that he walked toed-in."

"Did you examine all the possibilities of someone coming into town, committing the murder, and then making an escape?"

"We did. There was reason to believe the drummer from Monroe may have committed the murder, so we followed him up to Hatch and questioned him."

"And what did you find as you interviewed him?"

"We found he was there in Hatch when the murder happened, and that he has size ten feet."

"So there's no way he could be the culprit?"

"That is correct."

"So you turned back to Orderville and started to investigate those who lived in town?"

"Yes."

"And did you find someone in town with a size six shoe, who walks toed-in?"

"We did, just Alvin Heaton, Jr."

"And does he have an alibi for the time of the murder?"

"Not that anyone can prove."

"What is the timeframe of his alibi that he cannot

substantiate?"

"From the hour of five to six in the evening."

"And remind us what time Merlin heard the gunshots."

"Right around half past five."

"Thank you, I have no further questions for you at this time; you may be seated."

The bailiff called for Doctor Moir and then swore him in. He was seated on the stand.

"Now, Doctor Moir," Harmon began, "how are you related to the defendant?"

"The same as Sheriff Brown; knew him on sight and saw him around some church functions."

"Did you accompany Sheriff Brown on his trip to the hollow?"

"I did indeed, sir."

"And you conducted the autopsy on Mary after you arrived in Orderville?"

"Yes, I did," Andrew confirmed.

"Tell us about your findings. Were you able to determine her cause of death?" Harmon inquired.

"Upon the first examination, I found vaginal secretions that showed she had had intimate relations before she was killed."

"Were these relations with the killer, and was she forced?"

"She was not forced, and there is no way to determine how soon before her death the intercourse occurred," the doctor stated. "Unfortunately, science can't agree on a timeframe, so I can't tell you how soon before her death this happened. I also cannot conclusively testify as to whom she had those relations with. However, according to the report of her actions before she was killed, it's likely it was with whoever killed her."

"Tell us about the cause of her death."

"The killer shot her in the back four times with a .38 caliber revolver."

"Did you retrieve all four bullets and positively identify them with the gun?" Harmon asked.

"No, we did not," Andrew answered him. "Sarah Foote found one bullet stuck in her clothes, and I retrieved two from her body."

"So, how do you know they were all .38 bullets that were shot into her back?"

"Well, assuming that the killer did not carry two different caliber revolvers with him and shoot one with his left hand and one with his right, they would have all come from the same gun. It was obvious, upon a medical examination, that all the wounds were inflicted at the same time. Upon visual inspection of the holes, they all appeared to be the same size. The two I retrieved that did not pass all the way through her body were also .38 caliber. While we only recovered three of the four fired bullets, as a medical professional conducting the autopsy, I would have to say with one hundred percent certainty that the fourth one came from the same gun."

"All right," Harmon said. He paused because he wanted to separate that autopsy question from the next one in the mind of the judge. "You mentioned that was the first examination you did. Does that mean there were more than one?"

"Yes, upon the second examination with Doctor Robert Garn, from Panguitch, we dissected the uterus and found she was six or seven weeks pregnant."

It was obvious that Edith was mortified by the public revelation, even though she had prepared herself for the information being made public. While the expression on her face did not change, her countenance did, and we could all tell how it affected her. Ezra remained stone-faced, but we could see fire in his eyes. He sat rock still and made no indication that he heard what Andrew had said. He had already steeled himself for when the news would come out for everyone to know. He wouldn't give the community the satisfaction of seeing his reaction.

Alvin's parents hung their heads in shame as their son's indiscretions came to light in front of the entire county. His mother looked as if she wanted to slide down in her seat and disappear.

"And if this intimacy and pregnancy was caused by the defendant," Harmon asked, "what would happen to him?"

"That's more of a matter for someone such as yourself and the court system to answer. But as I understand it, since the State of Utah outlawed relations with single women under nineteen years of age, he would have gone to jail."

"Thank you, Doctor, that's all I have for now."

Andrew stood up and left the witness stand.

Harmon turned to the judge. "Your Honor, that is all we have to present at this hearing. We trust we have shown sufficient evidence to warrant going to trial."

"Very well," Judge Ford stated, glancing over his papers. "I would say you most definitely have enough to proceed to trial, even if the defense had joined in the proceedings. Let me look at my books here, we will set the trial for Sept...."

"Your Honor," John Brown said, standing up to address the judge.

"Counselor?"

"We wish to have the charge changed from first degree murder down to second. We feel that the defendant's youth and extenuating circumstances warrant the lesser charge."

"This is a decision for the prosecution. What say you, Counselor?"

"No, Your Honor. The prosecution will let the charge stand at first degree murder," Erickson said.

"Then, Your Honor, I move for a change of venue," John said without batting an eye. "It is obvious the community is polarized toward my client's guilt or innocence. I am convinced he cannot receive a fair trial in Kane County, because everyone has already made up their minds one way or the other."

Judge Ford turned to Harmon and James. "What say you, Counselor, and you, Sheriff Brown? Is this something you are in favor of, or do you want to fight to keep it here locally?"

"One moment, Your Honor," Harmon stated as he and James put their heads together to discuss the situation.

"What do you think, James?" Harmon whispered. "We have the advantage here, and I'm sure we can get a solid conviction, even without his confession."

"But it won't be a fair trial," James responded with a whisper as he shook his head.

It was obvious to us that Alvin's lawyer was concerned about the outcome of the trial and, as he sat there, he almost fainted when he saw his brother, the sheriff, shake his head. Alvin, on the other hand, looked like he was waiting for a picnic to start. None of us could ever figure out what was going on in his mind, not even to this day.

"So you think we should agree to this change of venue?"

"Unless we want to railroad Heaton right into the hangman's noose, I do. I believe we have him dead-to-rights on this, but I'd rather see him free than take away his fair trial."

"You realize we might let him walk," Harmon cautioned, "if we can't convince a jury of his guilt in a different part of the state?"

"If we stay here, we risk a mistrial or lose on appeal," James pointed out and then asked him directly, "What if it were you? Would you want a change in venue to make sure you received a fair trial to determine whether you lived or died? I know I sure would. Let's give him what he is due. We have enough solid evidence stacked against him that we don't need to railroad him into a conviction, even without his confession."

"Where would you suggest we go?" he asked. "South is out of the question, and going east doesn't seem to make much sense. We could either go west to St. George or we could go north, but how far?"

"Panguitch is too close," James pointed out. "We would have the same situation there that we have here, I'm sure of it. Salt Lake is no good, it is too far away and too many city folk. There is no way we could find a panel of his peers up there."

"Provo? Nephi? Gunnison?"

"Richfield."

"Agreed. We can most certainly find twelve jurists who will be his peers and can better understand the situation. Besides, it is as far away as we can get and stay within the Sixth District," Harmon said. He turned back to Judge Ford.

"Your Honor," he began, "thank you for your patience as we discussed the matter. In the interest in justice, we agree that a change of venue is the proper course of action. However, we are concerned it may be moved out of the sphere of the defendant's peers. Therefore, we stipulate that the change be made to Sevier County."

Without missing a beat, Judge Ford lifted up his gavel, "Richfield it is." He casually held the gavel in his hand for a moment as he continued speaking. "You will have to coordinate the trial date with Judge Chidester and his Sixth District Court." He raised his gavel up to shoulder height and brought it down on its base with a bang. "This hearing is dismissed."

A visible wave of relief came over Alvin's mother. Her hands had been clutched so tightly they were white from lack of blood. As she relaxed, you could see the color return. Alvin Sr. had hardly moved. As a matter of fact, I could not swear I even saw him move once, but I know I saw a change in his demeanor.

John Brown walked over to the prosecution's table and extended his hand. "Thank you for agreeing to the change of venue, gentlemen. After I had the confession thrown out, I was afraid you would become vindictive and seek your revenge at the expense of my client."

"Well, I firmly believe your client should hang from the roughest and most painful rope that can be found in Zion, for what he's done," James said to his brother with a fair amount of snarl in his voice. "But we also feel the rule of law is supreme, and even the devil himself deserves a fair trial. You damn well better remember this, if it turns out we need a favor when we get to trial."

"Harmon," John said with a tinge of humor in his voice, "you need to quit feeding vinegar to my brother before we go to trial."

"He's just saying what we both feel, John," Harmon responded in a softer tone than James had.

"I won't be forgetting what you did for us here," John said. "It was a fair thing to do, and I will return the favor when it is the fair thing to do…. All joking aside, we are very grateful."

"Rule of law, John," Harmon mentioned as they shook hands in parting.

"All right, Alvin," James said, "Are you ready to go?"

"Back to the jail, then?"

"For now, but then we're moving you up to Salt Lake until the trial. Kanab just doesn't have the ability to hold you that long."

"How am I going to get up there?" Alvin asked as James

started to put the handcuffs back on his wrists. He began to lead him to the courthouse door.

"I'll take you up to Richfield, and then the Sheriff up there will take you the rest of the way."

"Can't you take me all the way up there?"

James stopped and turned Alvin to face him.

"'fraid it's not in the county budget. We're too small to have a surplus that will let me do that. Your proceedings have already used up half of what we have for the whole year."

"Any chance my parents can ride up with me? I sure could use their support on this trip.".

"I'm afraid I can't allow that," James informed him. "Same kind of thing as the handcuffs. I hope you understand."

"Don't mean to be such a burden," Alvin apologized. "You could always let me go if I get to be too expensive."

"I could do that," James said with a little smile, "but then you'd have Ezra gunning for you, and I'm sure you don't want that."

"You do have a point there; I'm probably better off to take my chances in court. At least then I might have the chance to live."

"That's right," James confirmed. "If you ran, Ezra wouldn't give you that chance. You'd be meeting your maker quicker than butter melting in a hot skillet."

James started them moving toward the door again.

"Are these cuffs really necessary, Sheriff?" Alvin asked as he partially raised his hands before they reached the door. "Haven't I proven myself by now?"

"As far as I'm concerned," he responded, as he led Alvin through the door and out to the street, "you have. This is for your own protection. I don't need to be shooting someone who is trying to take revenge, because they think you are running around too loose and free."

"So these are for my protection, you say? Funny, they don't feel like it."

"How do you think a grave will feel? Maybe you could ask Mary," James replied, out of patience at Alvin's whining.

Alvin's jocular mood suddenly subsided as the sheriff put him back in his place. It had become obvious to us, as they walked out of the courtroom that day, that Alvin was feeling more like the king of the county than a murderer on trial. That is, until the Sheriff's comment. Then, much to our delight, he began to look like the wounded dog we expected to see.

There were a lot of hateful stares toward him as the sheriff walked him out and down the street to the jail. There were some jeers from unidentified crowd members, calling him a woman or baby killer and such, but I was relieved to see that no one became physically violent toward him. My pa explained to me that we wanted justice through and from the Lord by his laws, for what Alvin had done, but not unrighteous vigilante justice.

Mamie tried to walk alongside Alvin as he was escorted down the boardwalk, but the sheriff waved her away.

"I'll be right here for you, Alvin, and I will do whatever I can to help," she called as they continued on their way. "Write me when you can."

Alvin was consumed enough with his sudden grief that he hardly noticed her, but when she told him to write her, he raised his cuffed hands to the side and gave a half wave of acknowledgement.

"I wonder if he'll be able to get a fair trial in Richfield." I heard one of the crowd members say.

"I certainly hope not," another one said. "He killed her and is guilty as sin. The poor girl, and her with child, makes it all the worse. He shattered our peaceful Zion with her death, and he deserves to swing for it."

"Yes, that poor girl," the first one said, "and her poor parents. Ezra and Edith from Mt. Carmel, right?"

"Yes, and they always seemed like such fine people," the other one replied. "It's a shame this had to happen to them."

"Maybe we should stop by sometime, give them our condolences, and pay our respects."

"Absolutely," the second one agreed, "the next time we're headed back up that way."

"Now, what are you going to do?" the first one asked him.

"I have a water turn this afternoon, so I need to clear out some ditches. The wife's favorite milking cow got out and caved a bunch of them in and, if I don't get them cleared out, we'll have irrigation water all over creation."

"That would make a muddy mess. I need to head over to the Co-op and pick up a couple of tools. I busted some trying to get that old tree trunk out of the field, and I can't do anything around the place until I replace them."

I was surprised at how quickly the conversation turned but, as I look back now, these two men were perfect examples of this whole situation. Alvin was a big sensation throughout the state for a short time. Then, all of a sudden, he was gone. Everyone moved on, and no one was talking about him anymore.

"I'm looking for Sheriff Myron Alma Abbott," James said as he escorted Alvin into the Sevier County Courthouse. "I have a prisoner I need to transfer over to his care to be taken up to Salt Lake City. Can you tell me where to find him? I am scheduled to meet him here today."

"He's expecting you," the county clerk said, "but he got called back to the sheriff's office for some pressing business. He wasn't sure what time you would be here, so he asked me to send you across the street to have lunch, while I ring him."

"Do you know how long he'll be?" James inquired. "I would just as soon get this transfer over with, so I can be back on my way home. My wife gets rather cranky when I'm gone too long."

"You have to eat," the clerk said, "but if you want to wait for a moment, I will see if I can catch him."

James nodded his appreciation.

The clerk picked up the earpiece to the phone, rattled the cradle, and listened. "Lottie, this is Frederick over at the courthouse, I need you to ring me over to the sheriff's office...is that a fact? Do you know how long he's going to be? No, those dogs can be dangerous...Is there anyone over at the jailhouse? Okay, ring me through then."

"Out chasing dogs?" James asked with a smile. "One of the fun jobs of a sheriff."

"David, this is Frederick over at the courthouse. The Sheriff from Kane County just made it up here. Will you let Myron know he's here when he gets back? Thanks, Lottie already let me know. Oh, is he? Well make sure he comes by here before he runs out to Central. The sheriff is anxious to be back on the trail. Thanks."

"Sounds like we're going to have that lunch after all," James said. "Alvin here's pretty peaked anyway. Just across the street, you say?"

"That's right," Frederick responded. "There are other places to eat, but this one is the best and it's close. If Myron gets back before you're finished, I'll send him over."

"We're much obliged."

Across the street, they entered the restaurant and took a table. They looked at the menu and found several choices, which made the decision more difficult, especially after being out on the trail for several days. They finally made their decisions and sat back to wait for their food to arrive. They visited about insignificant things then, when it came, Alvin dug in with gusto and ate several mouthfuls before he spoke again.

"What do you think will happen to me now?" he asked, chewing on a mouthful of food.

"I think you will get to meet that new lawyer your father hired for you. I guess he didn't have too much faith in my brother."

"Father said he was too small-town, and I need a big-city lawyer who knows all the tricks," Alvin informed him.

"It will take a lot of tricks to get you off from this one. You realize, don't you, now that we're out of the hearing and you have a new lawyer, the district attorney will reintroduce your confession at your trial?"

"Hadn't really thought about it, but I guess it makes sense. I wish I hadn't said anything. It's caused me nothing but grief ever since."

"Grief, like Ezra's been feeling?" James asked.

"More like aggravation," Alvin stated without even acknowledging the barb James put into his comment.

"If you're so sorry, why did you confess in the first place?"

"President Carter was putting too much pressure on me, for me to resist. I fought it as long as I could but, in the end, he made me do it."

"Is that you talking," James asked, "or your big-city lawyer?"

"It doesn't really matter, you see," Alvin commented as he took another bite of his food, "it's all one and the same at this point. Don't be surprised if you see me back home before long. Father says this city lawyer is also a judge and one of the best around. If anyone can get me acquitted of these charges, he can."

"Don't put too much faith in maybes," James cautioned. "Your lawyer would have to change the past for you to get away with what you've done. I'd hold on if I were you. It's going to be a rough ride, no matter how you look at it."

"Perhaps…"

"You must be Sheriff Brown from Kane County," a voice said from near the door.

James and Alvin turned to see a large man walking toward them.

"I'm Sheriff Abbott, and I'll be taking charge of our prisoner from here on."

"I'll be happy to turn him over to you," James said. "We are just finishing up here. If you want to give us a minute, we will come right over to the courthouse and meet you there."

"That'll work fine," Myron said. "Come on over when you're done then."

After he had walked back out of the restaurant, Alvin turned to James. "I don't think I've ever seen a man as big as that before. He's like a walking mountain."

"He is quite big, isn't he?" James agreed.

"There is no way I could ever dream of escaping from him. He could stomp on me, and I'd be finished."

"Then don't escape."

"I don't think I will," Alvin replied. "Not only am I scared of him, but I don't know if he will be as fair with me as you have been."

"He measures up to be someone who will be fair with you," James corrected. "He just may not be as understanding with you as I have been. You need to remember, he doesn't know you. To him, you are just another man arrested for a crime, and a dangerous crime at that. He will be treating you that way, like someone who could kill him if he's not careful."

"I hadn't thought about that," Alvin admitted.

"So keep that in mind when you feel he's not treating you

fairly. Ask yourself, if you were the sheriff and you were tending a dangerous killer, how would you act? See if that doesn't help you understand him better as you stay with him."

"That's a good idea, Sheriff, but do you think I'm a dangerous killer?"

"No, of course not, Alvin," he answered without hesitation. "I think you found yourself in a very difficult situation, and you chose the wrong way to handle it. I don't think you are a killer. I think you are a man who has killed someone."

"Thank you, Sheriff, that makes me feel better."

"Don't get too excited," James cautioned. "I still think you are a man who committed a cold-blooded murder. We could almost call it a double murder because she was pregnant with your child."

"I wish I could take it all back."

"I wish you could, too."

With his signature still drying on the document of transfer, James commented, "He's all yours now. He's a good boy who took a wrong turn. Keep that in mind as you're housing him before the trial. I'm not saying to give him his head and let him run, but I am saying don't shoot him because he sneezes."

"Are you worried I might not treat him well?" Myron asked.

"No. I'm worried you might treat him like a cold-blooded killer."

"Isn't that what he's charged with?"

"Yes, but he hasn't been convicted yet and, as you know, his new lawyer, Samuel Thurman, is going to take him to an alienist to check his state of mind. He thinks he might have just cracked under pressure."

"What more pressure do you think he's going to be faced with than being on trial for murder?" Myron pointed out. "I don't know that a psychiatrist is going to be able to do anything to help him. Desperate men do desperate and dangerous deeds."

"Exactly," James confirmed, "but I'm saying I don't think Alvin is desperate."

"Hmm."

"What I'm trying to say is, be careful and vigilant and watch your back, but don't be too hard on the boy," James clarified.

"You could have just said that at the beginning and saved us a bunch of time. I could have been halfway to Salina by the time you got all that explaining done."

"Sorry, I've known this boy for most of his life, and want to see him treated right. I also want to see that he gets what he deserves…one way or the other."

"I understand. I'll be careful."

"What are you planning to do with him once Samuel Thurman gets him to the city?" James asked.

"First, we will get him all set up in the holding area of the State Penitentiary, and then we have an appointment for him to see the doctor."

"I didn't realize he was ailing," James said, surprised. "He didn't say anything about it all the way up here."

"No, he's going to see the crazy doctor at the asylum."

"You mean the alienist?"

"That's it, precisely. As I understand it, Mr. Thurman wants to try for an insanity plea."

"Yeah, I've been thinking about that. Do you think it will work?" James asked him.

"I don't think so, at least not from what I've seen so far. I've dealt with some loonies in my time, and they always give me a creepy feeling. The kid out there makes me feel easy and comfortable. I think he'll do the same thing with the doctor, and he'll come back down here with a clean bill of health."

"That's what I would guess," James replied. "After all the time we spent on the trail coming up here, I'd say he's good and sane. I think he just got himself twisted around so badly that he lost sight of which way was up. You know, if he'd only taken his lumps and gone to jail for having relations with her, he'd be out already and living his life."

"Yes, but with a fathered child, whose mother he didn't like."

"What makes you think he didn't like her?" James asked, surprised.

"Because he killed her."

"Oh, yes," James stated in sudden realization of the obvious. "I get so caught up in the small details at times, I tend to lose sight of the bigger issues at hand. My wife is always getting after me for it."

"And wives are good at that, aren't they?" Myron smiled.

After the documents had been signed, the two men returned to the holding room where Alvin was waiting.

"Well, Alvin," James began, "I guess this is goodbye."

"I suppose so, Sheriff."

"I will be at the trial. I will see you then," he assured him.

"To testify against me."

"There is that. However, I will do whatever I can for you outside the courtroom to see to your comfort. I spoke to Sheriff Abbott about your situation, and he is fully aware of my feelings. As long as you behave for him the way you have for me, you'll be fine."

"Thank you, Sheriff," Alvin said, "and I'm sorry about the comment I made; I'm really scared. Even if you are there to testify against me, I will feel better having you there, as odd as that may sound."

"It doesn't sound odd at all," Myron interjected. "As a matter of fact, it is quite understandable. He has been your protector through all of this, even though he is the one who arrested you. Now his protection will no longer be with you. You can rest assured that I will put forth every effort I can to keep you as safe as he did. Of course, my job may not be as hard, because there aren't many people this far north who have the strong feelings about you as they do down south."

"That does make me feel better," Alvin assured him.

"As it does me," James said just to help Alvin feel better.

"We'll lock you in the cell tonight and start out in the wagon first thing in the morning," Myron said.

"With the cell door closed?" Alvin inquired.

"Excuse me?" Myron asked, baffled at the question.

"Back in Kanab," James explained, "we left the cell door open for him as long as there was an officer in the jailhouse."

"Now I understand. No, boy, we will have to keep it locked. Everybody would be screaming for my badge if they ever found out I did that. However, I will do everything I can to make your stay as comfortable as I possibly can."

"Are you going to handcuff me in the wagon?"

"I'm afraid I'm going to have to. Sheriff Brown has told me some good things about you, and if I could do it safely, I would let you ride without them."

"Not to worry," James mentioned. "He rode up here with them on. One thing we did to make them a little more comfortable was we took a couple pieces of sheepskin and wrapped his wrists with them, so the shackles didn't hurt so much. I have them in my saddlebags if you would like to use them on the way up."

"I certainly think we could do that," Myron said. "We're not trying to torture you here. We just need to make sure you don't get away."

"So, did you do it?" Myron asked as they drove up the long road between Gunnison and Levan. "I know I'm not supposed to ask you things like that, but the trip is getting long. I waited as long as I could before I asked, but the drive finally wore on me."

"I guess we'll find out when we go back to Richfield for the trial," Alvin said without admission.

"What about your confession?" he asked him. "I read it in the *Reaper.*"

"Coerced."

"Are you kidding me?"

"No."

"How did that happen?" he asked, astonished. "Did they beat you, starve you, and put you on the rack?"

"I don't know what the rack is, but I'm pretty sure they didn't do that to me."

"The rack is a torture device from the old country," Myron explained. "They kept them in castle dungeons and used them to stretch people out until they confessed."

"Confessed to what?"

"Anything the accusers wanted."

"Even if they were innocent?"

"Especially if."

"I don't like the sound of that," Alvin stated, "but no, they didn't hurt me."

"How did they coerce you then?"

"They brought in a member of the Stake Presidency," he said. "President Thomas Carter."

"Ah, yes, I've heard of him," Myron said. "What did he do to you?"

"Threatened me with Hell."

"Literally?"

"No, but he told me confession was good for the soul. He knew Mary was carrying my child, and he kept pressuring me until I gave in."

"So you lied to make him stop pressuring you?"

"I didn't say that."

"Then I'm confused," Myron stated. "Maybe I shouldn't have asked."

"Maybe not."

"However, this does answer another question I had that I've been waiting to ask as well," Myron taunted.

"What question is that?"

"Doesn't matter now. I found out the answer through the other question."

"Now you have to ask me, it's only polite."

"No, I don't."

"I'll tell my lawyer you tormented me on the way up here, and they will have to get another change of venue before he will let it go to trial."

"No, he won't, there's nowhere else to go."

"Of course there is," Alvin demanded. "We could go to Nephi, Provo, or even to Salt Lake."

"No, you can't," Myron said, enjoying his little taunts.

"We'll ask my lawyer when we get there."

"Fine."

"He'll tell you that we'll move the trial again."

"Nope."

"Oh, for hell's sake, why not?" Alvin nearly yelled.

"Because Richfield is the only place in the Sixth District Court you can go to get a fair trial. They're not going to take it to another district, because then you won't be getting judged by your peers. Didn't they explain that to you at the hearing?"

"Hard to say," Alvin admitted, settling down a little bit. "I may not have been paying the closest attention. I suppose we could have gone through the Second Coming, and I might not have noticed."

"That's about what I figured when you answered my second question."

"I never answered it because you never asked it," he claimed in mounting frustration.

"I didn't have to; you told me everything I needed to know."

"And what exactly is it I told you?" he demanded.

"Why you were going to see an alienist."

"And what exactly is it I told you?" he demanded once again.

"That your lawyer thinks you may be partially crazy, and he wants to use an insanity plea to get you acquitted."

"You're out of your mind, Sheriff."

"No, but you might be," he responded, "if you're lucky."

"You look like you're scared there, young man," Warden Arthur Pratt observed when he first met Alvin.

He was in the prison's holding area to wait for final introductory processing.

"This is his first time to the city," Sheriff Abbott said as he stood close to Alvin. "He's seeing a lot of things for the first time and, added with his circumstances, he's somewhat afraid. I'm sure once he's settled down and gets used to the routine, he'll be just fine."

"I'm sure you're right, Sheriff," Arthur said. "I've seen a lot of young men come through here, and each one finally learned how to feel comfortable. With any luck, your trial will go well and you won't be back here again. I must say, it's not very often we get someone your age coming here, especially for murder. If you were a sailor, I'd say that once you get your sea legs, you'd do just fine. Maybe instead, I'll say that once you get your prison-legs you'll do fine."

"He's a good kid, Warden," Myron said, "I don't think you'll have any trouble with him."

"All right, young man," Arthur said, "on the sheriff's recommendation, I will treat you as a good man. As long as you work with me and behave yourself, that treatment will continue. If you don't behave, then I will treat you as the cold-blooded murderer you've been charged as. How your time is spent here will be strictly up to you."

Alvin, looking at the ground, nodded but still said nothing.

"I have rewards for the prisoners I trust. They become trustees with extra privileges, which makes their time spent here much more comfortable. For those who don't work within the system, they find themselves doing hard labor."

Alvin nodded again, still looking at the ground.

"It's all up to you."

Alvin started to tremble and shake a little bit as quiet tears rolled down his face. He could not stop himself from crying, but he was doing everything he could to minimize it, especially in front of the warden.

"It's going to be all right there," Myron said to comfort him. "I know it seems scary now, but it will get better."

"I'll put you in a room by yourself tonight," Arthur said. "And we'll see how you feel in the morning. I'll even have one of my trustees bring you dinner in your room, how's that?"

Alvin silently nodded again.

"You best not let anyone else see those tears in here, or they will eat you alive," Arthur cautioned. "You'll have to become stronger than you ever thought you could."

Again, Alvin silently nodded.

"I guess this is where I leave you until November," Myron said. "I'll be back up to get you for the trial."

He started to leave when Alvin spoke for the first time since arriving at the prison.

"Do you have to go, Sheriff?" he asked as he fought to choke back the sobs.

"It's all right, son," he assured him. "I'll be back before you know it. Warden Pratt here will take fine care of you, and your parents can come and see you as often as they want."

Alvin nodded, tears still rolling down his cheeks.

Myron took a step toward Alvin and extended his hand. Alvin quickly grabbed it and held it tight with both hands as they shook. For Alvin, it was a lifeline he did not want to release. He knew he would have to, but he held on for a few extra moments in quiet desperation.

Myron patiently waited.

Finally, Alvin let go and stepped back, allowing him to leave the room.

Arthur placed his arm around Alvin's shoulder and walked him to his new cell.

Chapter Seven
The Trial Begins…

"Are you ready to select your jury?" Myron asked District Attorney Joseph Erickson.

"Yes, I have a list of questions a mile long I will be asking. I hope our pool is large enough, because I have no doubt the big-city lawyer over there has a list twice as long."

"Is there anything I can do to help?"

"I don't suppose you could arrest him for something and just hold him for a day or two, until the selection is completed, could you?" Erickson joked.

"Do you dislike big-city lawyers that much?"

"Not at all, and I don't dislike Samuel Thurman in the least. He's a very skilled lawyer and judge, that's why I would like a little time without him to get the jury squared away. He will be a strong opponent once we get to the trial, but I still think we've got all the cards in our favor."

"Maybe I could plant some evidence on him and arrest him for that?" Myron jested.

"Not that I'm even considering your proposal, but what did you have in mind?" Erickson cautiously joked again.

"Someone could actually steal one of the statues from the courthouse lawn and hide it on his person, and then when we searched him on an anonymous tip, we could find it."

Erickson laughed. "Those statues are six feet tall, how would you ever do that?"

"I didn't say it was going to be easy," Myron laughed. "By the way, did you ever find out why Judge John Booth from the Fourth District Court in Provo came down to sit over this case?"

"Yes, Judge John Chidester had unfinished business and couldn't clear his schedule in time to hear this case. He sent an official letter to Judge Booth asking him to fill in."

"I see. I figured it had something to do with Judge Booth's aspirations to higher offices," Myron commented.

"Perhaps his aspirations had a lot to do with John Chidester having unfinished business. Maybe John persuaded John to let John sit on this one for his career. Because John lives up to Provo, he has hopes to move up the state ladder, and because John lives down here in Richfield, I think he's happy where he's at. It's no skin off of John's nose to let John take over, and it is great press coverage for him as well."

"That was confusing," Myron said. "If I didn't know better, I'd say you did that on purpose."

"Maybe I did. I have to do something to relieve the anxiety over choosing the jury. This is always the hardest part for me because there are so many unknowns. The rest of the trial is pretty straightforward; I know my arguments, and I know most of Samuel's too. The only other nerve wracking unknown is the jury's verdict."

"Looks like they're about to begin," Myron observed. "I'll leave you be."

"No, I want you here to give me another opinion on the options. You know these people better than I do and certainly better than Samuel does. You've dealt with them as sheriff for years and can give me some valuable insight to their character and which way you think they'll vote."

The jury selection bantered back and forth until twelve men were finally chosen. They consisted of B. W. Hopkins and W. E. Hyatt of Joseph; Joseph R. Hooton of Central Valley (Central); Peter Christiansen, John Anderson, Hans Tuft, David Collings and Ole Larson of Monroe, F. P. Anderson and J. B. Sorenson of Redmond, and Soren Sorenson of Elsinore. As kids, those from Joseph, Central, and Elsinore, would have all gone to school with the kids in Monroe, so they would have all known each other.

Once the jurors had been formalized, Judge Booth began the lengthy process of reading them their instructions.

"In the District Court of the Sixth Judicial District of the State of Utah, in and for Sevier County. State of Utah, Plaintiff, vs. Alvin F. Heaton, Jr. Defendant," he began, "these are the instructions to the jury."

He paused for a moment as he looked up at them.

"Gentlemen of the Jury," he continued. "You are called upon as a part of the Judicial machinery of this state to assist by your judgment in determining the issues of this case, which are presented to you by an Information filed by Joseph H. Erickson, the duly elected qualified and acting District Attorney for the Sixth Judicial District of the State of Utah, which Information was filed in the County of Kane, in this State, on the 7th day of July, 1908, Kane County being one of the counties of this Judicial District. The said Information, which being legal in form and substance, charges Alvin F. Heaton, Jr. with the crime of murder in the first degree, the charging part of which is as follows, to-wit:"

As the information and instructions were being read, Alvin sat and gazed at the judge without sign of emotion on his features. He showed mild curiosity as they were being read but, beyond that, he appeared to be about the most unconcerned person in the building.

"The said Alvin F. Heaton, Jr. on the 20th day of April, A.D. 1908, at and in the County of Kane, State of Utah, unlawfully, willfully, feloniously, and of his premeditated malice aforethought did make an assault in and upon the person of one Mary Stevens, with a certain gun, to-wit, a revolver, which said revolver was then and there loaded with gun powder and leaden bullets and, by him, the said Alvin F. Heaton, Jr., then and there held in his hand; and he, the said Alvin F. Heaton, Jr., did then and there unlawfully, willfully, feloniously and of his deliberately premeditated malice aforethought, shoot off and discharge at, against, and upon, and into the body of the said Mary Stevens, and thereby and by thus striking the said Mary Stevens with the said leaden bullets, inflicted in and upon the back and internal vital organs of the said Mary Stevens mortal wounds, of which said mortal wounds the said Mary Stevens then and there instantly died. And so the said Alvin F. Heaton, Jr., did in the manner and form aforesaid feloniously, unlawfully, willfully, and of his deliberately premeditated malice aforethought, kill and murder the said Mary Stevens, contrary to the form of the Statutes of the State of Utah in such case made and provided and against the peace and dignity of the State of Utah."

I was absolutely mystified by what the judge read. About the only thing I understood in there was the name of Alvin and Mary. Beyond that, I was lost.

I turned to my father and whispered, "Did you understand any of that?"

"Shhh," he responded. "You shouldn't be asking such

questions like that in court."

I found out years later, after I had grown into an adult, that indeed he had not understood much more of what was read than I had. He just didn't want to admit it to me at the time.

The judge continued.

"The Defendant was duly arraigned before the bar of this Court in said Kane County and there formally and properly entered his plea of "Not Guilty," and on the case being regularly set down and called for trial it was then on proper motion and proof changed from said County of Kane to this, Sevier County for trial, and in pursuance of such proceeding and orders the case is now presented to you for your consideration and decision."

Is this process never to end? I wondered to myself as I tried to sit still in my seat, but boredom was making it increasingly difficult. *I'm going to die of old age before the trial even gets started.*

The instructions went on for what seemed like an hour to me. In reality, it was only about twenty minutes as each instruction was read to the jurors, as if they would be able to understand and remember all the judge said.

Still, the judge continued.

"The burden of proof rests upon the state to prove all the essential acts constituting the offense charged to your satisfaction, beyond a reasonable doubt. The manner and cause of death as alleged in the Information is an essential element of the charges against the defendant; as also are the charges stated in the Information: (1) That the killing occurred in Kane County, State of Utah; (2) That the killing was unlawful; (3) that the killing was willful; (4) That the killing was felonious; (5) That the killing was deliberate; (6) That the killing was with malice aforethought on the part of the defendant; (7) That the killing was premeditated by the defendant; (8) That the killing was the result of a specific intention on the part of the defendant to take life; (9) That the life so intended to be taken was the life of the person named in the Information. It is not enough that one or any part of these charges be proven beyond a reasonable doubt, but it is necessary in order to justify a verdict of guilty of murder in the first degree that each and every one of the allegations of the Information here enumerated be proven to the satisfaction of the entire jury and beyond a reasonable doubt."

I'm dying here. I wonder if I can charge the judge for that. I'd rather be at home doing chores.

Still the judge continued. After reading several more instructions, he finally paused.

"Do you, gentlemen of the jury, have any questions?"

Finally!

The jurors had a glassy look in their eyes after this initial reading, but none of them made any indication that they had a question for the judge.

"Bailiff, this seems like a good time to break for lunch," Judge Booth stated, feeling the jurors could use some time away after the selection process and instructions. "We will break for ninety minutes and then reconvene for opening arguments. Just a reminder to the jurors, you are not to discuss this case with anyone outside of yourselves. If you do, there could be criminal charges brought against you and a mistrial declared."

"All rise," the bailiff ordered as the judge stood up and walked out of the courtroom.

"Well, that was fun," Myron said to Erickson sarcastically as they gathered up their papers and belongings. "I'm afraid I will be leaving you after this."

"That's right, you need to sit with the defendant and his attorney."

"Yes, and I should have been over there during the selection process, but I think Judge Booth realized why I was at this table.

I'm glad he accepted my deputy as sufficient, while we went through the names."

"I don't think the judge saw him as a flight risk," Erickson commented, "especially in a crowded room like this."

"Was it this crowded down in Kanab?"

"Even worse, because the courtroom was smaller. This case is so sensational; it has really captured the interest of people throughout the state."

"Yes, I've noticed there are reporters from everywhere. There is even one here from the *Ogden Standard Examiner*. That's quite a ways away. As far as I know, this is the first case of its kind here in Zion."

"As far as I know," Erickson concurred, "you're right."

"That would explain the interest," Myron observed. "I wonder how long the interest will hold."

"I don't know, but the vast majority of spectators here were men. I only counted about ten or eleven women. I would suspect that the wives back home will get after their men for skipping out on chores and make sure they stay and work tomorrow."

"I suspect the women are anxious to hear a report on what's going to happen here from their husbands, after the children are in bed," Myron replied and then changed the subject. "I have lunch back at the Sheriff's Office, so I'm going to go eat and then tend to the issues that came up while we were here. Telephone me if you have any further questions before I return."

"I can't think of any," Erickson said, "but I will let you know if any come up."

"All rise for the honorable Judge Booth."

With a single movement, the over-packed courtroom arose to

await the judge's entrance. There were so many people that the rush of air blew some of Samuel Thurman's papers off the table onto the floor. Even though it was January of 1909, the combination of the coal fire and all of the people made the room quite warm. So warm, as a matter of fact, that part way through the afternoon we had to crack a couple of windows open to allow some heat to escape.

My parents brought me here, which was exciting for me, because I'd never been out of the county before and certainly never to anywhere as big as Richfield. We came up a few days early so we could do plenty of shopping for items that were difficult to get back home. We also wanted to sit in on the jury selection, because we did not think we would ever get to see one of those in a big case like this again.

After the judge rapped his gavel several times, we all sat down. I was surprised that I was a bit more nervous about testifying here than I was at the hearing. Maybe it was because I was so far away from home, and this time my testimony might get a man hung.

"Pa, maybe I shouldn't testify because, if I do, it might get Alvin into a whole lot of trouble."

"It's not your words that will get him into trouble," my father assured me. "It will be his actions. You tell the truth, son, and let justice take its course. Do you remember that he confessed to killing Mary?"

I nodded yes.

"Then it's not your words that will hurt him. It was his choice to kill her, not yours. Get up there and tell the truth when it is your turn, and I will be very proud of you."

"Your father and I are very proud of you, no matter what you do," my mother added, always making sure I understood what father was saying. "What your father means to say is that we are very proud of the young man you are growing into and, by the choices you've made in the past; we know you will do the right thing when it is your turn to testify."

"He knows what I mean, Mother."

"How would he know if you don't ever tell him?"

"All right, woman, I'll tell him right now." He turned to me. "Son, I love you, and I'm very proud of you. Your ma doesn't think I say it enough, but I am, and I show you every day."

"I know, Pa, and I love you too. I'm just a little scared. I sure wish I could have Griz up there on the stand with me."

"You'll be fine, and we'll be right here for you," he responded.

I was glad they were there with me.

Alvin was seated next to Sheriff Abbott and, as I recall, was described in the papers as a mere stripling in appearance, a schoolboy with regular features, with no signs of abnormal proclivities. He certainly did not look like someone who would take another human's life and, indeed, looked just like any other farm boy in the territory.

His parents wrung their hands in anguish and worry while Alvin appeared as the most calm and unconcerned person in the courtroom. They were intelligent people with a pleasing appearance. They, of course, realized the gravity of the charge against their boy and did their best to maintain proper decorum during the proceedings. As you could imagine, it was very difficult for them to sit and to listen to the damning things the prosecution and its witnesses brought out in testimony.

"We will begin with opening statements from the defense," the judge said, bringing us back to attention.

"Mr. Thurman?"

"Thank you, Your Honor."

There was a hush throughout the courtroom when Samuel

began to speak. Everyone was straining to hear every word he said. There were so many more spectators than before lunch, at this first-ever murder trial, that they flowed out into the lobby and into the clerk's office.

"Gentlemen of the jury, I commend you for coming out and doing your civic duty today. I am especially grateful because, as we conducted our selection process, I noticed you are discerning men who will fight to get to the truth."

"My client has been charged under the weight of circumstantial evidence, because no one saw the murder taking place, nor did anyone see my client go into or return out of the clearing in Gardner Hollow. As you were informed in the jury instructions, the burden of proof lies directly on the prosecution. Since they don't have any witnesses, or directly linked evidence, they will have to create a mosaic of possibilities they hope, when you stand back and don't look too close, will look like the picture they want you to see. However, what you need to keep in mind, is my client has an alibi and can account for his actions at the time poor Mary was killed."

"We will rely much on the same evidence, which the prosecution will offer, such as the frankness of the defendant. Also, he willingly submitted his clothing and shoes to the officers for testing and furnished the officers with a statement of his whereabouts on the day of the tragedy. We will use evidence that shows the defendant left the school house about four o'clock, went to the store, and spent some time there with his companions, eating candy and laughing. He left there, went home and arrived there a little after five o'clock. His mother was there, saw him and requested of him to drive some cows from the lot. Then he ate something and spent some time at the barn. From there, he went to his aunt's to see his cousin, Charlie Esplin, but he was not home."

"The defendant went back home and saw some people at about five-thirty in the evening. He called at a house that was being erected by his uncle and was seen by the victim's brother, Joseph Stevens. At that time, he went home, changed his clothes, and went out, cleaned out a stable, and was seen there by his little brother. It will also be testified to the reputation of this young man for truth, sobriety, morality, and right living that has never been questioned."

"The death of this girl was an absolute travesty; let us not diminish that fact in any way or fashion. And I absolutely believe that the killer of this lovely young lady must pay for his crimes, but that killer is not my client. As you listen to the testimony from the prosecution, be mindful for the holes they have covered up to make their argument look solid. Then pay particular attention to the defense witnesses, and these holes will become even broader and easier to see. We must bring the killer to justice; it just isn't young Alvin Heaton. It is imperative you find him not guilty to preserve and to protect justice in this case. I thank you for your time, and I am relying on you to make the right decision."

Samuel walked slowly back to his table, so his words could sink in before his opposition stood and began his opening statement. Erickson, well aware of what Samuel was doing, patiently waited for him to make his way back to his seat.

Ezra, who was seated at the prosecution table with Erickson, followed Samuel's movements with a look of disgust on his face for all to see. Samuel ignored him. Ezra looked very haggard and seemed to be about ten years older than he was the previous spring, before his daughter had been killed.

"Mr. Thurman, if you are done lollygagging in my courtroom, I will turn the floor over to Mr. Erickson."

A chuckle rippled through the courtroom as Samuel's delaying tactic backfired on him. However, this actually allowed for more time between presentations, so he took it as a victory instead of defeat.

"Thank you, Your Honor," Erickson said. He stood up, walked over to the jury box, and then stood and faced them for a moment before he spoke.

"Defense Attorney Thurman wished to put as much distance between his opening comments and mine as he possibly could. I paused when I walked over here, because I'm happy to oblige him. You see, his case is without foundation, and he is hoping his fine speech will convince you of his client's nonexistent innocence. And if his client was innocent, I would be happy to pause all day. As a matter of fact, if his client were innocent, then we wouldn't be here at all. Unfortunately, his client not only committed the murder of the beautiful Miss Mary Stevens, but he also confessed to it."

"During the month of April and previous to that time, Mary Stevens, the girl who is alleged to have been murdered by the defendant, was attending school in Orderville. Her home before that time was at Mt. Carmel, a little town just two or three miles south of there. While attending school in Orderville, she made her home with her brother, Joseph Stevens, his pregnant wife, and their two small children who resided there in Orderville. Bear in mind that on the 20th day of April, 1908, during the time the examinations were being held at the public school for the eighth grade students, Mary was among the students taking these examinations. On the day mentioned, she had been at school all day until four o'clock, except the noon hour. Just before she left the school, she was standing on the outside platform of the school building talking or, in company, with the defendant, Alvin Heaton. He was also there that day and had started to take the examinations, but decided not to finish. Mary went back to the schoolhouse after lunch to study and talk with the other students.

Mary Stevens, eighteen years of age, after leaving the schoolhouse the second time, went home to her brother's house. After remaining there for a short time, she went out of the house and started up the hill just north of where her brother, Joseph, lived. The last time she was seen alive by her family she was going up the hill from which she did not ever return."

"We will prove, beyond a shadow of doubt, that Mr. Alvin Franklin Heaton, Jr., lured Mary up to a clearing in Gardner Hollow under false pretenses, tried to convince her not to press charges against him or force him to marry her and, when she insisted, he retaliated. When her back was turned to him...did you catch that gentlemen?...When her back was turned to him, he pulled out a .38 caliber Smith and Wesson revolver and cowardly shot her twice in the back...an unarmed woman carrying his child. This drove her to her knees while she screamed, but she was still yet alive, so he took a couple of steps closer to her. He raised his gun once again and shot her a third time...her back still turned to him...in her back. This shot knocked her face down on the ground and, as she took her last desperate breaths of dust mixed air, he walked over, stood above her, and again, cowardly shot her a fourth and final time in the back. This spattered her life's blood onto his coat and shoes."

"Mary Stevens was now dead."

"Having completed his dastardly deed, he dragged her lifeless body to the preselected ravine and dropped her in face down. Reaching across the ravine, he dislodged rocks and dirt, which fell down on her, to conceal his crime from the world. He also gathered loose brush from around the area and tossed it into the ravine, further to hide his actions. It was the perfect crime; no one would ever find her there...at least so he thought. Once his task was completed, he dusted off his hands with approval and then turned around and noticed Mary's hat, still on the ground. In his haste to return to town to regenerate his alibi, he had completely missed it. He quickly grabbed the hat and tossed it down into the ravine. He knocked more dirt and rocks from the opposite ravine wall to conceal it, and, as the ensuing dust cloud kicked up, it appeared to him as if he had completely covered it. He instantly ran back down toward town, taking a different trail than he and Mary had taken on their way up and slipped back into his life, without anyone being the wiser."

"Two critical things Alvin the killer did not take into account and these two things are what led to his downfall. First, in his haste, he did not completely bury Mary's hat. He left the dust-encrusted blue ribbon partially exposed, which led to the discovery of her body's location."

"The second thing he did not take into account was young Mr. Merlin Brinkerhoff. Mr. Brinkerhoff was out tending sheep in the fields near the mouth of the hollow and heard the mortal shots fired by Alvin Heaton, Jr. This allowed authorities to establish a timeframe when the killing took place and a specific time they needed to look at his alibi. Upon closer inspection, the Kane County Sheriff found Mr. Heaton had no eyewitness alibi for the time the shots were fired."

"After her body had been discovered and a fair amount of investigation had occurred, all suspicion pointed to Alvin and only Alvin as the perpetrator. Human bloodstains were found upon his coat and shoes that could not be explained away. He subsequently confessed to the crime and made separate statements to several parties wherein he acknowledged the crime. He killed her to cover up the fact the girl was in a delicate condition, and that he, Alvin Franklin Heaton, Jr., was the author of that condition."

"There is so much evidence, and proof, stacked up against Mr. Heaton, I am convinced there is no way you will find any other way than guilty of murder in the first degree." He paused for a moment as he stood there and looked into the eyes of each juror and then repeated. "Murder in the first degree." He walked slowly back to his seat, much as Samuel had done after his statement. When he reached his table, he slowly turned to the bench and said, "Thank you, Your Honor."

"Maybe we should call this the lollygagging trial instead of Mr. Heaton's," Judge Booth stated with a bit of a barb in his voice. "Perhaps we can move the rest of the proceedings along a little quicker, gentlemen?"

"Of course, Your Honor," they both mumbled. Despite the reprimands, both attorneys would go back and do things the same way if they had the chance, because they both felt their delays had benefitted them far greater than it hurt them.

I was ready for another recess after those long introductions and being singled out by Mr. Erickson like that, but I was forced to sit there for several more hours. This was worse than being stuck out tending sheep on a cold day or sitting next to Claudia Barlow in church.

"That was certainly a solid picture damning Alvin that the prosecutor just brought out," my father said, as he leaned over me to make the comment to my mother. "I don't think he has a chance."

"I wish we could just go home," I whispered to my father.

"As soon as we can, son. We can't leave the animals in the neighbors' care for too long."

"Your first witness, Counselor?" Judge Booth asked Erickson.

"The prosecution wishes to call Ellen Jorgensen to the stand."

The bailiff called for her to come forward and then swore her in.

"Mrs. Jorgensen, you were born and have lived all your life in Orderville, is that not correct?" Erickson asked her.

"That is correct."

"Now, you told Sheriff Brown you saw Alvin near the Esplin barn some time after three o'clock on the day of the murder. Is that correct?"

"Yes, it is."

"Can you show me on the map where you live and where you saw the defendant?"

"Most certainly." She reached over and pointed out their locations.

"Thank you, no further questions."

Samuel stood up, walked over to Ellen and stood before her.

"Mrs. Jorgensen," he began, "are you absolutely positive that it was three o'clock when you saw my client walking along?"

"Pretty sure."

"How sure? A hundred percent? Ninety? Sixty-seven? How sure?"

"Eighty percent, perhaps."

"A man's life hangs in the balance, Mrs. Jorgensen, you need to be sure. What time was it? Could it have been earlier or perhaps later?"

"It certainly wouldn't have been earlier, so if I'm mistaken, it would have been later."

"What were you doing that afternoon when you saw him?"

"I was hanging laundry. I had been doing the washing all day and was getting near completion."

"How long does it usually take to do all your laundry?"

"All day most of the time," she said as she paused to think about it. "I got an earlier start that day, but I stopped to have lunch with my sister."

"So what is the absolute latest you could have seen him?"

"I don't think it was too late," she stated as she thought.

"That's not what I'm asking," he pinned. "I want to know the absolutely latest it could have been."

"The sun was still pretty high in the sky, I needed it to be so the sheets would dry, and I could make the beds that evening. I still think it was around three, but the absolutely latest it could have been would have been around five or five-thirty."

"Five-thirty, you say?" he pounced. "That is right in the middle of the hour the prosecution claims the victim was killed."

"I suppose."

"Thank you, Mrs. Jorgensen, that is all."

Joseph Heaton was called to the stand and sworn in by the bailiff.

"Mr. Heaton," Erickson began, "you were raised in Orderville, were you not?"

"I was."

"Are you familiar with the defendant?"

"I should be; we're kin."

"Did you see him on the afternoon of the murder?"

"I did, I saw him about six o'clock that night near the Jorgensen home, going at a fast walk."

"Did you see where he went?"

"He turned into his house and then came out again after a few minutes. He walked back to the Chamberlain's house, took a magnifying glass out of a small box, and looked through it. After a few minutes, he walked across the street to his father's barn. He was walking fast when he started and then broke into a run."

"Any idea why he was running?"

"None whatsoever. It's not like him to run a lot of places, so it must have been something important."

"Did you see him again after that?"

"Not that night. I had chores to do that took me away from

that side of the house. I didn't know what had happened up the hollow, so I didn't think to go back and check on him to see if he had left the barn."

"Thank you, Joseph, no further questions. Counselor?"

Samuel raised his hand and shook his head to indicate he had no questions for this witness.

"Your Honor, next we would like to call Doctor Robert Garn."

Robert walked forward, swore his oath to tell the truth, and took his seat.

"Doctor Robert Garn," Erickson began, "you are a resident in the town of Panguitch, are you not?"

"That is correct, I am."

"And you are a medical doctor, correct?"

"That is correct, yes. I earned my medical degree from the College of Physicians and Surgeons in Baltimore, Maryland."

"Were you in Panguitch at the time of the murder?"

"I was."

"Were you called down on orders to conduct a post-mortem examination?"

"I was so ordered by the Sixth District Court District Attorney."

"Which is myself."

"Correct."

"And did you complete the so commanded examination?"

"I did. On April 29, 1908, Doctor Andrew Moir and myself conducted an examination on one Mary Manerva Stevens, once her body had been exhumed from her grave."

"Why did you exhume her and what did you find?"

"We examined her to ascertain the condition of her body to furnish a motive for the crime. As determined by Doctor Moir, I found the cause of death to be four gunshots to the back. Beyond the obvious and on to the point of the post burial examination, we examined her abdominal cavity and her uterus. We found her uterus was impregnated, and she was around eight weeks along at the time."

"This would corroborate the evidence of sexual activity found by Doctor Moir upon his initial examination, yes?"

"Objection," Samuel stated as he stood. "We have not heard testimony from Doctor Moir yet, so the witness cannot testify as to what he will testify to."

"Overruled. I have seen the autopsy report, and it is spelled out very clearly. The witness will answer the question."

"Yes, it did," Doctor Garn continued. "Doctor Moir was correct in his findings."

"Thank you, Doctor, for your testimony. I have no further questions at this time. Counselor?"

Again, Samuel had no questions for this witness. He was an expert in his field, and his findings were based on scientific fact and could not be disputed...especially because they were testified to by two professionals.

I certainly wished they had asked more questions however, because my name came up next as a witness. One thing I was glad about them not asking any more questions however, was because my mother kept gasping each time the men used the word pregnant. We just didn't use that word in polite society.

"Your Honor, we would like to call Merlin Brinkerhoff to the stand."

Told you.

I froze.

I didn't want to go up.

My father squeezed my arm in a show of support, and my mother patted my hand...the one that was shaking so badly from fear. My feet felt so heavy, I feared I would never get there.

Finally, after what seemed to be about a week and a half, I made it to the stand.

"Please place your left hand on the Bible and raise your right hand," the bailiff ordered. He seemed so big to me at the time. As I look back now, I realize he was normal height, but quite round in the girth, making him seem much larger.

I raised my right hand and placed my other one on the Bible. Suddenly, he was talking like an auctioneer, "Do you swear to tell the truth, the whole truth, and nothing but the truth, so help you God?"

I paused for a moment, because all I understood from him was the word "God." I thought quickly back to the other times he had said it in the trial and what had been said at the hearing, and I pieced together what the oath was. I stated, "I do." The next time I would make that oath would be when I married Elsie Viola Jones, another decade or so later.

"Be seated," he ordered and walked away.

I was very glad to be able to sit down. I just knew everyone in that over-crowded courtroom could see my knees knocking together.

Mr. Erickson stood up from his table and walked over to the witness stand.

"Will you please state your name for the record?"

"Merlin Brinkerhoff of Glenside, sir."

"Are your parents here with you today?"

"Yes, sir, Silas and Elizabeth. There's no way they would let me come all the way up here from home by myself; it must be a hundred miles."

A ripple of laughter spread throughout the courtroom at the comment. I noticed even the judge chuckled at the comment, and I worried I might be reprimanded for making him laugh. I didn't mean to. I didn't try to make anybody laugh, I was just so nervous

I gave the first answer that came to mind. However, their laughter helped me to relax, and I felt much calmer during the rest of the interview.

"Where were you on the day Mary was killed up in Gardner Hollow?"

"I was out herding sheep about a mile from Orderville."

"Had you been there for long?" Erickson inquired.

"I was camped there with my dog and the sheep."

"You were camped there alone with no adults around?"

"Yes, sir."

"Well, Merlin, I'd say if you are responsible enough to camp out there and protect the sheep all by yourself, you could find your way to Richfield alone, too."

"And my dog."

This time the courtroom erupted with laughter. I figured I'd get it for sure from my folks when I got back to the hotel.

"When you were out camping and tending to your sheep on the day Mary was killed, did you hear gunshots coming from the direction of Gardner Hollow?"

"I did."

"How many did you hear?"

"Four. Two right together, then a third and then, after a moment, the fourth one."

"Did you see who fired the shots?"

"No, sir, I was camped up on the side hill above some cottonwoods and across the canyon from where the shots came. My view was blocked, so I could not see anyone over there."

"Did the shots concern you in anyway?"

"No, sir, like I said, they came from the canyon and there were always men up there hunting. I didn't think about who it was up there shooting. I thought, 'I wonder what they're hunting and if they got it?'"

"Thank you, young man, you were a very composed witness."

I sure didn't feel composed, but I was glad he thought so.

"Does the prosecution have any questions for the witness?" the judge asked.

"Yes."

Samuel Thurman stood up and looked like an angry giant as he walked toward me. He wasn't angry, but that is what he reminded me of.

"What time did you hear the shots?" he asked.

"About five-thirty," I responded through a dry mouth and burning throat. I was afraid he was going to yell at me.

"How sure are you that was the time?" he asked.

"Ma had just sent out supper."

"Excuse me?"

"Ma always sends one of my brothers or sisters out with supper if Pa doesn't bring it. She makes it up around five and then sends it out. My brother had dropped it off and had run back off to home before I heard the shots, so it was about five-thirty."

"I see," Samuel said and then paused for a moment.

He looked at me and I knew he had more on his mind he wanted to ask me, but he finally exhaled and relaxed. He turned around, walked back to his table and picked up some papers. I think he wanted to challenge my testimony, but was afraid of the damage it would do to his case. If he bullied a 10-year-old boy, then the jurors may see his case, and position, as weak. He shuffled through the papers for what seemed like an hour before he turned back toward me.

"You may go back and sit down with your parents."

I was never so glad to be released from anything in my life.

When I sat down, my father wrapped his arm around my shoulder and squeezed hard to show how proud he was of me and how much he loved me. My mother just cried into her handkerchief. I asked my father about it later, and he said it was because I looked so grown up on the stand, and she knew I wasn't a little boy anymore.

I knew that; I was ten.

After I sat down, they called Ezra to go up and testify. Because he wasn't there at the time of the murder, I wasn't sure what good he could do up there but, by now, I was fascinated with the trial process and couldn't wait to find out.

After he had been sworn in and seated, Erickson approached him.

"Will you state your full name for the record, sir?"

"Ezra William Stevens."

"And will you state your relationship to the victim?"

"I was her father. Her mother, Edith, is here too."

"Do you live in Orderville?"

"I do not, but my son Joseph does. I live a couple miles down the road in Mt. Carmel."

"Were you in Orderville at the time of your daughter's murder?"

"No, I was working in Mt. Carmel there in town when I was hailed to answer Joseph's phone call. I immediately rode as hard as I could to his house when I found out she had been killed."

"What did you do once you arrived?"

"I had my son take me up the hollow to where she had been killed and where the posse had lost the killer's tracks."

"Did you start to look for the tracks yourself?"

"I did. I found his tracks, size six, and followed them on the soft ground. Once they reached the rocky ground, they became much more difficult to follow. Joseph and I had to spend quite a bit of time looking each time we lost them."

"How hard were they to reacquire?"

"At one point I had to scale the ledges to get a bird's eye

view, so I could see them again."

"Were you able to follow the tracks to the murderer's home?"

"No, we lost them in all the traffic on the streets when we got back to Orderville."

"Did you notice anything else particular about the tracks?"

"Yes, that when Alvin walked alongside Mary, he tended to walk toed-in."

"Well, that's what we are here to determine, whether it was Alvin or not. Do you mean to say that when the killer walked alongside Mary, he tended to walk toed-in?"

"Yes."

I noticed how anger crossed his face when the prosecuting attorney made him take back that he said Alvin did it.

"Is there any other testimony you would like to add at this time?"

"No, sir."

"Thank you."

"Does the defense wish to cross examine the witness?" Judge Booth asked.

Samuel took a minute to look over his notes and then said, "Yes, Your Honor."

He stood up and walked over to Ezra. "You said each time you lost the killer's tracks, you were able to reacquire them, correct?"

"That's the word District Attorney Erickson used, but yes, that is what happened."

"How can we be sure the tracks you reacquired each time were that of the killer?"

"Two reasons, sir. First, they were always a size six and walked in the same manner. There was no question, it was the same man."

"And second?"

217

"There were no other tracks up there. He came back off the trail through the brush and grass clumps. Nobody else went that way."

Samuel paused for a moment longer as he tried to determine if there were any other relevant questions he could ask, that would shed some doubt on Ezra's testimony. Try as he might, he could not think of anything.

"That is all, thank you."

"You may be seated," Judge Booth stated.

Ezra stood up, still looking ten years older than he was, and walked back to the prosecution's table to sit down.

"The prosecution would like to call Miss Stella Stout."

Stella was brought forward and seated in the customary manner.

"Miss Stout, do you live in Orderville?"

"Yes, sir, I do."

"Did you know the defendant while you were living there?"

"I most certainly did."

"Did you see him in town on the day of the murder?"

"Perhaps earlier in the day, but I'm not sure."

"Did you ever see him with Mary?"

"Yes, I did. One night about three weeks before the murder, I saw Alvin go to the Stevens' place and call on Mary. He was seeing her on the quiet."

"About what time was this?"

"I'd say about eleven o'clock at night."

"Did you ever tell anyone else they were seeing each other?"

"Didn't really occur to me to do that."

"What else did you see there?"

"Mary came out, and they passed around the west side of the house. After that, I couldn't see them anymore."

"Where were you when you saw this?"

"I was on the clay point across the bridge."

"Did you ever see them together again after that?"

"No, sir, I did not."

"Thank you very much. Counselor?"

Erickson walked back to his table and sat down as Samuel stood up to approach the witness.

"Where is it you were going when you saw the defendant and the victim?"

"I was on my way to Mrs. Esther Paine's, who had been sick. I had been staying with her to help her out. My father had walked with me from home as far as the post office and then turned back."

"Talking with Mrs. Paine, who is too sick to come here herself, she stated that you told her it was Hyrum Mower you had seen with Mary. Is that not what actually happened?"

"No, sir, she was confused when she said that. What she is referring to is another time, before that, when I saw two boys at the Heaton house, and I thought one of them was Hyrum Mower, and I think the other one was Jackie Adler. I don't know if this has any connection whatsoever with the trial, but Hyrum and Alvin palled around a lot with Jackie, so it was not an unusual thing to see. Because Mrs. Paine is housebound, she loves to hear what everyone around town is doing."

"Thank you very much, young lady. No further questions."

Stella and Samuel sat down and Erickson stood back up.

"We call for John W. Healy to come to the stand."

After he had been seated, Erickson began to question him.

"Do you live in Orderville?"

"Yes."

"Do you know the defendant?"

"Yes."

Erickson produced a revolver from the evidence table and

showed it to Johnny.

"Do you recognize this gun?"

"I do. It is mine."

"Can you explain to the court how it came to be in the possession of the defendant?"

"Back when I was shearing sheep last April, Alvin approached me and offered to rent the gun from me for a deck of playing cards."

"How long was this rental to last?"

"Just for a month."

"For the record," Erickson said as he took the gun back from Johnny, "let it show that the firearm in question is a Smith and Wesson revolver of .38 caliber. Counselor?"

Samuel walked over to him and looked at the revolver, read the manufacturer's name on it and the caliber stamped on the barrel.

"Agreed," he said.

"How did this trade come about?" Erickson asked, as he turned back to Johnny.

"I was up playing cards with Alvin and Joseph Stevens after I finished shearing for the day. Alvin said he wanted to borrow the gun, so he could shoot rabbits during the spring roundup coming up soon. I saw no reason not to let him take the six-shooter."

Erickson handed him back the revolver. "Will you open it for me?"

Johnny pressed the release latch that held the cylinder in the frame, and it swung out.

"How many chambers does the cylinder have?"

"It has…I never noticed that. It has five. I always thought it was a six shooter."

"Thank you. Counselor?"

Samuel stood up and approached the witness. "When you

bought this, you bought it for a six-shooter?"

"Yes, sir, that is correct."

"Then you were cheated out of one hole in the cylinder," he said, slightly mocking the witness.

This caused a titter from the spectators.

"Your Honor, I have no further questions for this witness but I would, however, like to recall Miss Stout to the stand. I do have one more question for her."

"Bailiff." Judge Booth said.

The bailiff recalled Stella and reminded her that she was still sworn in. She confirmed she knew that.

"Why is it you stopped by the bridge to watch what was happening at the Stevens' house?" Samuel asked.

"I was curious to know who was calling on Mary Stevens."

"Why so curious?"

"Because not many fellows called on her. As a matter of fact, I would have to say that I don't know of any that went calling on her."

"Thank you."

"Your Honor," Erickson stated, "it is getting late, I move that we adjourn for the night and reconvene in the morning."

"Granted," Judge Booth agreed. "I'm also sequestering the jury in the custody of two bailiffs, Albert Olsen and R. H. Barney. You two will be sworn in to take charge of the jurors."

They both nodded.

"Court adjourned until tomorrow morning at ten o'clock," the Judge announced as he rapped his gavel on its base.

What a relief! We could finally get out of there. As fascinating as I found the legal process, it was still hard for me to sit still all day long.

My father turned to me, "You held really still in here. Why don't you go out and run around the building three times, and then we will find some grub for dinner."

I was only too grateful to do as he suggested, so I slipped out past everyone as politely as I could. Once I escaped the crowded throng gathered around the doors, I started to run as fast as I could. I circled the building the first time and was going for my second when I heard someone call, "Here comes Merlin on the outside; he looks like he's left his competition behind, but the race isn't over yet."

I thought it was awfully strange that this person would say anything at all, as I ran by. When I circled the building the second time, I heard him again. "Merlin, still in the lead, rounds the last corner for another lap."

I almost stopped to tell him it wasn't really a race, but I was running so hard, I couldn't even tell who was saying it. I ran around the building the third time and stopped in front of the main entrance.

"And he took them by a mile," I heard the voice say.

Panting for breath with my hands on my knees, I looked around and found it was Wilford Heaton who had been "calling my race".

"Hello, Brother Heaton," I said as I fought to catch my breath. "I didn't realize it was you who was talking as I came around."

"I'm not surprised. By the way you were moving, I think you could have outrun a wildfire at that speed."

"I couldn't stand to be cooped up in that building any longer. It was worse than trying to sit still in church."

Wilford laughed. "I understand. If I were younger, I probably would have been running right along with you. Lucky for you, there wasn't more snow on the ground or you'd have looked like a fawn on the ice trying to get around."

"I'd probably run in a straight line if that was the case. Then

I'd of stopped and turned around and run back the other way."

"You and your folks headed out for dinner now?"

"I reckon so, sir, but here comes Pa. You can ask him yourself."

"Hello, Silas. How did you fare today?"

"Much better than poor Merlin here. I didn't think he was going to be able to sit still for another minute in there."

"Headed back to the hotel?" he asked.

"Pretty much. We need to get this one fed before he faints over dead on us from all the running around. I suspect we'll eat there because it's handy."

"I have some errands to run before I can eat, but maybe I'll see you there."

"We'll keep an eye out for you."

Joseph Stevens was the first witness of the day. He was called and sworn in, like those before him.

"Joseph Stevens, how long have you lived in Orderville?"

"About seven years."

"What is your relationship with the victim?"

"I'm her brother."

"Can you tell us why Mary was living in Orderville with you at the time of her death?"

"She moved up from Mom and Dad's place so she could go to school for the year of 1907-08."

"Where were you when you last saw her?"

"I was at home working in the garden when I saw her going up the hill a short distance from our place."

"What time was that?"

"Seems to me it was about four or five in the afternoon."

"Did your sister return home that night?"

"Not that I could tell."

"Is that a no?"

"Correct, she did not come home that night."

"Did that concern you?"

"Not at the time. We thought she might have gone over to a girlfriend's house to study all night. She was a good student and got good marks in school. I went down and checked at the school, but David Smith said neither he nor any of the students had seen her that morning."

"So you did not find her at any of those places?"

"No."

"Then what?"

"I went to the Co-op and called home to see if she had gone there for the night."

"And?"

"No. So I headed up the hill to look for her."

"Did you find her up there?"

"Not exactly. I found where something had happened. It wasn't until later I found out it was where she was killed."

"How did you find out?"

"I went back to town and got the constable. He got a posse together, and we went back and found her buried in the ravine."

"How had she gotten there?"

"She had been killed and buried there, so we wouldn't find her."

"But you did."

"Yes. He left a little bit of Mary's ribbon showing, and that's how we found her."

"Who accompanied you in the posse that afternoon?"

"Ed Carroll, who is Justice of the Peace, Wilford Heaton who is the constable, Wallace Adair, Nevin Luke, and David Esplin."

"What did you do once you uncovered her body?"

"We carefully lifted her out and conducted a coroner's inquest to determine the cause of her death."

"You didn't believe she had tripped and fallen into the ravine on accident?"

"And have all those rocks and dirt fall from the side wall, and then the brush blow in and cover her up overnight? No."

"What did you find?"

At this point, Joseph paused and looked down. When he looked back up, we could see there were tears in his eyes, and he was fighting back the sobs that wanted to erupt from his body.

"Your Honor?" Erickson asked.

"Take a moment, Mr. Stevens. Compose yourself and we will proceed," Judge Booth instructed.

"Thank you," Erickson stated on behalf of Joseph.

The courtroom anxiously sat silent, waiting for more of his story. After a few minutes, he had regained his composure and was able to continue.

"We found she had been shot four times in the back. Someone had murdered her."

"How did you get her home?"

"I carried her. The other men offered to help, but I felt it was my sacred responsibility to bring her home, one last time. I had failed her in life; I couldn't do the same in death."

"Is there anything you would like to add to what your father has already testified?"

"No, sir, everything else happened pretty much as he stated."

"Thank you."

Erickson turned toward Samuel and raised his eyebrow in a question to see if he had any questions, but he did not.

"Why don't you ask him questions?" Alvin asked him in a whisper.

"Because he did not testify to anything that mentioned you. Everything he said was his experience of finding the body, but not at any point did he mention or implicate you. What questions would you have me ask?"

"None, I guess, I didn't think about it like that."

"Your Honor," Erickson said, "I would now like to question Constable Wilford Heaton."

Wilford was called, sworn in, and seated.

"Wilford, you are the constable of Orderville, is that not correct?"

"It is."

"Did you lead the posse that found Mary's body?"

"In a manner of speaking. One could argue that Joseph Stevens was the leader."

"But you were present and acting as constable?"

"Yes."

"You were there when the body was found?"

"I was, that is correct."

"You examined the body personally and found the bullet holes in her back?"

"Yes, we also found, after we had taken her back to Joseph's house that two of the bullets had exited from her chest."

"Did you happen to check the defendant's shoes to see if they fit the tracks?"

"I did. I looked at them after they were submitted into evidence here in the courtroom. As I recall, the tracks were somewhat larger than these shoes, but that's just my opinion."

"That is all I have."

"Thank you. Questions, Counselor?" Judge Booth asked.

"No, thank you, Your Honor."

"You may be seated, Constable. Your next witness, Counselor?"

"We would like to call Sarah Foote to the stand."

"Very good. Bailiff."

Sarah was called forward, sworn in, and seated.

"Sarah, you live in Orderville and were present when they brought the body down from the Hollow, is that correct?"

"Yes, sir, at least I was called over to the house when they brought her down."

"What was your role in the examination of the body once it reached Joseph's house?"

"I removed the clothes from her body and washed her for burial."

"And it was you who found the .38 slug stuck to her clothes?"

"Yes, it was stuck in the blood that had saturated her dress."

"What did you do with the bullet once you found it?"

"I turned it over to the constable, who turned it over to the sheriff when he arrived."

"Were you aware of any relationship between the victim and the defendant?"

"No, sir, I was not aware of any."

"Thank you very much, those are all the questions I have. Counselor?"

"None."

"You may be seated."

Next to be called and seated was Doctor Andrew Moir.

"Just for the record, Doctor Moir, will you please tell the court where you received your medical degree?"

"I went to school at the Michigan College of Medicine and Surgery in Detroit."

"And you indeed graduated, yes?"

"Of course."

"Did you examine the wounds on Mary's body in autopsy?"

"I did."

"What did you find?"

"I found her body was advancing in decomposition, as you would expect. I also found abrasions on her right arm and one on her right earlobe. There was a ragged scalp wound above and in front of her left ear about two inches long, and slight abrasions on both of her arms that could be explained by the rocks and debris dumped onto her body. I also found the previously mentioned gunshot wounds."

"What did you determine about the four gunshots?"

"They all entered her back, but only two exited coming out of her left breast; any one of them would have been fatal."

"What else did you find as you examined her body?"

"In looking for a motive for the crime, I did not find any evidence of vaginal violence, I did however, find vaginal secretions, indicating she had intercourse previous to her murder."

"Were you able to determine how soon and with whom she had relations?"

"No, sir, our modern science is not up to that point yet."

"Did you conduct a post-internment autopsy with Doctor Garn?"

"Yes, at your order."

"Do you concur with his findings as stated in these proceedings?"

"I do."

"Just to refresh the jury's memory, what did you find in that examination?"

"She was with child."

"Thank you."

Next to be called was the teacher David Smith.

"Did you see Mary with the defendant on the day of her

death?" Erickson asked.

"I did. I saw them on the schoolhouse porch around lunchtime on the twentieth of last April. I later saw Alvin about four o'clock and walked toward the store with him at that time."

"Do you know the nature of the visit between the two on the porch?"

"I saw Alvin give her a note."

"Did she read it?"

"Yes, she did."

"Do you know what it said?"

"I do not."

"Thank you."

Lunch was called and, when we returned, the courtroom was filled to suffocation by a larger crowd than any time previously. There were many more women in the audience this time than before. I guess they were not satisfied with their husbands' reports of the days' events.

Sheriff Brown was called to the stand to testify.

"Please state your name for the record."

"James Brown, Sheriff of Kane County at the time of the murder."

"Are you acquainted with the defendant?"

"Yes, I've known him all his life."

"You were in Kanab when you received the call that Mary had been killed?"

"Yes, it was the twenty-first of April of last year. I immediately summoned Harmon Cutler and Doctor Andrew Moir, and the three of us rode directly up there."

"While you were there, did you have contact with the defendant?"

"Yes, at various times."

"After you conducted your investigation, you arrested Alvin

for the murder of Mary Stevens, correct?"

"Yes."

"The defense attorney is greatly concerned for his client, as well he should be. He will no doubt ask if you warned him that anything he said in custody or confession, would be used to condemn him. Did you warn his client of this?"

"No, we did not. We did not realize someone who would commit murder wouldn't realize that if he confessed to it, it would be used against him. It is the sort of thing that any rational man would know."

"Are you saying you believe Alvin to be rational?"

"I do."

"Objection." Samuel stood up as he addressed the judge. "He is not qualified to make that kind of determination."

"Overruled," Judge Booth answered. "He is stating his opinion and has probably spent more time with the defendant than anyone else since the murder took place. As a lawman, he would have developed some sort of educated idea as to his state of mind."

Samuel sat back down without further comment.

Erickson continued.

"Did you offer any inducement to get the boy to make a statement at the time you had him in custody?"

"None, whatsoever."

"Did you ask the defendant about his gun?"

"I did. He admitted he had a gun in his trunk at home. He ran home and retrieved it at my request."

"And you offered no inducement to get him to do this?"

"No, sir, but then again, neither did we warn him that it would get him arrested."

"When you searched his possessions at his house later that day, did you find anything related to the murder?"

"We found blood on his shoes and his coat. He claimed it was from a chicken he killed for the roast the Sunday before the murder. When we sent them to the State Chemist, Herman Harms, he found it to be human blood, not animal."

"What did the defendant tell you about the bullets he purchased from the Co-op?"

"He told me he shot one in front of his uncle's place, two or three over at the Esplin barn, and one had been fired at the chicken roast."

"That accounts for five of the six shots, what happened to that last one?"

"He said it dropped out of his pocket and he lost it."

"Did you find any reason not to believe he lost the last one?"

"Not at the time, but since then, we believe he used two at the roast and four against Mary."

"It has been stated here on this stand, that the tracks on the ground going up the hollow with Mary Stevens were a size six. Did anyone ever verify that?"

"Yes, sir."

"Did anyone ever think to take these shoes," he picked up the pair of Alvin's shoes in evidence, "up into the hollow and see if they even fit the tracks?"

"Yes, sir, both Harmon and I tried them."

"And?"

"Harmon struggled a little bit to get a full fit. He could get the heel to fit perfectly, and then the sole perfectly, but never at the same time, due to the softness of the ground distorting the track when the killer walked."

"And did you have better luck?"

"Yes, I did, I was able to find tracks on harder ground where the tracks had not been distorted. They were a perfect match. Ezra had mentioned to us that the killer walked toed-in, or pigeon toed. We noticed he was correct as we followed the tracks. Later, when we had the young women of Orderville walk arm in arm with the boys, I found Alvin was the only one who walked toed-in."

"One last thing before I let you go," Erickson said. "The time of the murder was somewhere around five-thirty, is that correct?"

"Yes, it is."

"And what is the timeframe that you cannot corroborate the defendant's alibi with witnesses?"

"The defendant was able to provide witnesses for every hour except from about five to six o'clock the day Mary was killed."

"Sheriff, is it possible to walk from town, up to the murder site, spend let's say ten minutes, and then make it back to town in an hour?"

"Yes, Doctor Moir and I were able to walk it at a comfortable pace, with a ten minute stop at the murder site in fifty minutes."

"So, if a person were to run, he could spend longer at the site, let's say to engage in sexual relations, and still make it back after the murder and concealment in less than an hour?"

"Objection!" Samuel exclaimed as he jumped to his feet, almost knocking his papers to the floor.

"Overruled," Judge Booth stated. "The witness will answer the question."

"Yes, in my opinion, it would be possible for the killer to do that, if his dalliance didn't take too long. If there had to be prolonged conversation or something else involved, then no, I wouldn't think it possible."

"So if the conversation took place on the walk up the hill, then the act itself could take place immediately upon arrival?" Erickson asked. "Especially if the killer did all this under false pretenses?"

"I can't imagine the killer did it any other way than with false pretenses. Can you imagine him saying, 'Hey beautiful, how about meeting me up the hollow so I can shoot you in the back?' I certainly can't."

Once again, the courtroom erupted in laughter. I don't know that what he said was so funny, but with the tensions high in the room because of it being overcrowded, it allowed some of that tension to dissipate.

The judge rapped his gavel. "I expect more of you, Sheriff."

James winced and nodded his head as he gave his shoulders a slight shrug.

"I'm sorry, Sheriff," Erickson apologized. "That isn't exactly what I meant. What I meant was, if the killer spoke loving and romantic notions to a woman who was pregnant with his child already, she may be ready and willing to engage once they arrived, believing he had love and perhaps marriage on his mind?"

"I suppose it could happen that way."

"Thank you. Counselor?"

"Yes, thank you," Samuel said as he stood up and walked over to the witness stand.

"Sheriff Brown, I have some questions as to your statements about my client's whereabouts on the afternoon of the murder. Let's go over that again."

"All right…," Sheriff Brown stated as he paused to think back to what had been said earlier. "Let's see, he told me he was at school in the afternoon, and then from the school he went to the store, then he went up over the hill to a point of rocks and waited there for a while…"

"Hold on now, Sheriff. I do not want any statements by my client after he was arrested. Let's stick to his alibi."

"Well…he claimed he went to the house, then to his aunt's and called for his cousin Charlie, then to his house and cleaned the barn. Then to his aunt's place again, and then to the store, then back to his aunt's place where he spent the night."

"Do you feel like he covered the ground of his whereabouts all afternoon?"

"He gave me a plausible explanation as to where he was during every hour of the afternoon."

"What exactly does that answer mean?" Samuel pressed.

"It means, had there been no suspicion cast upon him by other evidence, I would have no reason to doubt his story. He has eyewitnesses to corroborate all of his story except between five and six o'clock, and because he confessed…"

"That's quite enough, Sheriff, thank you. No further questions."

Harmon Cutler was called to the stand. He testified that he rather thought he had told the defendant anything he said might be used against him. He also stated that even if he had not warned him about his statements, his father, Alvin Sr., had. He also corroborated the statement about procuring the defendant's coat and shoes with the bloodstains on them. He was turned over to the defense.

"You were present when my client was questioned about his alibi, correct?" Samuel asked him.

"Yes, I was."

"Let's go over his statement step by step, Counselor," Samuel stated. "We've heard bits and pieces along the way from Sheriff Brown and others. Let's take some time and put them all together if we can."

"All right."

"Start with the beginning of his alibi for us, if you would."

"First, he claimed he went from the school to the store and then went home. Once he arrived there, he found some cows in the yard that did not belong there, so he drove them out. When they were on their way, he went inside and ate lunch. After lunch was over, he claimed that he went out in the barn and watched a setting hen for a half-hour. He left that activity when his mother requested he fix the fence, but he decided he didn't want to do that. Instead, he went to his aunt's house and called for his cousin, Charlie Esplin. Since Charlie wasn't at home, he returned to the store but found nothing of interest there, so he returned home once again. He cleaned out the stable and then went back inside to change his coveralls. In his statement to us, there was some time around five o'clock that afternoon that was not accounted for."

Harmon paused for a moment as he struggled to remember the precise order of events.

"If I had my notes I took at the time, I could refresh my memory better."

"Fine, fine, but what I want to know is when in the afternoon did the defendant not fully account for his whereabouts?" Samuel pushed, starting to lose patience.

"Sir?" Juror Hans Tuft raised his hand from the jury box.

"Go ahead, Juror," Judge Booth acknowledged.

"I have a question for the witness. Did you, as prosecuting attorney of Kane County, ever try to substantiate the defendant's story?"

"I did, but I was not able to find any witnesses who saw him during the times he claimed to be working or sitting alone." He turned back to Samuel and continued. "I interviewed several people while I was there questioning witnesses, and they all said they saw the defendant at the times and places he mentioned seeing people, but I could not find anyone who saw him at the barn while he watched the hen or was cleaning stalls."

"Did you think to talk to his mother and ask her if she had seen him doing this?" Samuel pressed hard, obviously becoming agitated.

"I did not."

"And why not?" Samuel pressed harder. "Isn't that the sort of thing you would expect a skilled investigator to do?"

"Alvin said there was no one in the barn to see or to verify he was there. I saw no reason to upset her by asking her questions her son said she could not answer. If she had looked in on him, surely, he would have used her for his alibi, or she would have come forward to help save her son. However, because neither one offered this as substantiation of his story, I saw no reason to pursue it."

"That is all, Counselor," Samuel said with some frustration.

It was obvious to the spectators he was worried about his client's alibi, which could not be substantiated by witnesses during the time of the murder.

Jackie Adler was called to the stand.

"I understand you had a conversation with the defendant the January before the murder," Erickson began. "Please tell the court how that conversation went."

"We were walking by Gardner Hollow and Alvin made the comment there were lots of murders being committed. He also mentioned Gardner Hollow would be a good place to commit a murder. I had no idea at the time he was really going to go through with it."

"Objection, Your Honor." Samuel stated as he stood.

"Sustained," Judge Booth said. "The witness will refrain from assuming Mr. Heaton is guilty until it is so proven."

"Sorry, Your Honor," Jackie said, "just when he confessed and all."

"What was your reaction to his comment?" Erickson asked.

"I replied that I thought it would be a good place, just as part of the conversation. I also said I would hate to be the one to commit such a crime, because I would surely be caught doing it.

Alvin replied he was of the opinion he could commit murder there and not be found out, as all he had to do to escape suspicion was to act natural."

"Did you agree with that?"

"Most certainly not, sir. I said it would be all right to act natural and all, but he would get caught anyway."

"Is that all?"

"No, Alvin said he knew a place in the hollow where he could commit a murder and would not be found out."

"No further questions. Counselor?"

"You say the defendant made these remarks to you," Samuel stated as he stood, "but he denies he ever said it. Furthermore, he claims he confronted you and told you so."

"He denied to me that he said it, but he said it to me and I cannot go back on what I heard, unless I told people I dreamt it. I did not dream it."

"No further questions." Samuel released the witness from the stand.

Junius Heaton was called to the stand.

"How are you related to the defendant?" Erickson asked.

"We're cousins."

"Please tell the court where you reside."

"Alton, Utah."

"You had a conversation with the defendant about Mary before the killing, did you not?"

"I did, we were down riding the range in Yellowstone, Arizona the summer before he killed her."

"Objection, Your Honor," Samuel exclaimed.

"Sustained," Judge Booth said. "Witnesses, please pay attention. Please refrain from making statements that directly accuse the defendant with the killing, until it has been determined by the jury. Please disregard the fact that he allegedly confessed while he was under arrest in Kanab."

How were we supposed to ignore that?

"We were down riding the range in Yellowstone, Arizona, the summer before she was killed."

"And what did you two talk about?" Erickson questioned.

"I asked him what sort of girl Mary Stevens was. He replied that she was no good, and he could kill her as easily as he could a dog."

"Thank you. Counselor?"

"No questions at this time," Samuel stated.

Valentine Tate was called to the stand.

"Mr. Tate, do you reside in Orderville?"

"No, sir, I'm just down the road in Mt. Carmel where Mary's from."

"And did you have a conversation with the defendant about Mary before her death?"

"I did. We were at a dance in Orderville in February before he…before she was killed. I was standing near the window to get a little air, and Mary walked by. Alvin, who was standing near me, said someone ought to take her virtue and then take her out and kill her."

"Are those the exact words that he used?" Erickson asked.

"No, sir. He used much rougher language than that, I just didn't feel it necessary to use that kind of language in the courtroom in front of the women."

"I understand your concerns, Mr. Tate, however it is important for the case that the jury knows the precise words he used."

"Counselor," Judge Booth intervened, "I believe the court has a pretty good idea of the words that were used, and we feel the gist given by Mr. Tate is sufficient. Please proceed."

"Yes, Your Honor," Erickson said. "No further questions."

"Counselor?"

Samuel nodded to the judge in affirmation as he stood and walked over to the witness.

"You've said under oath that you had this conversation with the defendant."

"Yes, sir."

"Was there anyone else with you who heard this conversation?"

"No, sir, it was just Alvin and myself."

"So we need to take your word that this conversation happened?"

"Yes, sir, but I am under oath."

"No further questions."

"Ladies and gentlemen, the hour is getting late and, being as it is Friday afternoon, we will now adjourn for the weekend. We will reconvene on Monday morning at nine-thirty. Court dismissed."

"All rise."

"Can we go home now, Pa?" I asked. "I'm tired of this and want to get back to our sheep."

"You're not so worried about the sheep as just getting out of here and not sitting in that overcrowded courtroom anymore. I must admit, I've never seen so many people crammed into one room in my life. I think if we tried to fit one more in there, the building would burst off its foundation."

"We could start stacking people on top of each other toward the ceiling."

"I suppose we could try that, son," Silas admitted. He smiled and started the family toward the hotel.

Chapter Eight
How Find You?

Monday morning when court resumed, Thomas Carter was called to the stand.

"Please state your relationship to the defendant," Erickson instructed.

"I am in the Stake Presidency in Kanab, which includes Orderville. I was also the treasurer of Kane County about five years ago, and now I am one of the school trustees in Kanab."

"Please tell us about your involvement with Alvin on or about May twelfth of last year."

"I had a conversation with him on the subject of the Mary Stevens' murder. Harmon Cutler and Sheriff Brown were present for its entirety, and Doctor Moir arrived part way through."

Pay attention here. This was the critical point in the case for the prosecution. It is the alleged confession, which was the absolute final nail in Alvin's coffin that would send him away for life or death.

"Your Honor," Samuel Thurman stated as he stood up. "A

sidebar, please."

Both Erickson and Samuel approached the bar when Judge Booth nodded his approval.

"We request the jury be removed from the courtroom for a discussion of the confession's admissibility."

"Granted," Judge Booth stated.

He ordered the bailiff to remove the jury and stay with them until they were recalled. The District Attorney resumed questioning the witness as soon as the jury filed out.

"Were any promises made to Alvin to get him to confess to killing Mary?"

"No, there were not."

"Were you acting as a counselor to the Stake President of the Church of Jesus Christ of Latter-day Saints, when you had your conversation with Alvin?"

"No, I was not."

"Was there any appeal from the defendant for spiritual or other consolation, owing to church association?"

"No, sir."

"Did you make any kind of promise, threat, or inducement in order to get a statement from him?"

"No, sir."

"Did anyone else do it in your presence, or that you are aware of?"

"No, sir."

"How did the defendant's confession come to be in writing?"

"During our conversation, Alvin confessed his part in the murder. At that time, I called for the others to come in and join in the conversation. Sheriff Brown brought in a table, pen, and paper, and copied down the confession for him to sign."

"Are you saying Alvin did not write his own confession?"

"Correct," Thomas said. "As a matter of protocol, we figured it was better to have an officer of the court do it for admissibility's sake."

"Did Alvin read the confession before he signed it to verify the Sheriff had written it down correctly?"

"Yes, he did."

"And then he signed it?"

"Yes."

"Was there at any time, any threat or promise made toward the defendant to induce him to sign the statement?"

"There was not. Once he confessed, all resistance left him, and he became very compliant. He cooperated fully and no longer tried to hide his role in Mary's death."

"Here in my hand I have a document that appears to be the one you are speaking of. Will you look at it and confirm whether or not it indeed is his confession?"

"Of course," Thomas said as he took the document and looked at it. "Yes, this is the confession Sheriff Brown wrote out, and that the defendant and each of us present signed, too."

"Your Honor, we wish to submit this written confession in as evidence."

"Counselor?" Judge Booth asked Samuel.

"Not a chance, Your Honor."

"Do you have any questions for the witness before I decide on its admissibility?"

"I do, Your Honor," Samuel stated.

"Proceed."

"Mr. Carter, did either my client or his father ask you to visit him in jail?"

"No, sir."

"Then why were you there?"

"At about nine o'clock, I received a request from the prosecuting attorney to visit the jail."

"That was Harmon Cutler, correct?"

"Yes, sir."

"Did Alvin know you were a member of the Stake Presidency when you arrived there?"

"Yes, he did, but, as I said, I was not there in a religious capacity. I was there at the request of the prosecuting attorney because of my interrogation skills."

"Did you make it clear to my client that you were not there in a religious capacity?"

"The subject never came up."

"And you never brought it up."

"No, sir."

"Continue."

"I confronted him, saying I had believed him to be innocent, so I conducted an investigation of my own to clear his name. But at each step, as I looked deeper, things only looked blacker for him. So I told him it would be much better for him to tell the truth."

"Did you quote scripture to him, quote the case of David and Uriah, or use any inducement with the boy?"

"I did not. I talked with him about an hour and a half about the murder and other matters. Among them, we talked about the penitentiary and its rules and regulations."

"Did you at any time use your position in the LDS Church to leverage a confession from my client?"

"I did not."

"Much stress is laid on the Saints in their teachings to obey and to honor the Church leaders," Samuel stated. "Do you expect us to believe Alvin didn't see you more as a Church leader and not as a civic interrogator?"

"I cannot answer to his state of mind."

"Did you say anything about guilt to the boy?"

"I told him that whoever killed Mary would not be able to get out from the guilt of what he'd done. I also told him that if he was indeed innocent, then to stay with it; to hold out until the truth showed him to be free of the crime. But if he was guilty, I told him it would be better for him to tell the truth."

"You said Sheriff Brown wrote down the confession. Did he write it down word for word, or did he paraphrase?"

"He took the intent of what Alvin had said and wrote it down."

"So this statement isn't even in my client's own words?"

"Somewhat not, but as I previously stated, he reviewed the statement carefully before he signed it."

"How do you know he was careful?"

"Because he spent several minutes reading over it."

"Do you know he was reading it, or could he have been in shock over your coercion and merely been staring off into space? Do you know that he read it?"

"No, I suppose not. It appeared so to us, but once again, we didn't know his mind at the time."

"Your Honor, I would like to object to the admission of my client's written statement on the grounds that it was a confession made to a clergy member of the same religious denomination as my client. On further grounds, it was an involuntary confession made after undue influence had been used. Further, the witness was acting for and under the direction of the Prosecuting Attorney, and he was engaged in securing evidence against the defendant."

"Mr. Carter," Judge Booth began, "did you warn the defendant that any statements he might make would be used against him?"

"No, sir, I did not so warn the defendant. One thing however just came to mind. After signing the confession, Alvin requested we inform his mother and father of his statement first, before everybody else found out."

"Did he say why he requested that?"

"He didn't want them to find out about it from the neighbors or newspapers. He wanted them to have time to figure out what they would say to everyone, when they were asked about it."

"How did the talk about the penitentiary come about?" Samuel asked.

"Alvin brought it up. We were talking about moving him to Sugarhouse, and he wanted to know what to expect when he got there. I explained the rules and regulations of the prison the best I could for him."

"Thank you, Mr. Carter, I believe that will be all, at least for now."

"We are well into the noon hour now," Judge Booth stated. "So court will recess for ninety minutes for lunch. I will rule on this when we return."

"Please be seated."

"Your Honor," Erickson stated, "the prosecution would like to withdraw the alleged confession which we had offered into evidence."

"What is he thinking?" I asked, as I turned to my father. "We all know he did it, and we all know he confessed to it. Why don't they make them use it?"

"I don't know, son, but I suspect they are playing a chess game here."

"You don't know how to play chess, Pa," I reminded him.

"I know a little bit," he informed me. "I know enough to realize the withdrawal is a strategic move."

"How so?"

"I don't know but, if we watch long enough, we may be able to figure it out."

"Very well, Counselor," Judge Booth stated. "Bring the jury back in, Bailiff."

Once the jury was reseated in the box, Sheriff Brown was recalled to the stand.

"Can you tell us about what happened with the defendant, subsequent to May 12th, 1908, the day of the confession?" Erickson asked.

"Alvin was warned by his father and his attorney, John Brown, not to make any statements as to the killing of Mary Stevens."

"Objection," Samuel stated as he took his feet. "We already covered this."

"All right, Counselor. The jury will be removed once more while we try and sort this out again."

After they had been removed, the witness continued.

"I heard John tell Alvin to not talk about the killing of Mary Stevens. A few days after his confession of May 12, his father also warned him not to talk about it. After the preliminary hearing, where Judge Ford ruled his confession inadmissible, Alvin was once again warned not to talk any more about it."

"Just out of curiosity, Sheriff," Judge Booth asked, "is there any relation between you and the defense attorney, John Brown?"

"Yes, sir, he is my brother. We have the same father, but come from separate plural wives."

"Has this relationship in any way affected your judgment or performance during the course of your investigation or testimony?"

"Not at all, sir. I've been very careful of that."

"Good enough."

"Your Honor," Samuel said as he stood near his table, "these statements the Sheriff is bringing up cannot be admissible in court because they took place after the alleged confession."

"What exactly are you speaking of?" Judge Booth asked.

"The comments that Sheriff Brown is about to make."

"How do you know what he's about to testify about?"

"He's about to make comments regarding conversations had by my client after May 12th."

"Well, how about if we hear them first, and then you can object?"

"But, Your Honor, they should not even be brought into the courtroom. Therein lays my objection."

"Putting my personal feelings aside," Judge Booth said, "because the prosecution withdrew the alleged confession from the table, you don't have any grounds for an objection on these because they were made afterward."

"But, Your Honor," he repeated, "these comments were made as a result of the alleged confession. It is the fruit of the poison tree; anything that comes afterwards is inadmissible."

"That is true, Counselor, but if the prosecution doesn't submit it as evidence, I can't rule on its admissibility. If I can't rule it inadmissible, it doesn't become a poison tree. However, your client was already under arrest, and those comments may or may not have come without the confession. Unless you can show me direct correlation between the events of May 12th and these other statements, the court must assume there is not one. Can you show me that?"

"No, Your Honor."

"Then we will proceed with the understanding there is no direct correlation between them. I caution the witness and the others in the courtroom not to refer to the events of May 12 in your testimony. However, you may speak freely of any other events that happened after that."

"Did the defendant make any other statements as to his involvement with Mary?" Erickson asked him.

"Sometime around July or August of last year, he asked me about a young man who happened to pass by us. He asked if he had been in jail for some time, and I informed him that yes, he had indeed been in jail for two or three months. Then he said, 'I would have been out of this if I hadn't done what I did.' I said, 'Yes, if you hadn't killed the girl, you would have been out of here now.'"

"What did he say to that?"

"Nothing."

"Your Honor." Samuel stood again. "Is there no way we can connect this to the original admission?"

Erickson stepped in, "Your Honor, I repeat, the alleged confession has been withdrawn and is no longer a matter for the court. This last statement had nothing to do with the first confession but was simply an implied admission."

"Then I wish to offer the alleged confession to the court to secure a ruling on its admissibility," Samuel stated.

"That's fine, if that is what you want to do," Judge Booth said. "However, the court will not rule on the confession until it is offered as evidence to the jury."

"Any confession obtained from the defendant by illegal means," Samuel stated, "either threats or promises, cannot be admitted in to evidence, and any subsequent confessions or admissions which are made under the same influence cannot be admitted."

"I've made my ruling, Counselor," Judge Booth said. "We refuse to rule on the admissibility of the confession without it being brought before the jury. However, for the purpose of ruling on the present evidence offered, we will assume that the first confession was inadmissible, but the evidence now offered is not under the same influence, and therefore it will be admitted."

"I take exception to that, Your Honor," Samuel said.

"Duly noted," Judge Booth said and then continued. "Bring in the jury."

Once the jury had returned, Erickson continued with the witness.

Sheriff Brown repeated everything he had previous testified to without the jury present. Then he continued on, "Alvin and I were out hauling hay and another young man passed by where we were working. Alvin asked, 'That fellow's been to jail, hasn't he?' I told him yes, he had been to jail. 'What had he done?' Alvin asked. 'Oh, he got into trouble with a girl,' I informed him. 'How long was he in?' he asked. 'bout two or three months,' I told him. 'Then I'd been out by this time if I hadn't done what I did?'"

"Sheriff," Judge Booth interjected, "let me caution you that at this point you cannot say anything else."

"Understood."

"That will be all," Erickson said.

Junius McAllister, a seventeen-year-old boy, was called to testify.

"How do you know the defendant?" Erickson asked.

"Knew him while he was in jail down in Kanab."

"Did you ever have occasion to converse with him?"

"I did on several occasions. On one such occasion in September or October, we talked in the presence of George Swapp on a Sunday afternoon about the killing of Mary Stevens."

"Your Honor," Samuel stated again.

"Jury?" Judge Booth asked.

"Yes, sir."

"Bailiff, please retire the jury once again."

As soon as the jury was retired, District Attorney Erickson

stated that the witness would testify that young Heaton said that on that occasion, he had shot Mary Stevens. He told him that she started to run, so he shot her again and she dropped, and then he shot her again.

"It sure took nerve to do it, he told me," Junius stated as he verified what the district attorney said.

"No further questions. Counselor?"

"Just one question," Samuel said. "What was it that was said that started you three on this subject in the conversation?"

"I honestly don't recall."

"Your Honor, you can't allow this testimony to stand since the witness can't remember all of the conversation."

"I will reserve judgment until we hear from the other boy."

George Swapp was called forward.

"Were you present for the conversation referred to by Junius McAllister?" Erickson asked him.

"I was."

"Is there anything you would like to add or take away from what he said?"

"Just that Junius and I frequented the jail because Alvin often played his harmonica, and we went there to hear him."

"I've decided to allow the testimony," Judge Booth stated. "Bring the jury back in."

I leaned over to my father and whispered, "How is the jury supposed to keep anything straight with all this back and forth?"

"I don't know, son. The other thing I don't know is how they are supposed to find him guilty if they won't let them hear his confession."

"It doesn't seem right to me, Pa," I whispered. "If he said he did it, then the jury should be able to know that before they make their decision. I sure would hate to be them, if they said he was not guilty and then found out he'd confessed."

"I'd imagine most of the jurymen know about the confession already," my father whispered back. "It was printed in the newspaper here in town, and I'd imagine all the county was talking about it."

"That makes me feel better. I'm hungry."

"Me too. We'll eat as soon as the judge calls another break; it shouldn't be too long now."

Junius and George repeated their testimonies before the jury. Then Junius added, "I never told anyone about this conversation. As I understand it, a kid had been hanging around the jail and heard our conversation. He went and told the sheriff what he overheard that day. The sheriff then came to me and inquired about the story, so I told him. I was never looking to get Alvin in any more trouble than he was already in."

"Thank you," Samuel stated as he indicated to the judge that he was finished.

"The hour has grown late, ladies and gentlemen," Judge Booth finally stated. "This is a good time to adjourn for the evening. The witness is excused."

The bailiff walked behind the bench and bent over to whisper in the judge's ear. He listened intently for a moment and then nodded his head up and down in affirmation.

"It would seem there is a desire on the part of the jury that they be able to attend the theater tonight," he announced. "Does either the prosecution or defense have any issue with them going?"

Both Erickson and Samuel indicated that neither of them minded. They stood together, discussed it with each other and then turned to the judge.

"The only stipulation we have, Your Honor," Samuel stated, "is that they be escorted there by three bailiffs or deputies."

"We want to be sure they don't discuss the case with anyone

while they are out," Erickson added.

"Seems a reasonable request, so let it be," Judge Booth said. "We will reconvene tomorrow morning at nine-thirty."

The gavel dropped.

Sixteen-year-old Carl Ramsey of Richfield was called first to the stand when court resumed the next morning.

"You say you had a conversation with the defendant at the jail, here in Richfield?" Erickson asked him.

"That is right, sir. It was me and Louis Bean, when we visited the jail window. We were visiting with him about a mandolin pick when I got kind of brassy and said, 'Well, I'd hate to be you, if you done it,' and Alvin replied, 'Well, I done it all right.' Then I asked him if anyone saw him do it and he said, 'No, no one ever saw me within three miles of that damned place.' That was all."

"Thank you, young man. When I bring Louis up here, will he tell me the same thing?"

"Pretty much, sir. We were so scared to come up here and testify that we discussed it to make sure we could remember correctly what he said to us."

"Kind of like rehearsing lines to a play," Erickson stated to prevent the defense from destroying the boy's testimony for that reason.

"Yes, sir, I mean no, sir, not like a play. We only wanted to make sure we had our facts straight and didn't come up here and embarrass ourselves. We wanted to tell the truth, correctly."

"Thank you, son. That will be all."

Louis Bean was called to the stand and, just as predicted, his statement matched very closely to that of Carl.

At this point, the prosecution rested.

Now it was time for the defense to take over and start calling their witnesses.

Samuel Thurman called Augusta Anderson first to the stand.

"Mrs. Anderson, you live in Mt. Carmel, yes?"

"Yes, I do."

"Were you in Orderville the day Mary Stevens was murdered?"

"I was. I was in the Co-op store that afternoon, and I saw Alvin there in the company of Hyrum Mower."

"How long were you there?"

"I was there for over an hour, and Alvin was there the entire time. There were also a number of schoolgirls present at that time, and some boy companions. The boys and girls were passing candy and nuts and such stuff."

The prosecution cross-examined her in the most rigid way, but he failed to shake her testimony, except to draw out from her that she had had some trouble with the Stevens family, and she was particularly friendly to the Heaton family.

Alvin's eighteen-year-old girlfriend Mamie Robinson was called to the stand to testify for the defense.

"Miss Mamie Robinson, you are well acquainted with the defendant, are you not?" Samuel asked her.

"It's actually Mary, sir."

"I beg your pardon?"

"My real name is actually Mary. Everyone just calls me Mamie. It's something my folks started when I was a kid and it stuck."

"I see," Samuel said. He debated for a moment which name he should call her. "Do you mind if I call you Mamie to help avoid confusion?"

"I would prefer that, sir."

"All right, Mamie, you are well acquainted with the defendant, are you not?"

"Yes, sir, I am. I've known him most all my life, living down in Orderville."

"Did you see him on the day of the murder?" Samuel asked.

"I saw him at school in the morning and then at the store later on."

"In Orderville, correct?"

"Yes, sir. I left the schoolroom there about one o'clock before I went home for a while. Later, I went over to the store and he came in about five minutes after I arrived there."

"How long was it that you were there in his company?"

"We were there from around four o'clock until about five o'clock in the afternoon."

"What was it you were doing during this hour at the Co-op?"

"We were eating candy and nuts."

"Did you see him again later that evening?"

"Yes, he returned to the store after six o'clock."

"Thank you. Questions, Counselor?"

"Miss Robinson...Mamie, you were there with other teenagers that afternoon, is that correct?" Erickson asked.

"Yes, I was."

"And there were adults there in the store as well?"

"Yes."

"Can you identify for us who some of those adults were?"

"Mrs. Anderson was there, so was Edward Carroll, and Ella Chamberlain as I recall."

"You were keeping company with Alvin at the time, were you not?"

"Yes, we are sweethearts."

"And you would do anything you could to help him, correct?"

"Yes, anything at all."

"Including lying?"

"Objection," Samuel stated. "Witness has done nothing to warrant such an accusation."

"I withdraw the question. I understand you quarreled with the defendant because of his attentions toward Mary Stevens."

"Absolutely not. We never quarreled over her, and I was never aware of his attentions toward her."

Edward Carroll was called to the stand.

"Miss Robinson stated you were in the store at the time the defendant was there on the afternoon Mary Stevens was murdered. Is that correct?"

"Yes, sir. I saw him there about four or half past on that day, then I saw him again just before we closed the store at seven o'clock."

"Did you notice him acting at all out of the ordinary?"

"Objection, witness is not an expert on the defendant's state of mind," Erickson stated.

"I'm not asking to his state of mind, Your Honor," Samuel said. "I'm asking about his outward actions. Was he acting in a manner unusual for him? Being the witness is the defendant's uncle, he would be able to testify to that."

"Overruled."

"No, I did not notice any unusual behavior in the defendant."

"Thank you."

Ella Chamberlain was called to the stand.

"Mrs. Chamberlain, you were in the store on the afternoon Mary Stevens was killed?"

"Yes, I was one of the clerks working at the Co-op that day."

"Did you see the defendant there on that day?"

"Yes, I did. He came into the store around four o'clock. He was with a crowd of schoolboys and girls."

"Did you notice what time he left?"

"No, sir, but I did notice him again around six thirty later that evening."

"Thank you. Counselor?"

"Mrs. Chamberlain, you say the witness did not return to the store until six thirty?" Erickson asked.

"I did not say that. I said that was the time I noticed him back there. I was working in and out of the back room. He could have come in at any time before that for a while, and I wouldn't have known it."

"Thank you."

Mrs. Jane Heaton, the defendant's mother, was called to the stand.

"Mrs. Heaton, we are sorry for the reason you have been brought here today," Samuel began. "Will you please tell us when you saw your son on the afternoon that Mary Stevens was killed?"

"He came home from school that afternoon, stayed there for a while, and ate lunch. Then he drove some stock out of the lot and went to the barn. He came back out of the barn later on and came into the house. I saw him walk east later on along the sidewalk, and then saw him again about twenty minutes later, looking through a magnifying glass in front of the Chamberlain's house. He came home again after that, then went back out and cleaned the stable."

"Thank you. Questions, Counselor?"

"Mrs. Heaton," Erickson said, "are you sure about the times you saw your son doing these things?"

"Absolutely."

"How long was he gone when you saw him looking through the magnifying glass?"

"Only about fifteen or twenty minutes."

"And you say you are absolutely sure about that?"

"Yes."

Alvin's uncle, Wilford Heaton, was called to the stand.

"You saw the defendant that afternoon, did you not?" Samuel asked.

"Yes, sir, I saw him somewhere around five thirty that evening."

"Was that down at the store?"

"No, sir, I was working on my new house at the time when Alvin came to the open window and looked in. He made a comment about how well it was coming along."

"How long was he there?"

"Only for a minute."

"Thank you. Your witness, Counselor."

"Constable, how sure are you that it was five thirty when the defendant stopped by?"

"Somewhat. I looked at my watch later on, and it was about six o'clock. I estimated he stopped by about a half hour before that."

"So, it could have been later?"

"Yes, I suppose so, but I wouldn't think by too much."

"Fifteen minutes, maybe?"

"Maybe."

"Thank you."

Court was adjourned that evening until ten o'clock the next morning.

The next morning, the defense brought up a dizzying roster of witnesses to state they had seen the defendant at any particular time, to try to solidify his alibi. They also testified to his good character and reputation. After the parade of witnesses, the defense rested.

We were all very disappointed when Alvin didn't take the stand. We really wanted to hear what he had to say about the day's event, and how the prosecuting attorney would break him in his testimony. But then again, that's the heart of it right there, isn't it? The defense attorney must have known that his conscience would get the best of him, and he would confess again, and there would be no way Thurman could take that back.

Soon, the defense took the floor to give his closing statements.

"Gentlemen of the jury," Samuel began, "the state has presented you with the mosaic of circumstantial evidence that we mentioned to you last week when this trial started. Unfortunately, for them, it was all a façade and has no real substance to it, as I have shown here these last few days.

"The defendant's actions and whereabouts have all been accounted for on that horrible day, and his own mother showed there was not enough time for her son to make it up to the clearing in the hollow and back. His uncle, Orderville's own constable, testified that he conversed with the defendant at his new house in town…at the very time he was accused of killing the girl."

"Unless the defendant has found the ability to be in two places at one time, there is no way he could have committed this most horrible crime. The town has testified in aggregate that he had a reputation in the community for peace, sobriety, quietness, morality, and virtue."

"Look to your hearts and consciences, and you will see there is no way he could have done this. Look at the evidence, and you will see scientifically that he could not have committed this crime. What happened to Mary Stevens that afternoon was absolutely horrible and inexcusable, and the man who killed her must be brought to justice. It just wasn't my client who did it."

His summation was much longer than that, but I fell asleep somewhere in the middle of it. My father said it lasted for two and a half hours and was a magnificent address and a skillful plea for Alvin's defense. His appeal to the jury was remarkable for the acquittal of the boy defendant.

It may have been magnificent, but I was glad I fell asleep. I just wanted to go home.

Joseph Erickson, for the prosecution, then stood up and began his summation. I wished I could have gone back to sleep.

"I have been deeply interested in this case from the very beginning," Erickson began, "and I gave it my very close attention. From what I discovered, there is not a shadow of doubt in my mind as to the guilt of the defendant. I've seen the atrociousness of this crime up close and first hand, and I'm about to convey to you, once again, what it was like."

"What I have learned, and what we've shown you, is that Alvin Heaton, Jr., member of Orderville's community, did lure Mary Stevens up the canyon to a preselected clearing, and he did deliberately and with malice of forethought, shoot her in the back four times, because she was in a delicate way at his hand."

"She did nothing wrong to warrant such a violent end. She was a promising student who was receiving high marks in school and had her whole life ahead of her. She was about to become a mother, have a child to raise, and teach it right from wrong. Granted, the actions that led to this child's coming were illegal and may have landed her in jail for a time, but again, it did not warrant death from behind."

"The defendant had her blood on his coat and shoes, which he feloniously claimed was from a chicken. He had one of the few .38 revolvers in town and had just purchased six bullets, only one or two of which could be accounted for, because the other four were discharged into the victim. His shoes fit perfectly into the killer's tracks, and he is the only one in town who walks toed-in with size six shoes. There was also an absence of witnesses who could solidly corroborate his whereabouts at the time of the shooting. Most importantly…pay attention now…he confessed to others that he killed her."

"He…confessed…to…others…that…he…killed…her."

He paused a moment for dramatic effect and then continued.

"Mary was a promising young girl with her whole life ahead of her," he repeated for effect. "This was ripped away in a most brutal fashion by the defendant, and this is something that can never be replaced. Think of your own children, of your own daughters. How would you react if someone attacked them in such a cowardly manner by shooting them in the back…four times…while they were unarmed? Bang, bang….bang…and finally bang!"

"She deserves justice; she needs justice. Your children would need and deserve justice. Look at the evidence, it is all there, plain as can be. You must find the defendant guilty of *this most horrible crime*, so that it does not go unpunished. So that Alvin Franklin Heaton, Jr. does not get away with the murder of this wonderful young lady and their baby."

He made a dramatic show of finishing his statement as he slowly walked back to his table.

I must admit Mr. Erickson fairly outdid himself as he reviewed the case for the state. He cleared up many points that may have been a little misty, and those in the courtroom were agreeably surprised at the masterful presentation of his case against Alvin. His address lasted but an hour yet, in that short time, he carried conviction to the minds of the spectators that the state had made no mistake in the prosecution of Alvin Heaton. It was a compelling argument, and I was glad it was all over; all except for the jury's decision.

They were given over the case at about three o'clock that Thursday afternoon. It was about half past eight when word was passed around town that the jury had agreed upon a verdict. There was a rush to the courtroom to hear the verdict. Every day, the courtroom had been filled to capacity, with every seat taken, and every inch of floor space stood upon, so it was quite a movement for us all to get back within its confines.

Alvin and his parents were present when the jurors came back into the courtroom. He presented the same stoical front that he had maintained since the trial began. He was the coolest and, apparently, the most disinterested person in the room, as the jurors took their place in the box.

As soon as court was formally opened, the jurors were asked if they had agreed upon a verdict. The foreman, B. W. Hopkins, rose and said, "We have."

"What find you?" Judge Booth asked.

"We find the defendant, Alvin Franklin Heaton, Jr., guilty of murder in the first degree with a recommendation of mercy."

"Objection, Your Honor," Samuel stated as he stood, "that is not one of their options."

"I must admit I've never heard of that before," Judge Booth said. "We will take a short recess while we confer with the law and see what the jury can come up with."

There was an audible sigh of disappointment by those in attendance, who anxiously wanted to know this young killer's fate.

After about fifteen minutes, the jury returned.

"What find you now?" Judge Booth asked.

Mr. Hopkins stood up and said, "We find the defendant guilty of murder in the first degree with a recommendation of life imprisonment at hard labor."

Alvin made no outward sign of having heard the verdict, nor the fact that he had escaped the noose. He sat in his place as utterly unmoved as was possible to imagine.

I guess the defense attorney should have stayed his objection to the recommendation of mercy. His client would have been better off than the verdict with which the jury returned. I guess he should be grateful he was not sentenced to hang; it would have shortened my story, and made it not nearly as interesting as it's still going to get.

"Jury members, do each of you agree with this verdict? Mr. Hopkins?"

"Yes, guilty."

"Mr. Hooten?"

"Yes, guilty."

"Mr. Christiansen?"

"Yes, guilty."

"Mr. F. P. Anderson?"

"Yes, guilty."

"Mr. John Anderson?"

"Yes, guilty."

"Mr. Tuft?"

"Yes, guilty."

"Mr. Soren Sorenson?"

"Yes, guilty."

"Mr. J. B. Sorenson?"

"Yes, guilty."

"Mr. Collings?"

"Yes, guilty."

"Mr. Larsen?"

"Yes, guilty."

"Mr. Gardner?"

"Yes, guilty."

"Mr. Hyatt?"

"Yes, guilty."

"Thank you, gentlemen of the jury."

Alvin heard each one of these twelve affirmations without displaying as much interest as the most disinterested spectator. He was stoic and indifferent during the entire proceedings. It was almost beyond conception that a young man could listen to the verdict, placing the guilt of the most horrible crime ever heard of in these parts and remain so indifferent.

Yet, he was unmoved.

"Will the defendant please stand and approach the bench?" Judge Booth commanded, disguised as a polite question.

Alvin stood up and walked toward the judge.

"Do you have anything to say for yourself, young man?"

Alvin shook his head.

"Nothing as to why sentencing should not be passed?"

"No, sir, I have nothing to say."

"Then I hereby sentence you to imprisonment for life at hard labor, in accordance with the verdict and recommendation of the jury."

Even with the sentence of the court passed upon him, and the gates of the penitentiary yawning for him, the young convicted murderer evinced no emotion.

We expected a scene between Alvin and his parents, but there was nothing of the kind. He seemed to be the most unconcerned of everybody in the courtroom, even me, and I thought he got what he deserved…maybe he did too. As best as I understand, or understood at the time, Alvin's youth kept him from the rope. Had he been a little older, he would have surely swung.

Outside, while we were all inside listening to the verdict and sentencing, there was a large crowd gathered around the courthouse. There were far too many people fascinated with the trial to get them all inside to see what was happening.

As soon as the verdict was announced, one of the local

Richfield people stepped out of the door and shouted, "Guilty! They found him guilty and gave him life imprisonment with hard labor!"

A cheer arose from the crowd in jubilation at the announcement. Several men turned and patted each other on their backs in congratulations, because they felt justice had been served. They had all read Alvin's confession and were convinced of his guilt. Inside, we could hear the cheer and knew what it was for. Even that did not stir Alvin to show emotion; he was a rock.

We started to exit the building in a slow and orderly fashion, much as we did every Sunday after church.

As soon as the sentence was passed, Alvin was returned to his cell. He was escorted out of the building by Sheriff Abbott, who returned him to handcuffs for transportation. His parents and Mamie followed right behind him.

When we all got outside, I saw Ezra and his wife, Joseph and his wife, and their three children walk outside and over to Harmon Cutler, and Sheriff Brown and his wife.

"Thanks, Harmon," Ezra said when they were all together. "I would hate to have risked my salvation if they had found him not guilty."

"You don't mean to tell me you would have killed him if they found him innocent?"

"I think that's exactly what he means to tell you," James said. "I'm glad we'll never have to find out. I hate the idea of arresting good people I know."

"What makes you think you would be able to arrest me?" Ezra asked in a cryptic tone.

Edith looked up at her husband, trying to decide if she should say anything or let him have his say unencumbered.

"One advantage I would have," James stated, "is we're out of my jurisdiction here, so I wouldn't be the one doing the arresting."

"As long as it didn't happen back home," Pearl added as a warning.

"I'm sure after all we went through back home…," Harmon questioned, "I'm sure Ezra wouldn't go back to Orderville and kill Alvin, right?"

"That's right," Ezra stated. "I wouldn't go back home to do it."

Edith slid her arm into his. I think she was quietly reassuring Ezra that he would have her support if it came down to that.

We all took it that Ezra was talking tough because his beloved daughter had been killed by this boy. We found out how wrong we were in '22 when he shot and killed his brother-in-law, Andrew Siller, at Mt. Carmel, after a prolonged quarrel over financial matters. I was a grown man at the time and tried to follow the case with some interest, but the details were so meager that we really never knew anything of what had happened.

Over at the escort wagon, the deputy who was driving, helped Alvin up onto the seat. His mother was hanging onto his father's arm, crying. Alvin seemed to be at peace. Mamie walked over between the wagon wheels and reached her hands up toward Alvin. He turned in his seat to face her and reached out both of his cuffed hands to hold hers.

"I can't believe your lawyer was going to try and declare you insane. Why, everybody knows you are just as sane as the day is long."

"He was just trying to get me a not-guilty verdict, that's all," Alvin said disinterestedly.

"Well, I'm glad it didn't have to come up in court, I would hate to have people thinking you were crazy."

"The alienist doctor didn't think I was, so that's why it never came out. It would have been mentioned if Samuel thought it would have done some good. The prosecution's case was so strong that he was trying anything he could to keep me out of jail or being hanged."

"You know I love you and would do anything for you, don't you?"

"Sure, I do."

"You never loved *her*, did you?" she asked, scornfully.

"No, I just used her for intimate relations," he assured her. "She meant nothing to me. I wanted yours and my relationship to stay pure until we could get married."

"You did this for me then?" she asked as stars began to appear in her eyes.

"Among other reasons, yes," he confirmed.

"I will leave home and move to Sugarhouse, so I can visit you at the penitentiary all the time...I will wait for you."

Alvin gave himself a half smirk and then, without emotion, stated, "Didn't you hear? They gave me life in prison with hard labor."

"But if you're good, they might let you out early, and then I could be right there waiting. We could get married and go somewhere new to make a home."

"They're not going to let me out early. Remember, I killed a young girl who was carrying my child."

"Once you get up there they'll be able to see the real you, and they'll let you out, I know it."

Tenderly, he gave her hand a light squeeze. "Forget about me."

Sheriff Abbott stepped over to Mamie and gently put his hand on her shoulder. "I'm sorry, Miss," he said with great understanding, "but it's time for him to go."

The tears she held back could be controlled no longer, and she began to sob. "But I'm not done yet."

Sheriff Abbott gently pulled her away from the wheels as the wagon started to pull away. "It's time."

She wheeled around and wrapped her arms around the sheriff, burying her face in his chest before he could react. As she cried violently at the all-too-premature departure of her beloved, Alvin Sr. stepped over and tenderly removed her from the grateful sheriff, turning her to face him. He wrapped his arms around her and allowed her to bury her face into his chest and cry, until she was finished.

"Are you doing all right, son?" Sheriff Abbott asked as he rode his horse beside the wagon.

"Just kind of thinking," Alvin responded.

"Anything in particular? You're quieter than usual."

"About the trial and all," he replied. "I guess I have to admit that I got what I deserved."

"If you did it as you say, then yes, you did."

"I guess I should consider myself lucky. I could have received the death penalty for this."

"That is a fact."

"Then, why don't I feel so lucky?"

Chapter Nine
Hard Time and Making Time

"How are you coping with prison life?" Warden Arthur Pratt asked Alvin. "You've been here for a year now. Have you been able to adjust?"

"I suppose so," Alvin responded. "I'm still not used to being around so many people. There are more people here at the prison than in my home town."

"I doubt that, but I can see how it would feel that way."

"Anyway, I've started to get used to the rest of it. I've settled in enough that I'm not crying myself to sleep every night anymore."

"I've given you your space this last year," Arthur stated; it was obvious he had something on his mind.

"Yes, and it sounds like you're about to either take that space away, or to step into it. Which is it?"

"I hope I'm just stepping into it for a moment."

"All right, then, what's on your mind, Warden?"

"I followed your trial in the papers with great interest," he began. "I even subscribed to the *Richfield Reaper*, so I could read everything that was going on, especially with the trial."

"Yes...?"

"Dag nab it, Alvin, did you do it? Did you kill that girl?"

"Yes."

"Why? How? It doesn't fit your character. I've dealt with hardened criminals my whole career, and they have a certain bravado or swagger to them. You have none of that."

"I've been giving that a lot of thought," Alvin said after a short pause, while he decided on how much he wanted to share with the warden.

"Any conclusions?"

"Yes. Since I've been here, I've seen and gotten to know many of those hardened men. The only conclusion I can come to is that Sheriff Brown was right. I'm not a killer, I'm just a boy who killed someone."

"You were a boy. Would you do it again?"

"Do you mean, with all I know now, would I go back to 1908 and do it again? Or do you mean would I do it again if you let me go?"

"Okay, let's answer both of them, starting with the first one."

"All right, I've also given this a lot of thought over the last year. I decided that if I could go back to that April afternoon and could face Mary again, I would put my arms around her, give her a deep embrace, and tell her I would help take care of the baby, but I didn't want to marry her."

"So you would do the time in jail instead of killing her?"

"Yes, that's exactly what I'm saying. A few months of jail would be a drop in the well bucket compared to the stretch I'm doing now."

"And what about the other question?"

"As to whether I would do it again, if I got out of here?"

"Sure, would you do it again?"

"There would be no need to. I'm not going to have intimate relations with an eighteen-year-old girl again, so it will never be an issue."

"What about if you get angry with someone, I mean plumb dog mean angry, would you do it then?"

"No."

"How can you be so sure?"

"Because when I killed Mary, it ripped something out of me. I felt like a man who's been attacked by a mountain lion or a bear and had a leg bit off…scarred for life. The only difference is my damage and scars are on the inside, and I did them to myself."

"So you haven't had any desire to kill anybody else?" Arthur asked him, point-blank.

"No. As I told you, I'm not a killer. Why do you ask? They seem like awfully nosy questions for a warden to be asking a convicted criminal."

"I want you to become a trustee and be a waiter for my family in my home."

"You what…?" Alvin asked, shocked.

"I want you to come and buttle for my family."

"Why would you want me to do that? I'm in here for first degree murder."

"I watched you carefully when you were here before your trial, and the year since you've returned. I feel you are spot-on in your explanation about who you are. You are not a killer, and I'll put my family's life in your hands to prove it."

"I can't imagine your wife and children will approve or feel comfortable with it."

"I already talked to my wife, and she is fine with the idea."

"What about your children?"

"They're excited, believe it or not. They're anxious for me to ring over there and tell them whether or not you've accepted."

"Can I have some time to think it over?"

"Sure. One thing to keep in mind as you are mulling it over, you were sentenced to hard labor for the rest of your life. This would be much easier and hopefully much more enjoyable than that."

"I don't know anything about being a butler or a waiter."

"There's not much to know. Don't spill the food when you're bringing it. Serve from the left and take from the right. Answer the door when someone rings the bell. The rest is just common sense."

"Why me?"

"I think you've earned it."

You'll never guess what happened to Alvin after he'd been in prison for eight years. We were all shocked when we found out. I'm not bashful about saying there were many of us here who thought all involved had lost their minds.

In November of 1916, Alvin applied for early release, because he had been such a model prisoner. I'm sure the warden had a lot to do with that. The Board of Pardons deliberated over it and, after several months of contemplating the decision, finally agreed to let him go. He was scheduled to be released in November 1917. It was going to be very interesting to see what kind of reception he would receive once he returned home, especially after only eight years in prison.

"Well, it's been seven years now that you've been buttling for us," Arthur said. "It's been a good run, but we need to talk."

"Are you sending me back to hard labor?" Alvin asked him. "Have I done something to anger you or something wrong?"

The two men were in the warden's office. There was a guard standing lazily by in the back of the room in case of a disturbance. Both the warden and the guard knew Alvin would not cause any problems, but the guard was always there on call.

The warden was seated behind his desk, and Alvin was seated in the chair directly across from him.

"No, no, you haven't done anything wrong. I've decided it's time for me to retire."

"I knew you were thinking about it," Alvin said, "but I didn't know you had finally decided to do it, or so soon."

"Yes, I'm getting older, and there are certain things I want to do before I die."

"Like what, sir?"

"Relax."

Alvin laughed at the warden's comment. "I certainly can't blame you for wanting to do that. I'm sure there are other things you would like to do as well."

"Yes, of course. The wife has a list of things a mile long for me to do. Come to think of it," Arthur mused, "I may want to come back to work just to get a rest from those chores."

"I may well be here."

"Maybe not, I've heard hopeful things about your parole hearing to be released early next November. You have a surprising amount of people working on your behalf. I can't imagine that the parole board will keep you in here for the rest of your life."

"That would be nice," Alvin mentioned.

"I know your mother has been writing to Judge Booth on a regular basis to have him write a letter on your behalf."

"She wrote me about that," Alvin said. "She mentioned the judge had been resisting her for quite some time."

"Yes, I'm aware of that," Arthur chuckled. "I'm also aware

she refused to let up on him until he agreed to do it."

"What are you saying?" Alvin asked him in bewilderment.

"I'm saying your mother's constant supplication has finally paid off," Arthur stated. "Judge Booth finally relented and wrote the letter to the Board of Pardons on your behalf. He wrote that, in his contemplation of writing the recommendation, he had taken your youth at the time of the crime and your family's standing in the community under consideration. He also wrote he trusted the Board of Pardons would see their way clear to agree to his recommendation. Plus, I've continually been giving my recommendations to the Board as well."

"So my sentence has been commuted down to November?"

"It looks that way. By the time 1918 comes around, you will be living in Orderville with your family, never to see us again."

"It will have taken me a year to get through the pardons process," Alvin said with obvious relief, "but it will be well worth it. I can't believe I will finally be going home."

"I thought you might like to see this letter from District Attorney Erickson."

"You mean the man who put me here in the first place?"

"No, that was you, but yes, the man who prosecuted your case at the trial."

"What does he have to say?"

"Let's see…Erickson wrote that you have successfully been reformed by the judicial system, and there was no reason to continue keeping you incarcerated. He requested the Board consider your time served as adequate for your rehabilitation and for leniency and understanding toward you."

"What made him decide to write that letter on my behalf?" Alvin asked him.

"Your lawyer wrote him a letter, asking him to do it for you, and to send it to the Board of Pardons."

"Is that the letter you have in your hands?"

"No," Arthur answered. "This is a copy Samuel sent to show you."

"So let me see if I have this right, I have the lawyer who prosecuted me at my trial, and the judge who presided over it, both writing letters of support to get me released early? Did I fall off the rock pile and hit my head? Because I must be having hallucinations."

"No, son," Arthur informed him. "This is real, and it is really happening."

"So, how long until you make your retirement official?" Alvin asked.

"Are you worried the new warden might not want you as his personal family waiter?"

"Yes, I'm worried I might end up on that pile of rocks, breaking them down for the last months of my sentence," Alvin stated, obviously concerned.

"I can't imagine that would happen," Arthur assured him, "but if it will make you feel better, I will speak to the new warden on your behalf."

"It would make me feel better, and I would appreciate it. One of the worst things about being in prison is you lose all control over your life. The things I used to do, you know the things I used to take for granted, I can no longer do. For those I can still do, I can only do them by your leave."

"I know, and that's why I want to do everything I can, to get you out of here," Arthur pointed out. "You are not a hardened criminal, and you don't belong here. As far as I can see, you've paid your debt, and you should be given a second chance."

"Don't forget me when you retire. You never know, I may need a job as a family waiter when I get out in November."

"Look us up, son."

You're probably asking, how on earth did Alvin convince the Board of Pardons that he had reformed in eight short years of a lifetime sentence? You're in good company, because I don't think there was a person in Orderville over the age of twelve, who wasn't asking themselves the same question. I was the same age when he got out as he was when he killed Mary. He was looking forward to getting out that coming November, but the twists and turns kept coming.

"Sit down, Alvin."

"This seems oddly familiar. Isn't this where I ask if I'm in trouble?"

The two men were in the warden's office as before. The warden once again was seated in his large chair behind his desk, and Alvin was seated in the chair directly across from him. As always, there was a guard standing quietly in the background.

"It's been eight years since you came to us here at the state prison."

Alvin nodded his head.

"Like I told you before, after that first year, I could see you weren't a hardened criminal."

"But I did kill that girl, like I told you."

"I know, and you know that's why I let you serve my family. You were straight forward and honest; that carries a lot of truck with me."

"I'll always be grateful for that, sir but, begging your pardon, why are we having this conversation again?"

"I'm getting to that," Arthur assured him. "You know I'm retiring in a couple of days, yes?"

"Yes." Alvin nodded his head.

"I've grown to think of you much as a son, and I want us to walk out those doors together."

Alvin was obviously confused.

"I value your friendship, so I called an emergency meeting of the Board of Pardons to get them to release you on the day I retire."

"I don't understand," Alvin stated as he tried to sort out his confusion. "What is it you're saying?"

"You were already slated to be released in seven months or so, so I had them push your release date up. My last day of work will be your last day in prison. When I walk out of here for the last time as warden, you will walk out at my side on your last day of being a prisoner. I think you've done enough time and should be a free man."

"May…," Alvin's words were choked off as his emotions got the better of him, and he began to cry. Tears flowed freely down his face as he bowed his head, and his shoulders began to shake.

The guard looked inquisitively at the warden to see if there was something he should do for the weeping prisoner, but Arthur shook his head slightly.

"Take your time, son," Arthur said. "We have plenty of it. This has been a long time coming. I'll bet this is the best news you've received since you were arrested all those years ago. Now you can go home and be with your family again."

There was a pause in the room as the warden patiently waited for Alvin to work through his emotions.

When his sobbing subsided and he regained control, Alvin was able to finish his comment. "May the good Lord be willing." Then he paused for a few minutes as he took in the enormity of all that had transpired.

"But what will I do?" he asked. "I haven't been able to come up with any kind of plan or arrangements for work. This is all so sudden, I thought I had another seven months to figure all this out."

"That's the best part," Arthur said with some excitement. "I've procured you lodging and a job back down in Orderville, so you can go home to your family."

"I can't believe you really did that," Alvin stated, shocked. "I am so grateful, but I can't go back down there. I can't stand to face all the looks of accusations or pity, I will see on every face from Panguitch to Kanab."

"I hadn't thought about that," Arthur said. "I figured you'd want to go back down there to your family and friends. I do have a friend who owns a restaurant in Provo. How about if I give him a call and see what I can work out?"

"I don't know what to say, other than thank you, and may the Lord bless you a thousand times over for what you've done."

"You've earned it. Go pack because we leave tomorrow."

"Good glory, so soon?"

The following day around noon, there was no fanfare. It appeared to be just another quiet day at the State Penitentiary. The doors slowly opened to allow Warden Pratt and Alvin Heaton to walk out together, side by side. Alvin was wearing a brand new suit and carried a bundled package under his arm. There was a black automobile waiting on the street for the two men. It was a new Ford, a Model T, with a driver sitting inside, and the engine turned off. There were three men standing near it, waiting for Arthur and Alvin to walk over. When they approached the three men, the two could see the paper badges the men wore. One was from the *Ogden Standard Examiner*, one from the *Salt Lake Telegram*, and the other from the *Salt Lake*

Tribune.

"Mr. Heaton," one of them said, "how does it feel to be free so many years earlier than you expected?"

Alvin hung his head and shrugged his shoulders. It was obvious to Arthur he did not want any publicity or notoriety. This was a day he had planned to share only with Arthur.

Arthur stepped in and said, "This young man has been a model prisoner, and he has come up to the mark in every manner. As you may know, his sentence was already commuted down because of his good behavior, and he would be released in November later this year. Since that date was only seven months away, I wanted the Board of Pardons to release him earlier, so we could walk out today for the last time, together."

"What will you do now?" another of the reporters asked him.

"Gentlemen, please," Arthur stated, "we've already said all we're going to today. Catch us another day. Today is about family and friends."

The three reporters mumbled acknowledgements and shuffled off to their next respective assignments.

Arthur turned to Alvin, "Now remember, I've secured you a waiter position down in Provo. The owner is a friend of mine and will take good care of you."

"Did you tell him why I was in prison?"

"No. I told him you had grown into a good man, and I trusted you with my family's care. I also told him you needed a fresh start. The rest of what you tell him is up to you."

"You don't think he already knows?" Alvin asked, concerned.

"Oh, I'm sure he does," Arthur stated straight. "I'm sure lots of people in Provo know about you because your story was in all the papers. I also think he will treat you as if he doesn't know, out of respect for me. So go down there and just pretend with him, start a family, and put all this behind you."

"That may not be as easy as it sounds," Alvin said as they stepped into the automobile. "Things didn't work out so well the last time I was with a girl."

Seven or eight years went by and we didn't hear much of Alvin. He got that job up to Provo at the Sutton Cafe there at 46 West Center Street and, by 1922, he had become the headwaiter.

His life was very different in Provo than it had been in Orderville. You can say that prison changes a man, and I'll certainly not argue the point but, not only did his time away allow him to mature, I think the change of environment did him a world of good. You see, as I mentioned at the beginning of the story, Alvin was from a prominent family, from a town that saw its role in the Mormon empire as probably larger than it really was. Even though we had no rich people in Kane County, you could make the argument that Alvin was a spoiled rich kid. After having everything stripped away from him and beat down by his prison stretch, he finally molded himself into the man he was meant to be.

They say that great adversity brings out the core of a person. Trials, adversity, loss, they all chip away at our presumed identity – the person we think we are – until our essence emerges with the person we truly are. We saw his essence emerge once he was released from prison, and he could once again make his own choices. Of course, he was able to make choices in the pen, but they were always tempered by rules, regulations, and armed guards. A nightstick and a '94 Winchester do wonders to help an inmate make the proper decision.

Once he was released, he lived his life as well as anyone could. Unless you knew his past, there is no way you would have pegged him for a man who brutally killed a woman carrying his child. As a matter of fact, you would see him as stable, dependable, and the sort of man you would want living next door to you…if you didn't know. Even if you did know, by the time you got to know him, it wouldn't matter too much, because you could see the caliber of the man by his actions of the present.

Shortly after he moved to Provo, he met Bernice Hindmarsh. I ran into her down in Orderville when she came down for the… well, I'd better wait until we get to that part. We had a chance to talk, and she told me a little bit of how she came to know Alvin.

"Are you ever going to come calling on me, Mr. Heaton?" she asked him one day while they were both at a church dinner.

"Whatever do you mean, Miss Hindmarsh?" he asked.

He had noticed her from time to time for several months, but the scars within him ran so deep he never pictured himself getting married. He kept his distance from her, never really giving her too much thought. One day at the ward house, they ended up sitting next to each other in services, and a conversation ensued. She found his quiet demeanor fascinating. She could tell by the way he carried himself that he had great depth and a story to tell. He just never told it to anyone. He had caught her fancy after that conversation, and she found reasons to be near him and to talk to him. After this had gone on for a couple of months, she felt they knew each other well enough they could start courting. She knew he wasn't calling on any other girls because of the time they spent together, and the conversations they had. She could never figure out why, though, when they got along as well as they did, he never asked to come calling on her. Finally, she'd waited long enough.

"Are you ever going to come calling on me?" she asked as they sat at the church dinner together.

"What makes you think you would enjoy having me do that?"

"How can you ask that, Alvin?" she asked point-blank. "We've known each other for months, talked extensively, and yet, you still haven't come calling. I know you're not calling on anyone else, so why not me? I thought we were getting along fabulously."

"We are," he said, "but this is neither the time nor the place to talk about it."

"Then when?" She put him on the spot with that direct question.

"I don't know, it's not a conversation I ever want to have with anyone, ever."

"You said that already."

"What?" he asked her.

"Ever."

"Get the point yet?" He was not trying to be rude, but he was trying to dissuade her from her interest in him.

"Sure, but that doesn't matter, I want an answer, and I won't give up until I get it."

"Yes, you will, or at least you should. Like I said, this is neither the time nor the place."

"Then give me the time and place, and I will be there ready to listen," she commanded, ignoring his warning.

"Are you telling me what to do?"

"Yes, I am. I like you, Alvin, and I want you to come calling on me. Because you won't do it of your own accord, then I will do all in my power to get you to do it."

"You'll wish you hadn't once you get what you want. How does the old Greek saying go? The gods punish us by giving us what we want? Be careful of what you want."

"I'll take my chances."

"Isn't that what Odysseus said in the Iliad?"

"It sounds like you've had far too much time to read."

"You have no idea," he agreed, wishing he could be anywhere but there at that moment.

"Give me a time and place."

"What?" he asked her.

"I said, give me a time and a place."

"For what?"

"For you to explain to me why you won't come calling. You told me this is not the time, nor place to do it, and I am going to get an explanation. I can tell you're dodging my questions, but I can't figure out why. I will come and sit on your front stoop until you give in."

"Fine. I work the breakfast and lunch shift tomorrow at Sutton's. Come by there about half past five, and we'll take a walk toward the mountain."

"And you'll tell me everything then?"

"I'll think about it, but no promises. I may begin the story, and then we'll see how far it goes."

"I'll be there."

"Oh, you made it."

"Did you think I was going to back out and not come?" Bernice asked him.

"I was hoping," he responded with a twinge of disappointment.

"There's no chance of that," she assured him. "The Almighty Himself would have a difficult time keeping me away today. Are you ready to walk?"

"Almost. I still have a couple at one of my tables. They're pert near finished and, as soon as they are, we can be on our way. Can I get the kitchen to put something together for you right quick?"

"Can I get a piece of pie and a glass of milk? I didn't get enough to eat at lunch, and I'm near to starving."

"We can stay here and eat dinner before we walk. I know the people who own this place, and I think I can get a pretty good deal."

She chuckled at his joke and then paused as she thought about it. "Are you trying to delay our talk?"

"Yes…no," he said. "I just thought it might be nice to talk without the pangs of hunger. I've been giving it a lot of thought since last night, and I've decided to be open and honest with you and tell you everything. I'll join you for that dinner, if you like."

"Wow, you spun me around with that last comment, from dinner to full confidence, back to dinner. I don't think any of these fancy new automobiles can turn around that fast. However, my father did have a cow horse that could do it."

"Dinner?"

"Does that mean you're sparkin' me, Mr. Heaton?"

"No…well, I'll let you know after dinner and our talk. There's a lot that has to be said before we get to the sparks."

"Why do you say that?" Now, he had her full attention.

"Because," he said, and then paused, "if our talk goes well, then I will be calling on you."

"And if it doesn't?"

"I will die of shame and most likely move away."

"Do you have any doubts it will go well?" she asked, now fully excited at the prospect she would be giving her heart away later that evening.

"More than you could possibly imagine," he assured her.

She paused for a long time, causing Alvin's heart to sink down into his feet. He had never given any romantic consideration to this woman he now found utterly attractive. She had awakened something deep within him he had dared not pursue; not since he was taken away from Mamie in Richfield. He had resigned himself to a life of celibacy and solitude and never had dared to hope for any kind of romantic companionship. He knew he would hate it if she stirred all those longings within him and then was repulsed by his past. He could have gone on forever the way he was but, now that his feelings and passions had been awakened, he couldn't go on living with them…not around her at least.

He shook his head to clear out the thoughts.

What are you thinking? he asked himself. *I can't resent her for this, she has no way of knowing, and if she walks away, I'll withdraw back into my shell and go back to things as they were.*

After his tumultuous storm of thoughts and emotions passed, he was drawn back to the moment by her voice.

"Dinner, then?"

"What would you like to order?" he asked out of habit, somewhat disoriented.

"You choose for us. Show me where to sit, and I will wait for you."

He glanced around the room and noticed the couple in his area was getting up to leave.

"Let me clear off the table they're leaving, and we can sit there. I'll go tell the cook to make us up something, and I'll be right with you."

She remained standing while he whisked into the kitchen for a moment and then returned with a bus tray. He quickly cleaned off the table and motioned for her to come over and sit down.

"Let me take this back into the kitchen, and then I will come sit with you."

"What did you order us for dinner?"

"I don't know," he confessed as he walked away.

Bernice sat there rather puzzled for a minute until he returned. "What do you mean you don't know?"

"Just that. I told the cook this was our first and maybe only date and to make us something special."

"How will you know when it's ready if you are out here with me?"

"One of the other waiters will bring it out to us."

"So, this is a date then?"

"I would like to think so, even if, like I told the cook, it's our only one. You pushed hard enough for this; I would like to enjoy it."

"A date it is then. You realize, of course, you have to take me home afterwards, don't you?"

"I would be delighted, but you very well may change your mind after you hear my story."

"Why, Alvin Heaton, if I am to go out on a walk with you this evening," she said with playful scorn, "I expect you to see me safely home afterwards, whether we're talking or not."

"Don't say that unless you mean it," he pled.

She could see the deep pain in his eyes, so she took a moment and thought about it to make sure that was what she really wanted.

"All right, Mr. Heaton, no matter what happens tonight, I expect you to see me home afterwards."

"Done."

"Besides, it's not like any of your dates never made it home after seeing you, is it?" she said playfully.

When dinner was over, they stepped out of the café and

turned east toward the mountain.

They strolled and talked of unimportant matters until they got away from the bustle of people coming and going in the downtown area.

Once they cleared past most of the houses and all the prying ears that may have overheard their conversation, he stopped and stood by a fallen tree.

"Perhaps this one?" he suggested as he motioned for her to sit down.

"Okay, what is this secretive past you won't tell anybody?" she asked, her eyes soft.

"First off, with this knowledge comes responsibility."

"You sound like a Sunday School teacher," she joked.

"You have to promise me you will never tell anybody what I'm about to tell you."

"Okay," she said lightly.

"No, I'm serious. Regardless of the outcome, whether you love me or hate me…especially if you hate me, you've got to promise me you will never tell anybody else, ever."

"Okay," she said more seriously.

"Promise me."

"I just did."

"No, say the words."

"Why so serious? You're starting to worry me."

"You have reason to be worried. Say the words if you truly want to know."

"All right, I Bernice Hindmarsh, hereby do promise regardless of what you tell me or how I feel about you, I will never divulge what you tell me," she said and then added, "without your express permission."

"Without my what…? Oh, I see. Yeah, if there is a reason to tell, if you give me your solemn oath, then you couldn't do it. All right, I'll accept that."

"So tell me this story," she said as she placed her hand on top of his.

He looked down at where her hand rested and debated on whether to make her move it or not. In the end, he decided to not say anything yet, because he liked how if felt. It had been a very long time since he had such feminine attention, not since Mamie...or Mary.

"First off," he began, "I want to explain that I've paid for my mistakes, and I am not that boy anymore. As a matter of fact, it's not so much a story about my past as it is about someone who used to be me."

"You've got me intrigued," she said with a broad smile and sparkling eyes. "Please continue."

"Speaking of continuing, feel free to stop me and have me take you home at any time during the conversation. If you get to a point where you don't want to hear any more, let me know and we'll quit."

"So cryptic." Her eyes were wide with anticipation.

"When I lived down to Orderville..."

"I didn't know you lived in Orderville. I thought you grew up in Sugarhouse."

"No, but we'll get to that. When I lived down to Orderville, I was almost finished with school. We were taking our final examinations and preparing for graduation. I had a girlfriend named Mamie at the time."

"Is knowing her name important to the story?"

"Only if you want to understand what was going on," he informed her. "We were steady sweethearts and were probably going to get married. However, she was a very proper Saint and refused to do much kissing, let alone anything more."

"And you wanted more than that?" Bernice asked, making

sure she was following the story properly.

"Yes, much to my regret."

"Are you trying to tell me you had intimate relations with a girl in your past, and that's why you act the way you do?" she asked, trying to figure out the end of the story and save him the discomfort of admitting to it.

"No, well, yes, but...," he answered, rather flustered. "Let me tell the story."

"Sorry, I'll try not to interrupt so much."

"Mamie wanted to wait until we got out of school and married, before we started engaging in matrimonial activities. I agreed, because I had to. However, there was this girl in town; she was sort of an outsider. She came from a town that was a couple of miles down the valley. Orderville broke away from that town, so they could practice the purer form of the United Order."

He continued, "She wanted to be liked, and she wanted to be one of us. She made some girlfriends there, but none of the boys would go calling on her. She wanted to be accepted into our fold so badly, that she offered herself up to me."

"You mean like a..."

"No, it wasn't like that. We just got talking one night, when no one was around, and things turned passionate. I wanted the passion, and she wanted to be loved. Of course, I do think she liked the passion as much as I did. It worked out for both of our benefits...in the short run. Since our relations were illegal, we told no one and did our best to make sure no one saw us together."

"One day, while we were taking our final exams, she said she just had to see me. It was an important matter that couldn't wait. We agreed to meet up at the hollow at the edge of town. We'd met there a time or two before, so we could engage in our passions. When we got there, she informed me she was going to bear a child and demanded I marry her."

He paused here for a moment and then reminded Bernice that he had paid for his crimes.

"I didn't want to marry her, nor did I want to be burdened with an unwanted child at that age. I had borrowed a gun from a friend, and had it with me. I pulled it out and shot her until she was dead."

Bernice gave an audible gasp as she finally learned the deeply buried truth he had tried so hard to keep hidden from the world. And why he never came calling on her.

He could feel her hand stiffen and could see she had been taken aback by his confession.

"This is why I made you swear you would never tell another soul. And remember, I've paid for my sins before you get mad and make me take you home."

"Is your story finished?"

"No, not yet."

"Then we're not going anywhere until you are," she said with genuine interest and compassion, having recovered from his revelation. "Why did you do it?"

"That's the big question, and I don't know if I have an honest answer for you. I don't know if I have an honest answer for myself."

"Give it a try."

"All right, but realize I'm figuring this out as I go along."

"Understood."

"The obvious answer and, of course the cheap-seat answer, is I was too young to really fathom the depth of what I was doing."

"Did you?"

"Yes…and no. I knew killing her was wrong but, in my youth, I didn't fully comprehend the finality of what I was doing. I thought I did, but until I got several more years under my belt, eight of them in prison, I didn't."

"So you understand better now?"

"Absolutely," he assured her. "The rest of the reason was complete selfishness. I was too big for my britches and, in my mind, I could do no wrong. I was from a prominent family, at least for the area, and she was not. Somehow, I had justified that she was less than the rest of us who were actually from Orderville. That thinking made it easier."

"What was her name?"

"Mary."

"Did you love her?"

"No."

"So she was strictly for pleasure?"

"Yes."

"Did no part of you care for her?"

"I felt contempt for her. I felt she was not as good as the rest of us, but she was good enough for pleasure."

"So you forced her to have intimate relations with you, so you could have pleasure?"

"I never forced her!"

"Would you talk to her otherwise?"

"No."

"And she wanted love, yes?"

"Yes."

"Then you forced her."

"No."

"Then at least let us agree that you coerced her," she said.

"Fine."

There was a pause as Alvin collected his thoughts and debated whether he wanted to continue the conversation. He decided he'd come far enough that he might as well finish and let the chips fall where they may.

"Were you angry at her?"

"No, I felt very little emotion toward her at all. She was merely an object for me to bring out and play with in the dark."

"Why didn't her father kill you?"

"He wanted to, believe me; and so did her brother. Her father, a man with many hard years behind him, realized I was better off left to the law and the Lord. He didn't want to risk his eternal salvation over me, *if* the law would take care of it."

"And if the law didn't?"

"Then he would have killed me."

"What about her brother, would he have killed you?"

"Her father wouldn't let him. He wouldn't let Joseph risk his salvation either. He figured only one of them needed to sacrifice eternal glory to avenge her death. Her brother took it hard, as hard as her father did. He would have willingly risked it to see me pay for what I did. Frankly, I don't blame him."

"What has it been like going back there after all these years?"

"I haven't been back. I was arrested in '08, and taken down to Kanab. After the hearing, they changed the trial location to Richfield. After the trial, I was taken up to Sugarhouse and started my lifetime sentence. After eight years up there, I was released, because I had been such a model prisoner. I had made friends with the warden and ended up being the waiter for his family, in his home."

"That shows a lot of trust."

"Yes, he said he knew I had changed and trusted me with their lives."

"I'm starting to get that feeling."

"What feeling?"

"That I can trust you with my life."

Alvin paused for a moment. He started to choke up from her comment. Of all possible things he had imagined she might say after his explanation that was certainly not one of them.

"Anyway, I've relived it over and over through the years, and I would give anything to go back and change the moment when I decided to kill her."

"When was that?"

"That's the trouble, and I think it's part of what bothers me the most. I don't know when that moment was. It had to have started with me. There was something in me that had an innate disregard for others and their lives; that's where it began. After that, my disdain for Mary fueled that feeling, and I began to make offhand comments to friends and cousins that her life was not worthy of living. Perhaps that was merely a reflection of how I saw myself and my life. Maybe it wasn't about Mary at all. Later, as she began to pressure me into marrying her, I felt justified in ending her life to preserve my freedom and selfishness."

"I sure hope you don't intend to do that to me if I ask you to marry me." She was unsure what to say in response to his confession, so she turned to humor to mask any awkwardness she might have been feeling. Still, the humor was awkward and inappropriate.

"No, I've learned to say no when I need to and not resort to violence."

"You're saying you would say no to me if I asked you to marry me?"

"We both know you're not going to do that, but that is not what I meant. I just mean I've matured tremendously since then, and I know how to react better to sticky situations, especially ones of my own making."

"Prison teach you that?"

"Yes. You learn that mighty quickly if you want to survive. There were plenty of real killers in there who would have gladly ended my life, if I had given them provocation."

"I don't think you're being honest with me."

"What do you mean? I've told you everything…things I've never told anyone or even admitted to myself."

"I don't think you're being honest with me and, more importantly, I don't think you are being honest with yourself. I think you loved her in some way."

"The hell you say."

"No, I'm serious. I think part of you cared for her, and that's why it's affected you the way it has."

"Then why did I kill her, if I did?"

"Like you said, you were selfish," Bernice stated. "There's no other way to put it."

Alvin said nothing as her pointed and potent statement made its way through to his heart. She said nothing as she could see the wheels of thought turning in his mind.

Several minutes went by before he finally spoke. "You might be right." Tears started to roll down his face as he admitted this fact to himself. *What an act of total selfishness,* he thought to himself, *what on earth was I thinking? How can I make this up to her?*

Compassionately, she slid closer beside him and wrapped her arms around him. This embrace served to release other pent up emotions, and he began to cry more forcefully.

He cried. He cried hard. He cried for himself but, for the first time, he cried for Mary. He now mourned for her as he never had before.

Bernice tightened her embrace, drawing him in closer. His shoulders racked with sobs so much that she feared she might not be able to hold on to him much longer. Finally, his convulsions stopped and settled to a constant flow of tears.

She lightly kissed the top of his head as it was bowed into her chest. He moved into her a little more seeking safety and acceptance.

When his tears finally subsided, she said, "It is time for you to take me home."

He looked at her with a puzzled expression. Then the truth of the matter dawned on him. She heard his story and wanted nothing more to do with him. She had pushed him into a corner, and now he was going to pay the price of it. Maybe it was time to think about moving to Idaho. He heard that Lewisville was a nice place to live.

"You'll keep your promise?" he asked her.

"Yes."

"Then I will take you home."

"Good, because it's getting late and, if you're going to come calling on me tomorrow, we need our sleep."

"What?" he asked in complete bewilderment, not daring to believe what he just heard.

"I said, if you are going to come calling on me, we need our sleep."

"You still want me to come calling on you then?"

"Of course."

"But what about all I told you, does it not give you pause?"

"No. Maybe if you had told me that story when we first met, I would have turned away, but I've gotten to know you over these last several months and, quite frankly, I've rather fallen in love with you. I've seen the man you've become, long before I discovered the boy you were. Besides, I trust you and I've come to feel safe with you."

She took his hand and stood up. She started to walk away, pulling him up with her. "It's time to go."

"I'm not sure what to say."

"Well, this is how I figure it. I have feelings for you and want you to come calling. You explained this painful and difficult history, which must mean you have feelings for me too. Otherwise, you'd never have revealed all this and made yourself vulnerable. You would have sent me away and gone on with your life."

"Hmm," he said.

"So let's just cut through all the pretense and call this what it is. We are now courting, and we will just see where it goes from there."

"Are you always going to run things between us?"

"If that's what it takes to keep us moving in the right direction, then yes, I am."

"What direction is that?"

"How about eternity?"

Chapter Ten
You Can Never Go Home

You thought you were ready for the end of the story? You're never going to believe this next part, but it's as true as the rest of it.

Alvin and Bernice got married and had a son, Ferron. That's not the part you're not going to believe. That part's coming up.

1924 came along, and Alvin and Bernice had been married for five years or so. Little Ferron was four-years-old when a call came to the house. It was for Alvin and, during the conversation, his tone was quiet and subdued.

"When?" he asked. "Are you sure? Can't you do it without me? All right, I'll be ready, just swing by and get me." Then he hung up the phone. His head and shoulders drooped down, and Bernice could instantly tell something was wrong.

"What happened?"

"Ma's about to lose the house."

"I'm sorry, what is it you have to do?"

"I have to go down and see about her sheep."

"Sell them?"

"I'm not sure, maybe find a new field for them to be in and someone to tend them for her."

"That means going back down there."

"Yes."

"But you said you'd never return."

"It's Mother."

"Yes, but can't your brothers take care of it? Isn't Franklin still down there?"

"She's not his mother."

"No, but he's still your brother."

"Half-brother," he corrected her. "I need to go. I need to see her."

"What about the café?"

"What's the good of being head waiter if I can't work the schedule around?" he asked her.

"How are you going to get down there?"

"My brother Gerald is going to take us down in his automobile. It sounds like Howard and Joseph Chamberlain are going to be joining us."

"Well, that's as good of a reason as any to go back there."

"I suppose. I tried to talk Gerald out of taking me, but he insisted that Mother needs us both."

"How long has it been since you've been back to Orderville?"

"Sixteen years, and I hoped I would never have to go back there again."

"When will you be going down?"

"This afternoon."

"That soon? Can't you wait a little longer to get ready?"

"All I need are some clothes, a Coca-Cola, and an apple for the road."

"Nonsense, you'll need more than that. I will pack you a

proper lunch."

Later that afternoon, Gerald's automobile ambled to the front of their house. Gerald sat in front, while Howard and Joseph Chamberlain rode in the back. They gave a quick honk to let Alvin know they had arrived.

The front door opened as Alvin stuck his head out long enough to give them an acknowledging wave and then disappeared back into the house. The three men sat outside and waited as Alvin said his goodbyes and gathered up his things for the trip. After several minutes, they became impatient, and Gerald honked the horn again.

OOGA, OOGA!

Alvin hurried out of the front door followed by Bernice and Ferron. He trotted out to the automobile, stowed his gear in the boot, and then walked back to his wife. He gave her a loving hug and a kiss. Ferron ran headlong into their legs and wrapped his arms around them both for a family hug.

"Come on, Romeo," Gerald said. "We still have a fair amount of driving to do if we're to get down to home before it's too late."

"I'm coming, I'm coming," Alvin claimed, still involved in the embrace.

"Bring them along, if you can't stand to be without them that badly," Gerald urged. "But come along."

"Yeah, but put them in the boot," Joseph said, laughing. "There's not enough room in the back seat for everyone."

Alvin slowly pulled away from Bernice and Ferron. "I hate to leave you."

"I hate to have you go, but it's only for a few days," Bernice assured him. "We'll be fine, and they have someone working for you down at the café. We'll see you as soon as you get back."

"All right, but I still hate to go."

"I know you hate to leave us, but you need to admit you

don't want to go back down there."

"I know, but that is only a small part," he insisted. "The bigger part is I don't want to leave you."

Alvin sat down in the front passenger seat and reached out to hold her hand.

"Drive carefully, Gerald," Bernice said, "and have Alvin call me when you get there. We'll have prayer for you while you're away."

"I'll be fine," Alvin assured her, "I'll call in the morning."

"How does it feel to be going back to Orderville for the first time since you were arrested?" Gerald asked him.

"I don't want to go. I wouldn't be doing it if Mother's house wasn't going into foreclosure." He turned to the men in the back and in a friendly tone said, "And what are the two Chamberlain boys doing going down with us?"

"Oh, you know," Howard said, "any chance to go home and see the family. Besides, we're pitching in for petroleum and agreed to ride back here the whole way."

"Sounds like a ball," Alvin said with a playful tone of sarcasm. "Let's get rolling."

"Hop out and turn the crank, brother."

Alvin got out, turned the engine crank and got back into the automobile. As they drove away, Alvin lovingly waved goodbye to his wife and son.

"I'll be back home before you know it."

"Boy," Gerald said, "you're not the same brother I knew back home. Who would have ever guessed you'd turn into such a family man? I'm surprised you don't have more kids with another one on the way."

"A lot's changed since back then." Alvin settled in for the long drive.

Hold on to your hat for this one.

Hours later, Alvin was driving the automobile down the road in the dark. The other three men were asleep, leaving Alvin to his thoughts.

They were just minutes outside of Orderville when Alvin began to quietly talk to himself. "This is a little too eerie. The last time I was near this canyon was when I killed Mary." He suddenly had a vivid flashback, remembering the events that led up to that fateful day, sixteen years earlier.

Jackie Adler, Hyrum Mower and he were sitting around a campfire, playing cards. They were up in the canyon a little way, and there was not another living soul around.

"Mary's pregnant," Jackie said.

"What?" Hyrum and Alvin both exclaimed, shocked.

"She told me last night."

"Poor girl," Hyrum said, "she desperately wants to be loved by someone. I think that's why she's been having intimate relations with each of us…searching."

"Because anyone of us could be the father," Jackie said, "whoever draws the low card will deal with the Mary situation."

"What do you mean 'deal with'?" Hyrum asked.

"I mean marry her or kill her."

"No!" Alvin cried.

"Mary is beneath us," Jackie said, "like the dirt under our feet. We will go to jail if something's not done."

"I don't know, Jackie," Hyrum said.

"Do you want to go to jail and have your life ruined?" Jackie asked.

"No, but I'm not too fond of your plan."

"It's not my plan," Jackie assured him. "It was Alvin's with all his talk about killing her all this time. That's where I got the idea."

"I was just fooling about," Alvin insisted. "I didn't mean any of it. There must be a better way."

"If you can come up with a better plan," Jackie said, "I'd love to hear it."

"No, no better plan," Alvin said after some thought, "but what if we get caught?"

"We make a blood pact right now," Jackie said, "that no matter what happens, we will speak of this to no one. Neither will we ever mention the others' involvement in this."

"So you're saying if you get caught," Alvin asked, "you'll never tell anyone that Hyrum and I had intimate relations with Mary and never tell anyone of this plan, ever?"

"That's exactly what I'm saying. Either we are all in this, or we're all going to the hangman's noose."

Jackie paused for a moment and then continued, "If whoever does this is dumb enough to get caught, he will never tell anyone the others were involved. That way, they can get on with their lives and not have them ruined by one impetuous girl."

"Of course, we don't have to kill her, right?" Hyrum asked. "We still have the choice to marry her, don't we?"

"That's right, the choice is yours. However, the pact still applies. Never tell anyone."

"Yeah," Alvin said. "Can you imagine how horrible she would feel if she knew about us drawing cards for her and this pact?"

Jackie shuffled the cards and then let Hyrum cut them. He shuffled them once again, and then let Alvin cut them. He shuffled them again and set the deck on the ground.

"Low card does it," Jackie said, as he looked each of the other two in the eye. Alvin and Hyrum both nodded in understanding and agreement.

Jackie nodded to Hyrum, who drew off the first card. Without looking at it, he held it close against his chest.

Jackie looked over at Alvin, who took the next top card. He too, held it up against his chest without looking at it.

Jackie reached down and drew off the next card and slowly pulled it up. He gave it a quick glance, and then turned it around for the others to see.

Seven of spades.

Hyrum slowly pulled his card out to where he could see it, and his head and shoulders immediately dropped. He turned the card around, defeated, for the others to see.

Four of clubs.

A shot of hope streaked through Alvin as he quickly pulled his card away from his chest and looked at it. With a petrified look on his face, he let the card fall to the ground.

It landed face up.

Two of diamonds.

"It's up to you now, Alvin," Jackie said. "Make the choice to marry her or not, but you need to follow through with it. Tell no one of what happened here today."

"Johnny Healy has a .38 I could use. Maybe I could trade him this deck of cards to use it for a while."

"Remember," Hyrum said, "the choice is yours. You still have the option to marry her."

"That would upset Mamie too much."

His mind came back to the present suddenly as he drove down the road in the dark. It dawned on him that it was July 2; Mary's birthday.

"Happy birthday," he said to himself and to the memory of

her. Then in remorse for what he had done, he continued, "It's your birthday today, isn't it? I'm afraid I didn't get you anything again this year."

He knew he had taken her life and everything she would have ever been, from her. He knew there was nothing he could do to replace that. Then his mind raced back to that April afternoon. He remembered when he walked out of the schoolhouse entrance and ran into Mary out on the grounds.

"I need to see you," Alvin told her. "Can you meet me up Gardner Hollow about four-thirty or five?"

"Yes," Mary responded with excitement and anticipation, "I can slip away. I will tell Joseph and Francis I'm going up to study. I will be waiting for you at the Point, where I go to read."

Alvin hesitated for a minute, then said, "If I'm not there by a quarter to five, head on up the canyon and I'll be along shortly." He slipped a piece of paper into her hand.

"I'll be waiting," she repeated and assured him with obvious anticipation and a little flirtiness. "I've been wanting to talk to you, too."

After she walked away from the school, she opened her hand to reveal the paper note. It read, "I can't wait to see you. Remember, mum's the word."

"I can't wait, either," she whispered to herself.

Mary was up at the Point later that afternoon, reading her schoolbooks. Alvin was not there yet, and she guessed it was about 4:45, so she decided to look for him. Gathering up her books, she slowly started up toward Gardner Hollow. She arrived at the place where another trail from town converged with the one she was on. Glancing over, she saw Alvin walking along. She paused for a minute and allowed him to catch up. When he got there, she took his arm and the two of them walked side by side up the trail to the clearing in the hollow.

"I've been watching for you," Mary said as she took his arm. "I was afraid Mamie might have tried to keep you from coming up."

"Don't worry, there was no way I was going to miss seeing you today," Alvin assured her.

"I could hardly concentrate on my examinations this morning; all I could think about was you. I wanted to see you, hold your arm as I walked with you, and be able to touch and kiss you."

"When we get up to the clearing we can do as much kissing as you want," he promised her. "We have all afternoon. My mom thinks I'm out working in the barn."

"I told my brother I was going to be studying, so I can easily stay out until after dark," she informed him as they continued to walk arm in arm.

"I'll try to make it worth your while."

"What do you see in that Mamie, anyway? I never thought she was all that special. I think you should stop seeing her and tell everyone about us. I love you and I want to be with you, and I want everyone to know about us."

They had reached the clearing and Alvin started to kiss her. The kissing became passionate and very physical. It was not long until they were fully engaged in physical relations. Once they finished, Alvin pulled away and rearranged his clothing.

"Alvin," Mary said, suddenly serious in a romantic way, "we need to get married, I'm going to have your child."

Alvin stood up with determination. "I know."

Mary continued without catching his reference. "It's going to be a beautiful child, and you're going to make such a wonderful father. Let's get married and we can raise a family. We can stay here, go to Mt. Carmel, or down to Kanab. We could even go somewhere else, if you wanted."

"Oh, no," he said, "I'm not ready to be a father, and I'm certainly not ready to be marrying you. Besides, I'm with Mamie."

"But what about all those things you told me on your late night visits?" Mary pleaded. "Did you not mean any of those things?"

"What things?"

"That you loved me and loved being with me. You promised when the time was right, after we finished school, we would be together. You promised Mamie was only for show, and you don't really care for her all that much. You promised your heart to me."

"I guess I also promised it to Mamie. I can't marry you, Mary, it just wouldn't look right."

"Did you have relations with Mamie?"

"No, of course not. Only you."

"Then, by law, you have to marry me. Besides, this baby deserves your name."

"What are you talking about?"

"The law. You can't have relations with a girl until she's nineteen. Marry me, or go to jail."

"Won't you let me off and not make me marry you?" he pleaded.

"No, I told you, I can make you marry me by law."

"Oh, I wish you hadn't had said that."

Mary burst into tears and turned away from Alvin to hide her shame and heartbreak as she fixed her clothes. Again, she had given herself to this man who she thought loved her.

"I'll be shunned and sent away," Mary sobbed, "and the baby will grow up without a last name."

"Don't be silly, you can give it the name of Stevens," he said as he drew out his rented gun and pointed it at her back. He had an angry look of determination on his face, almost as if he was possessed. He was still struggling internally with actually killing her, so the look momentarily faded as he let his arm, and the gun, droop a little bit.

When Mary turned and saw the gun, she immediately spun around and started to run away.

He quickly raised the gun and pointed it at her again and fired two shots in rapid succession, directly into her back.

She screamed, staggered two steps forward, and fell to her knees.

A look of evil took over his face as he stepped closer and fired a third shot into her back, causing her to scream again. This shot went all the way through her body and came out of her left breast, spraying blood on her face and hands. She fell forward, face down on to the ground as the life force bled out from her.

Alvin walked over, stood above her body, and shot her in the back one more, needless time, for good measure. This shot went all the way through her body again and spattered blood on his shoes and coat. He lowered the gun, moved away and turned back to look at her on the ground. Satisfied she was dead, he placed the gun back into his pocket.

As suddenly as it had come, the look of evil evaporated as the immediate realization of what he had just done filtered through. In a panic, he took the gun back out of his pocket and threw it away, down the trail. He spun around and began to walk rapidly back and forth, trying to decide what to do.

"Stick to the plan," he said to himself. "You have to see this through now." He grabbed her by her ankles and dragged her body over to the ravine he had previously scouted for this very purpose.

As he pushed her over he said, "You shouldn't have said I had to marry you."

She landed face down as he stood above and looked at her, "No one will ever find you down there. Goodbye, Mary."

The ravine was only a couple feet wide and about eight feet long, just big enough to conceal a body completely. He rapidly knocked dirt and rocks down on her from the ravine's sidewall to cover her up. Once she was buried, he brought over some brush and dropped it down on top to make it look natural and undisturbed. He turned to hotfoot it back down the trail to pick up on his alibi when he noticed her straw hat with a long blue ribbon tied around it.

"Damnit all to hell," he said "I don't have time for this."

He grabbed her hat, tossed it down in the ravine, and knocked some more dirt on top of it. This action created enough dust that he could not clearly see the ground or the partial ribbon still exposed. Instead of waiting for the dust to clear, he made the assumption all was hidden, ran over and picked up the gun, and trotted off toward town.

He took a shorter, more direct route instead of the trail for two reasons. One, he wanted to make better time. The other reason was in case anyone had seen him coming up the trail to meet Mary, he did not want them to see him coming back down alone.

He sprinted into town and ducked into his family's barn, where he immediately emptied the spent cartridges in a corner, and kicked some straw over them. He then began to clean out the stalls. After a moment of cleaning, he stopped to stand up and lean on the pitchfork. He was visibly shaken from his ordeal. He took several deep breaths to calm down. The callous look that had come over him when he was with Mary returned, and he went back to cleaning stalls for a minute before he walked out of the barn.

Suddenly, as he was driving, Alvin saw Mary standing accusingly in the middle of the road, wearing the same dress and hat with the blue ribbon she wore when he killed her.

He had been so deep in thought, remembering that day, that it took him a second to come back to his senses. The surprise was so complete that he swerved the automobile to miss running into her. Just as he swerved and saw the embankment coming at him, he knew his life was about to end. His final thought was, *what is Bernice going to think?*

He drove the car straight into the embankment, which threw him out of the automobile and onto the ground.

There was no movement from within the car.

With his last bit of life, Alvin dragged himself over to the embankment and sat up against it.

He looked toward the canyon, and quietly said, "I'm sorry, Mary, this should have never happened. If I'd of understood better…"

Then, with great tenderness, he said, "Happy birthday, Mary."

He closed his eyes.

Moments later, Gerald regained consciousness and stepped out to find Alvin against the embankment.

"I see you made it out all right. You could have come and helped the rest of us out, if you were going to wreck my car…"

He put his hand on Alvin's shoulder to get him to open his eyes.

Alvin was dead.

Gerald began to wail with grief.

Howard and Joseph slowly came to and carefully stepped out of the automobile. They walked over and put their hands on Gerald's shoulders to give him what comfort they could.

"What am I going to tell Mother?"

Chapter Eleven
Epilogue

Life in Orderville returned to normal. The loss of Alvin's life did not affect the community in any way that you could measure. He had been gone for sixteen years, and they had moved on. His mother was the only one in town who was actually affected by this. Mamie had long since married and had children of her own. She did not think about him very often but, when she did, it was wistfully about what might have been.

The murder and trial made a big impact in the news when it happened but, shortly afterwards, the state and the world moved on, and they were literally forgotten, except in the redacted memories of Kane County residents. It was not until 1940, when an article appeared in *Dynamic Detective* magazine, that this story somewhat resurfaced. Whatever impact it may have had, it was soon forgotten, once again.

Time continued on and left it in obscurity.

It was reported that since he had been released from prison,

Alvin had conducted himself in such a way as to completely justify his early release and return to society. Orderville had grown and changed many of their attitudes; they became a little more progressive than they had been.

One day, not too long after Alvin's death, an automobile bounced along the road as it drove into town. A twenty-three year old man was driving. Sitting next to him in the passenger seat was his very pregnant wife.

An aged Wilford Heaton walked to the car as they pulled over to the Co-op store.

"Evening, folks," he said. "How are you doing tonight?"

"Well, I'll tell you," the tired man said, "we're good, but we've been long on the road, and we sure could use a place to stay for the night. As you can see, my wife is very pregnant with twins."

Wilford stared for a moment, as he looked the car over, then he smiled and said, "You bet. There's plenty of room…for the four of you. Just drive up the road there, and you'll see a hotel on the right. After you are settled, come on down to the Co-op, and we'll buy you an ice cream. We may even have some peach cobbler left."

"Thank you for your hospitality," he said. "I'm sure you don't recognize me, but my name is Jack. I met you as a child. My sister and I were in the back of a wagon. My father was driving, and my mother was very sick from the flu."

"I do remember you now," Wilford winced. "Things were a bit different then. We were still hurting from the government and Gentile persecutions, and not too trusting of outsiders. How did your mother fare?"

"She died a week later."

"I'm so very sorry. I…"

"Not to worry, sir. Pa said that she would have died no matter what. The trip from back East was just too much for her.

He bore you no ill will. He said you treated us well enough."

"But we should have been warmer and more welcoming. We should have let you stay."

"We did make it to Kanab, on your advice, and she died comfortably in a nice room with lots of sunlight shining through the window. She's buried in a pretty cemetery east of town."

"Seems like I do remember hearing something about that now that you mention it."

Wilford turned and looked at the people around him until he spied the person he was looking for.

"Willy, come here," he said.

A young boy of six or seven went running over to answer the call. "Yes, Grandfather?"

"Willy, take these fine folks down and show them where the hotel is, and make sure they get checked in all right."

Willy turned to the couple in the automobile. "You can drive your machine and follow me. It's not far."

He turned and started to lead them away when Wilford called after him. "Be sure and bring them back for some ice cream and cobbler when they get checked in."

Willy stopped dead in his tracks at his grandfather's comment.

"Shouldn't they have dinner first?" he asked, in a bossy tone.

Wilford and the couple laughed. "Of course. We'll have dinner waiting for them, too."

We found that sometimes when you shut your eyes too tightly, or shut your gates against what you fear might be evil, you might find there is more evil within those gates than you realized. We fought so hard to keep the Gentiles out that we missed the deeds going on within our own ranks. Mary paid the price for it and, in some small part, so did we all. We never discussed it, but somehow we all decided we would never let that same evil creep back in, not while we were on the lookout. Now, when strangers come into town, we welcome them, unless they prove themselves to be unworthy of our trust. So far, things have been looking much better. We don't talk about Mary anymore, but you can still see her in our actions. And Alvin? If you ask me, I'd say he paid his penance, and he and the Good Lord will have a lot to talk about. But what do I know, I was only a ten-year-old sheepherder when it happened.

You wouldn't think that anything good would have come out of an untimely death, but the truth is those same four shots that killed Mary would eventually give a new, better life to a town called Orderville.

On July 2, 1924, Alvin Franklin Heaton, Jr., swerved off the road while driving at night and wrecked his brother's automobile.

He was thrown from the car and killed instantly.

It was Mary Steven's birthday.

Almost completely lost to history are the events of April 20, 1908, when Mary Manerva Stevens was brutally shot, and her body hastily secreted in a ravine to hide the crime. Precious little is actually known of Mary and other participants. This story has been hidden away and forgotten in the community and only whispered about by a few since its occurrence. Even many of the modern members of our small community have grown up without the story.

As time passes, those who do whisper about her mention she

had loose morals, but say nothing of the boys who were involved with her, as if to blame this on her.

Regardless, this, in no way, justifies Alvin and his actions that day. It seems this is more of an internal justification that has grown over the years than what was actually thought of her at the time. I would say Alvin was not a bad person. I think he was so focused on himself and the situation he got himself into, that he lost sight of the consequences. He lost all compassion and integrity at that moment when he lifted the gun.

As I look back now over the decades, it wasn't so bad being there in the Richfield courtroom but, at the time, it seemed like an eternal punishment once the fascination wore off. You wouldn't believe how much I wished I'd never heard those shots.

Only by those who choose to stop and listen hear the sound of those shots that still quietly echo through Long Valley. Beyond that, the world has forgotten Mary Stevens and her undeserved death.

My father kept reminding me that it was me hearing them that brought her killer to justice. I was like a hero, he would say, and that I was his hero. Knowing that helped a little, because I always liked Mary, but it was still difficult to sit in that court building, hour after excruciating hour.

Now, many years later, I'm so glad that I did. I often think of Mary and imagine her smiling at me for helping her get justice.

We miss you, Mary.

May your eternal rest be peaceful and surrounded by family.

Acknowledgements

This story could never have been told without the great help of the Mayor of Kanab, Nina Laycook, her cohort Linda Alderman, and their fellow Kanabite, Nathan Riddle. They were invaluable in their help and support in this project. I loved working with them on the *America's First All Women Town Council* documentary and look forward to many more projects with them in the future. I also had some other great beta-readers, Carolyn Blomquist and Bridget Williams, whose input made the story so much better. Also to Adam Mast, who provided some great ideas in the story arc, and to Linda Hansen, who once again worked her editing magic to make this incredible story read more as it should.

About the Author

Roger Blomquist Ph.D. was born and raised in the Wild West of Utah, Texas, and the deserts of Southern California. His mother and Grandparents grew up in Southern Utah giving him a special tie to this land. He served an American Sign Language mission during the era of eighteen-month missions, and returned home to finish school in drafting and design. After working for many years as an architectural designer, he found himself dressed as a cavalry soldier in Johnston's Army. He was ordered to report to Alpine, Utah, to be in the LDS film, *Mountain of the Lord.* That moment in time changed his life.

He worked on many historical and Western films after that and discovered a dormant love of history deep within him. He decided to return to school and pursue an education and career teaching history on the university level. He hoped he would be able to spark a similar love of history in his students, as had been awakened in him. He then earned his bachelor's and master's degree at Brigham Young University in American Frontier History.

While studying under the renowned Fred Gowans, Roger decided that since he could not afford the period saddles he needed for film, he would learn how to make them himself. Fred informed him of an old saddlemaker who had been trying to get him to come and learn, so he and Roger made all the necessary arrangements. They studied together under this saddlemaker and while in the process of learning, both made their own 1870's style saddle. Because of this, he did both his thesis and dissertation on these historical saddles and their makers. Roger then went on to earn his doctorate degree at the University of Nebraska-Lincoln, which is one of the top ranked universities in the country for Westward Expansion in American Frontier History.

His saddlemaking has continued and *True West Magazine* awarded him as the "Best Western Saddlemaker in 2005." He also continues to work in the film industry as a wrangler, actor, and scriptwriter/producer as the occasion requires. He wrote and produced the short museum film for the Camp Floyd/Stagecoach Inn State Park and Museum, which is available for viewing on YouTube under *Camp Floyd: Forgotten City in the Desert*. He also taught history on the university level for about eight years when he decided to turn his hand to historical fiction writing.

He has written a series called *South Pass* that begins with a family who suddenly finds themselves headed west with the first handcart company in history. Book one covers the family's conversion and their trek west; Book Two follows Steve and the handcart company after their split with Sarah's family, through their reunion and arrival in Lehi, Utah. Book Three looks at the origins of Johnston's Army, and the family acclimating to life in Lehi, Utah. Book Four follows the army through the Utah War and down into Utah Valley, and the family's progression in Zion.

Book Five takes place in the temporary military camp during the construction of Camp Floyd, and the nearby Mormon community of Lehi, introducing and intertwining the family with the soldiers. Book six looks at the permanent Camp Floyd with its diversions and relations with the local Saints, and Book Seven takes place in Frogtown with the Pony Express and other experiences. The other books in the series will sprout out from there following the demise of the Pony Express, Camp Floyd, Frogtown, and the nation's involvement in the Civil War, Transcontinental Railroad, and the Hole in the Rock Expedition. They will also check in on Max Parker, his wife Ann, and their son Robert Leroy, better known as Butch Cassidy. They will also return to an early time in Utah's history and cover more about the mountain men, rendezvous period, and the Native Americans who participated.

Follow his other books, including his *South Pass* series, on his author Facebook page under Roger Blomquist, as he completes more books and they become available.

Made in the USA
Middletown, DE
17 December 2020